The Windlands Tales

John Ernest Briggs

The Adventures of Window Breesian

Part One:
The Path To The Northlands

Part Two:
The Search For The Northlands Treasure

Part Three:
The Search For The Angels Of The Very East

Some of these adventures may not have been true at the time they happened, but most of them are true by now.

Book Three of the Windlands Tales

THE ADVENTURES OF WINDOW BREESIAN
Part Three:

The Search For The Angels Of The Very East

By

John Ernest Briggs

Illustrations by the author

Including a Reference Appendix

Willowix Publishing

The Adventures Of Window Breesian
Part Three:
The Search For The Angels Of The Very East

Text copyright © 2020 John Ernest Briggs
Illustrations copyright © 2020 John Ernest Briggs
Cover and interior design copyright © 2020 John Ernest Briggs

Willowix Publishing
WillowixPublishing@gmail.com

ISBN: 987-1-7325181-3-1

Library of Congress Control Number: 2019905745

Printed in Century Schoolbook font

To my nieces

Maggie Ryan [Vermillion]
and
Kelly Ryan [Tresette] –

Whose love of life and unbounded joy
reminded me
why I was writing this book

THE ADVENTURES OF WINDOW BREESIAN
Part Three: The Search For The Angels Of The Very East

+++++++++

+++++++++

INTRODUCTION TO PART THREE

Window Breesian, the young adventure-seeking man from the Windlands, is far, far from home. He and his friends have traveled all across the Northlands and then beyond to the east as they continued in their search for treasure and adventure.

But now, Panni, Rings, and Raine have all returned home. Still Window, and Circles, the silky-furred Deep Woods Woot, have decided to go on. They are traveling still farther to the unknown lands of the distant east in search of more treasure (which they don't need) – and, Circles wants to find another ocean (which must be there somewhere) – and he wants to find the Angels. Of course, the two travelers don't know if such creatures even exist.

Before Window and Circles lie more new friends and enemies, exciting and wondrous places, and the sharing of danger and discovery. Now, as their adventures continue, the two travelers are standing before a vast sea. Is it the Far Ocean of the Very East?

Some of these adventures may not have been true at the time they happened, but most of them are true by now.

John Ernest Briggs

PROLOGUE

+++++++++

[BEFORE THE SPARKLING SEA]

Tresette and Vermillion settled once again beneath the soft white covers of their bed and waited for their mother. Also, once again, the soft white moonlight came through their window and splashed across their tired but happy faces as they readied themselves. In just a few minutes their mother would, once again, read them another chapter of their favorite book.

"I love this part of the story, Mama," Veri shared with her mother.

"You like every part of the story," Tressi reminded her – Tressi's voice the exact same voice as her twin sister.

"I do not. I don't like the part when Window and Circles go to... Well, what if I do have lots of favorite parts? Window went lots of different places."

"Do you like this part, Tressi?" their mother wanted to know.

"Oh, yes, Mama, especially when..."

"Don't tell me, Tressi," Veri spoke up. "I want to be surprised."

"What is your favorite part, Mama?" Tressi wondered aloud.

Their mother thought for a moment and then replied, "My favorite part is when my darling daughters stop talking and I get to start reading to them."

"Oh, I guess that is my favorite part, too," Veri agreed.

The girls settled themselves under the covers.

"I like the name 'The Sparkling Sea,' Mama. It sounds pretty," Veri offered.

"When you think of a sparkling sea, Veri, you might think of what lies ahead of you and your sister. Your lives could be like sailing on a sparkling sea every day. Sometimes you know where you are sailing and sometimes you may get lost and be unsure of which way to go. Just remember, that just like Window and Circles, if you keep going, and never give up, you will someday find your way just like they did."

"Is that true, Mama," Tressi wanted to know, "or did you just make that up?"

"I guess both, my Dears. I did just make it up – but it is true. I hope that you never forget."

"We won't, Mama. We won't," the girls answered in unison.

"And, Darling Daughters, where are the two travelers going now?"

"To the sea, Mama! To the sparkling sea!" they again answered together.

"Okay. Let's go with them."

The girls nodded their agreement.

Their mother sat down on the edge of the bed and pushed some of her hair behind her ear. The bright light of the table lamp reflected from the jeweled pin in her hair and flashed on the ceiling like stars in the warm night sky.

The gentle night breeze came in the window and touched the faces of the girls as she opened the book.

Mama took one more glance towards the girls and sighed as she always did as she read to them.

"Chapter Twenty-One, Along The Laycellian Shore," she softly began. As she did, Tresette and Vermillion closed their eyes, joined Window and Circles far away, and imagined discovering a sparkling sea.

"There it is, Window! There it is – the Eastern Ocean!"

+++++++++

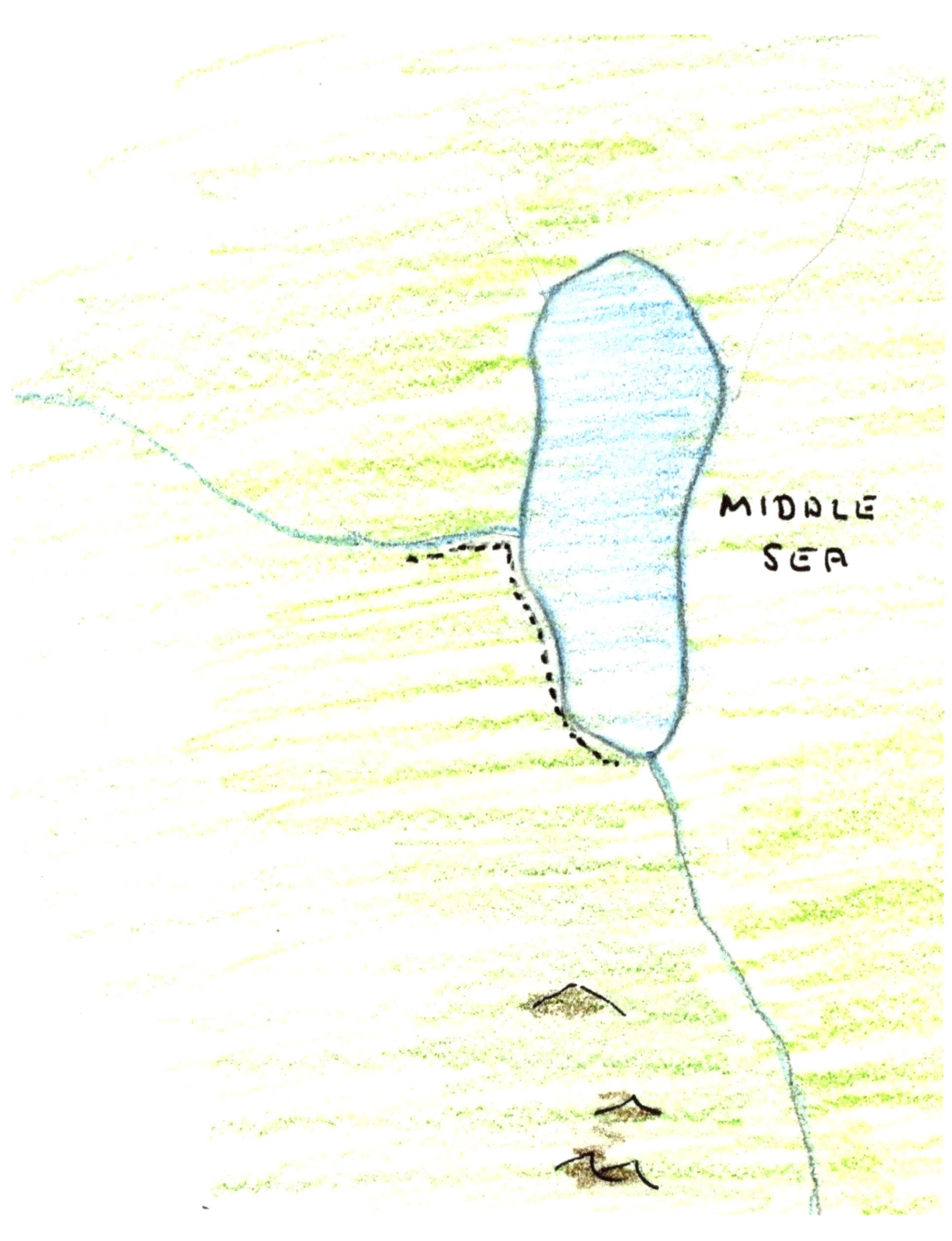

MIDDLE
SEA

CHAPTER TWENTY-ONE

ALONG THE LAYCELLIAN SHORE

"There it is, Window! There it is – the Eastern Ocean!" Circles happily announced as he pulled on his friend's arm. "I knew we could find it!"

"I'll bet your Mama Woot would be proud of you, if she knew that you have seen two oceans. You must be the only Woot in history to do that."

"I will tell her as soon as we get back. She will be surprised."

"I guess that my family will be surprised, too. I was only supposed to be gone for a couple of weeks, but now it has been a long, long time."

"Some adventures take longer than planned, I guess."

"Yeah, I guess. I am glad you are with me, Circles, or it would be a lonely adventure."

"How long do you think it will take us to get to the water, Window?"

"I'll bet we can make it by suppertime. Let's keep going."

"Do you think there are any Angels living down by the ocean, Window?"

"If there are, we will find them."

The two travelers climbed down a gentle embankment and once again hiked along near the edge of the river. Reeds and cattails grew everywhere in the soft ground. As they made their way across the ocean lowlands, soon Circles was calling out to the scores of sea-birds that were now overhead. He wanted to ask them about the ocean, but none would fly over to him.

"Raine forgot to tell me how to get the birds to talk to me, Window. Some of these birds don't seem very friendly."

"Try that one, Circles. He looks like a different kind."

"*Wet-i-wit, wet-i-wit,*" Circles whistled to the little feather-dove sailing across the grass in front of them. The grey-white bird turned and flitted down next to him and perched on the top of a water-reed that was bending in the breeze. "*Wil-a-wi, wil-a-wi,*" it replied to Circles' invitation to join them.

Apparently, this bird was not only friendly, but lonely as well. He offered to travel with the explorers for a way and tell them anything they wanted to know about the "Middle Sea" as he called the water before them. Window said hello to the bird, whose name, according to Circles, was Flitter, but it didn't pay much attention to him. It just gave Window a quick clicking sound in reply.

Anyway, it turned out that Flitter <u>was</u> very friendly but didn't really know much about much of anything. Well, he did know which direction the sea was, and other interesting things like where the trees were, but nothing more exciting than that. Circles was beginning to think that talking to birds may not be the great thrill that he had always thought it would be. Still, their bird friend flew overhead along with them as the travelers continued on their way to the water. It dipped and flipped and spun in the sky above them as they walked below.

"Do all birds have names, Circles? That would be an awful lot of names."

"I don't know, Window. Remember, I have only talked to a couple of them.'

"Oh, yeah, I forgot."

"I was just thinking, Window," Circles shared with him. "I'll bet that the Silkie would be very good at bird talk – since they whistle so well."

"You are doing a fine job of whistling, Circles, and chattering, too."

"I miss Raine, Window. I would like to hear him talk to birds. Well, I would like to hear him talk to anything."

"Maybe someday you will, Circles. Maybe someday."

As the travelers neared the ocean, the river widened and pushed across a delta framed by beautiful flowering reeds and water-grass. More birds were overhead and in the tall trees that approached the seashore across the river to the north. Billowing white clouds over the water finished the wonderfully pleasing view before them.

"Wow, Window. This sure looks like a place that beautiful Angels would want to live. This is a perfect spot. Well, except that I don't see any Angel castles."

"Maybe the Angels around here are the underwater kind of Angels."

"Yeah, maybe," answered Circles, not knowing if his friend was being serious or kidding him.

Just as the Atlandic by Meriselle, the Middle Sea was rimmed by a wide, flat, beach of soft sand. The two adventurers walked right up to the water's edge and stopped. Flitter, who had still been keeping them company from a distance, dived down past them, chatted something at Circles, and took off towards the trees.

Window and Circles dropped their packs onto the sand and Window pulled off his boots and socks. Then the two ocean hunters waded into the water. The cool of the ocean refreshed their feet as they kicked it ahead of them, and at each other. The travelers celebrated another treasure they had found together.

Then, after a few minutes of playing in the water, Window realized something important. "Hey, Circles. This isn't the ocean," he calmly announced to his friend.

"What do you mean, Window? It looks like the ocean to me."

"Yes, but it doesn't taste like the ocean."

Circles scooped a handful of water to his mouth and took a drink.

"Oh, Wow! This water tastes good. It's not salt water! It's not ocean water! It's not the ocean! Window, it's not the ocean," the disheartened Woot repeated to his friend.

"Looks like we have a bit more traveling to do, Circles – probably a lot more."

"I'll bet that if we found some Angels they would know where the stupid ocean is," countered Circles, somewhat angry, but more disappointed at their new discovery. His shoulders sagged along with his spirits.

The two disappointed ocean hunters dragged themselves out of the water and plopped down on the sand.

"Well, now what, Window? What direction should we go now?"

"I don't know, Circles. I thought that maybe there would be a city or something here where the river flows into the sea. But it doesn't look like any people live around here anywhere."

Circles looked at the sky overhead. "It will be dark in a couple of hours, Window. Let's just go under those trees over there and fix a camp for the night. Tomorrow we can decide what to do. We will think of something, I am sure. There doesn't seem to be any Angels around here anyway."

"Okay, Partner. You are right. Let's have a big fire tonight and enjoy the water. After all, we did find a really big sea. Maybe we can go fishing or something tomorrow.

The two campers chose a spot beneath some big fassa-trees and gathered enough wood to keep a fire going long into the night. Circles started to feel better as the sun went down and the fire jumped high into the darkening sky. Without Panni or Rings to join in, it wasn't as much fun to sing around the fire as they had done for so long, so the unsuccessful ocean-hunters just enjoyed the sea breeze and quietly watched as the moon began to rise over the water.

"Let's see what Charm has to say about this sea, Window. Maybe he knows something he can tell us."

Thinking rather doubtfully, Window pulled the faded blue light from is pocket.

"Hold him in the moonlight. He needs to wake up."

Window placed the faint, sleeping light in his hand and let the silver moonbeams wash over him. Almost immediately, Charm flashed a brilliant blue and jumped into the air.

"What do you think, Charm?" Circles asked him. "Where should we go from here?"

The lively light spun around in a circle in the air a few times then flew out over the water. He zipped back and forth across the small evening waves several times before he returned and landed on top of Window's food pack.

"But we have no boat, Charm. And we don't fly as well as you do."

Charm slowly flew over and sat on a rock next to Circles. The light remained there unmoving, as though embarrassed at the suggestion he had made. "I guess he hadn't thought of that," Circles shared with Window.

Then, to perhaps make the light feel better, Circles asked, "Do you think that Charm could learn to play Rainbow Chips, Window? We could use another player around here."

Upon hearing Circles' question, the friendly light-spark flashed bright blue, jumped up, and happily flew to the pack that held the chips. Before long, all three companions were placing and trading and winning the colored chips in the moonlight. Charm would jump on the chip he wanted to move, and then jump to the position where he wished it to go. Then Circles moved the chip for him. Although he didn't do very well this first time of playing, later on Charm became pretty good at the game. He especially seemed to enjoy winning the blue chips, even if he lost the other colors.

Then as the night grew longer, and the moon rose higher, the travelers ended their game playing and just quietly gazed out over the sea. The reflection of the moon on the water made a bright yellow path from the sky, across the water to them.

"I wish we could walk on that moon-path, Window. Then we could walk right over to the moon. I'll bet we could find those Angels under the mountains of the moon that Mellie told us about."

"Circles, if there are any Angels around here, I am sure we will find them. You are a fantastic Angel hunter."

"I hope so, Window. I hope so."

Then Circles saw something new in the water. "I wonder if those are Angel eyes, Window. But I really don't think so."

Window followed Circles' finger to where it was pointing, out into the water. At the end of the finger-path Window saw them, too – three sets of eyes, poking out of the water, about thirty feet from shore. They obviously belonged to some sea-creatures, apparently huge sea-creatures, whose bodies remained hidden under the water – only their bulging eyes stuck above the surface. The moonlight reflected brightly in their eyes and shined menacingly yellow in the direction of the surprised, and concerned, travelers.

Window immediately drew the knife from his boot. Circles reached over and readied an arrow in his bow. But, just as quickly, Charm jumped into the air and flew out toward the eyes. As he did, the creatures ducked below the water. Charm returned, but the eyes didn't. The Angel hunters saw no more of them that night.

The morning brought another beautiful day to the travelers. At breakfast, Flitter came back and again talked to Circles. The friendly, but less than brilliant, bird told him that it took the sky-terns a flight of an entire day to cross the sea, so it must big very large. He also was sure that the seashore to the north was extremely rough, but the sandy beach they were on now extended many miles to the south, so it would be much easier to travel that way.

"Let's check with a little vermillion, Window. I don't trust this guy."

So they did. Window used only about a dozen tiny sparkling flakes of the colored dust, which drifted off to the south. The Pixie dust agreed with the feather-dove. They would continue their ocean search along the edge of the Middle Sea to their right.

The travelers trekked along the water for most of the morning. Flitter followed in the sky above them, sometimes flying on farther down the beach and returning with reports of more trees and water ahead. Circles was beginning to really enjoy his conversations with the little bird. Flitter didn't have much of anything to say, but he said it with such happy enthusiasm that it lifted Circles spirits just having him around.

And the bird did enjoy fancy flying. He would spin and flip as he sped past the travelers or as he came to perch on Circles' hand. Window, too, appreciated having another companion, even one he couldn't talk to.

Window and Circles were no longer sure what they were searching for. Wherever an eastern ocean was, it must be a great distance from them. And they had found no Angels beyond the Gate To The Angels and had left the King's Treasure far behind them. Window's thoughts turned to Panni and Rings. Maybe he and Circles should end their adventure and return to the Northlands.

In the middle of the afternoon, the travelers stopped to rest. Well, Window wanted to rest, but Circles started tossing pebbles into the air for Flitter to try to catch – and they made a lot of noise. Circles was yelling to the bird, and Flitter was loudly trilling his replies. Window went farther down the beach so he could rest in quiet.

Window lay down in the sand along the water and looked across the blue of the sea. The sun was warm on his face and the gentle splashing of the waves on the sand seemed to be singing him a gentle lullaby.

"What a beautiful day, and a perfect place to relax," he thought. "Only one thing could make it better."

Window let out a wistful sigh, closed his eyes, and let his mind float on the waves. As he drifted off to sleep, he held one thought, "I wish Mary was here with me."

+++++++++

[BEYOND THE RIVER LANDING]

Hundreds and hundreds of distant miles to the west, Mary Collette Looking sat in the late morning sun and looked out across the river. Her beautiful light-brown eyes watched the beautiful blue water as it hurried past on its way to the sea – but her thoughts were far, far away.

Today she wore only her light-red summer-skirt and his favorite slippery, lace blouse. Today she had pulled the smooth curves of her light-brown, sun-streaked hair away from her face so she could feel the kiss of the breeze on her cheeks. And that is what she was thinking of – not the kiss of the breeze, but his kiss – and not a kiss on her cheek, but a kiss to melt her where she sat – a kiss like the last one they had shared – a kiss she could never forget.

Today was her day to do those things – to dress for him and to think of him. Most days she didn't allow herself to think of him – and the loneliness in her heart, and the sadness of her waiting, but today was the day she would give in to the temptation of her dreams.

Today she would forget about her work, undone at the river-house, and the chores waiting for her at home. Today she would not stop herself when thoughts of him jumped into her mind as they always did. Today, she would think of him all that she wanted – and that is all she wanted to do. She would remember his gentle caress and his compelling kiss and his comforting arms around her. She would read his letters again and try to feel his touch on the paper. She would remember his handsome face, his captivating smile, and the soft, hypnotic sound of his voice the night he whispered into her ear the words she could never forget.

Mary leaned back against a tree and pulled her feet up closer to her body. The wind fluttered her skirt and cooled her uncovered legs. She closed her eyes and ran her hand across the perspiration on her neck and her chest. She licked her lips and felt the breeze refresh them as the sun warmed her face. She let her dreams fly where they may.

And today, she would dream of when she would see him again. Just then, a willowix flew by above her as it soared across the river. She imagined that, if she could fly, she would speed to him just as quickly. She smiled, knowing that each day and each dream brought her closer to him.

Mary picked up a small stone and tossed it into the water. Her thoughts jumped to the night when they had fallen asleep on her living-room sitting couch. That was the night she knew she was falling in love with him.

And now, she would wait to see him again. Tomorrow she would not let her thoughts be of him. The next day she would not think of him. But today, Mary Collette Looking sat in the late morning sun and looked out across the river. Her beautiful light-brown eyes watched the beautiful blue water as it hurried past on its way to the sea – but her thoughts were far, far away.

+++++++++

In just a few minutes, Window awoke and opened his eyes to see the clear blue of the sky overhead. He expected to hear Circles still yelling to Flitter back up the beach. What he heard instead was something quite different – snoring.

Well, it was something like snoring, or deep, growling-like, heavy breathing. Window rolled his head to his right and froze. Asleep on the sand, just an arms-length from him, was a huge, slippery scaled, water lizard. The creature was about four feet long, and looked a bit like a wide river Radian-gator, from the marshlands of New South, but its scales were light grey and rougher.

13

The lizard had a fat tail and body, four short stubby legs, which each ended in four curved claws, and a long, long head, which ended in a wide mouth. Window felt certain that inside the creature's mouth would be more teeth than he cared to see.

Apparently, the lizard had simply crawled out of the water and fallen asleep next to him in the sun.

Window couldn't decide what to do. The creature looked extremely dangerous, but hadn't attacked him. If he had to defend himself from the lizard, his boot knife probably wouldn't pierce its body scales, so quietly sneaking away seemed by far the best solution.

Just then, the creature's breathing changed. He was waking up! Window was afraid to jump up and run. He didn't like the idea of being chased down the beach by a provoked sea creature.

Window stayed perfectly still as the lizard slowly opened his eyes. They were big and brown, and not menacing as Window expected. The creature just looked at Window for a moment and closed his eyes again.

Window was happily confused. It was as though the water creature only wanted company as he slept on the sand. It really didn't seem dangerous at all. Window lost most of his fear of the animal, and relaxed. He hoped he wasn't making a terrible mistake.

Window watched his new sleeping partner for a few minutes until it opened its eyes again. Then the creature's mouth slowly opened in a tremendous yawn. Its teeth were jagged and sharp, as Window had guessed.

After the yawn, the creature just looked at Window some more, but didn't do anything else but blink a couple of times. It was as though it was waiting for Window to do something – so he did something – something maybe Circles would have done. Window started quietly singing.

He couldn't remember many of the words, but he remembered the melody of a Windlands song his father had taught him about a ship sailing on a beautiful sea. So Window sang and bah-bahed his way through the song. The creature blinked a few more times but made no sound. Then it closed its eyes and appeared to be going back to sleep. So Window spoke to it.

"My name is Window. Do you have a name?" The creature opened its eyes again and looked at Window. Again, it seemed to be waiting.

A name jumped into Window's mind. I will call you Radio, after your cousins back in the Windlands. That is where I am from. It is a land far from here. Have you ever been there?"

Radio didn't respond. The bright mid-afternoon sun reflected off of his scaled back and into Window's eyes.

"I didn't think so. I have never been <u>here</u> before, either. My friend and I are on an adventure in your land. Do you know where the ocean is?" The grey-scaled Radio silently listened as Window talked on.

Window reached into his pocket and pulled out the medallion he had carried across so many, many miles. He held it out to the sea-creature and asked, "Have you ever seen this before? It is the reason I am here today. Without it, I would probably be back home hiking in the woods or building a house or something." Again, there was no reply.

Window continued to try to engage the Radian. "Are there any other people around here?"

Window was drawn to the creature's quiet calm and apparent contentment of resting in the sun. Then Radio shifted his body in the sand as if he might be preparing to move. Window decided to add still more to the story he would tell to everyone back at the Summer Breeze.

Slowly he reached his hand across to the creature to touch it. Radio closed his eyes and seemed to sigh in a sea-creature sort of way as Window rubbed his fingers over the lizard's head and the ribbed scales on the back of his neck. They were hot to the touch and oddly comforting.

Window slid his hand along the creature's back and then reached and carefully touched his nose. It was hot, just like the rest of his body.

"I wonder if rubbing a sea-lizard's nose is good luck," Window thought to himself. "I'll bet it doesn't happen too often."

Just then, Circles called to Window from far up the beach. Radio took one last look at his brief sunning companion and scurried into the water, sand flying behind him as he went. Before he disappeared for good, the sea-creature poked his eyes out of the water for one last look at the traveler. Then he was gone.

Window looked to his left. Circles was shuffling down the beach towards him.

"Hey, Window. Let's get going. Flitter is tired of chasing rocks."

"Okay, Circles. Hey, guess what I just did."

"What's that, Window?"

"I rubbed a sea-radian's nose."

"Did you also fall asleep? It sounds like you've been dreaming."

Window pointed to the trail in the sand where the creature had crawled to the sea. "My dream made that path as he went back into the water."

"Wow! Tell me about it."

And so Window did, as the two friends walked to the south, looking for Angels or anything else they might find along the shore of the Middle Sea.

++++++++

In a day or so, the sandy beaches at the edge of the Middle Sea were replaced by soft grass as the travelers continued on their way. The walk was easy and the weather, except for one rainstorm, was pleasant. But still, the travelers were getting bored.

"We need someplace definite to go, or something to search for, Window," Circles shared with his friend. "Adventures are a lot more fun when you know what they are."

Window felt it, too. When the most exciting part of your day is listening to wing-finches chatting in the trees as you walk by, it may be time to choose a new plan. Still, the vermillion had told them to go this direction, so they continued along the shoreline.

For three days, Flitter kept the travelers company on their way to the south. Then, one afternoon, he announced that he would go no farther. Circles thanked him for his help, and the little grey-white bird soared back to the north to his home in the trees by the sea. The last thing Flitter said to Circles, before he left, was that some cliff-birds from farther south told him that there were men like Window near the river. Of course, Flitter didn't know where the river was, but Circles was sure that if they just kept going around the sea, they would eventually find it.

"Let's go find the men by the river, Window. Maybe there is an inn we could stay at for a while."

"Okay, Circles. I hope you are right. I certainly would enjoy sleeping in a bed."

"And I haven't had any lemon-tea for weeks and weeks. Hey, Window, what kind of men would live way over here in the east anyway? We are far, far from home."

"I don't know, Circles. I have never heard anything of this part of the world."

"I will tell you if I find out anything."

"You do that, Circles."

"Oh, I will Window. I will."

The travelers' spirits were raised by their new goal and the thought of reaching civilization. Circles decided to make up a song about their travels to celebrate. He worked on it as they went along, and sang it for Window at the campfire that night. The moon was out so Window took Charm from his pocket to join them. The charming light flashed in the moonlight and zipped through the air as Circles sang.

"Twisting rivers grassy ways
Chatting birds and sunlit days
Cloudy skies and gentle breeze
Shining moon and sparkling seas

Treasure hopes and Angel dreams

Pixie dust in dazzling streams
Magic charm and sleepy nights
Near the fire's light"

Charm turned spirals above the campfire as Circles repeated
the part about the magic charm. Window liked the sleepy nights
part and soon lay down to accommodate.

++++++++

As Window and Circles followed the shoreline of the Middle
Sea it began to curve to the east. They would soon be on the sea's
southern edge. They had seen no more eyes in the water, or sea-
radians on the beach. Gradually, the grassy shore started to
occasionally turn a bit rougher as the travelers passed through
lightly wooded forests.

Window and Circles enjoyed their days together as always.
Circles spoke of finding the Angels, although, since leaving the
Moonlands, they hadn't seen any more Angel letters. Still Circles
believed that the vermillion was leading them in the right
direction.
"What will you do if we find the Angels, Circles?" Window
wanted to know.
Circles thought for a moment then replied, "I'll ask them if they
ever rode on the Silkie – like I wish we were doing right now."
The thoughts of both travelers briefly flew across the lands to
where they had met their Silkie friends. Then Circles asked,
"What about you?"
"I'll ask the Angels if they know where my medallion came
from."
After another thoughtful pause, Circles continued, "Do Angels
have medallions, Window?"
"I don't know, Circles. I don't think so."
Circles thought on, "Are there any Talkers in the east,
Window?"
"I don't know, Circles. You may be the only one."
"Wow! I guess that Raine was right. I am a special Woot."

"Yes, you are, Circles. You are a special Woot."

"You are special, too, Window – special to me."

Window smiled at Circles as the two friends walked on, along the waters of the sparkling sea.

The traveler's search for the men by the river only took one more day. In the middle of the next afternoon, Circles calmly announced to his friend, "I can smell them, Window. I can smell the men on the breeze."

He sniffed the air again. "But something is odd. They don't quite seem to be human – at least not human like you. Something is different."

In just a few minutes, as the two explorers emerged from an area of sea-bushes, they could see the men ahead of them along the shore. Several of them were in a lightly wooded area near the water. Window could see no buildings or boats or even any evidence of a camp. The men were walking down to the edge of the sea and looking out into the water.

Slowly, Window and Circles approached the group, of course, not knowing if they would be pleased to see two visitors from far away to the west.

"Maybe you'd better stay here, Circles. They may not be familiar with Woots – or any Talkers. I'll speak to them first."

"But, Window, what if they don't speak Atlan... – Oh, yeah, I forgot. With Raine's gift, you should be able to speak to any men."

"I hope so, Circles. I hope so."

Circles stayed hidden in the bushes as Window slid his pack to the ground and went on towards the men. As he got closer to them, he noticed they were all wearing odd, tight fitting, greenish clothing that brightly reflected the sunlight. Then, he noticed something much more surprising – they were not humans!

As Window came still closer, he could tell that the green of the men was not from their clothes, but from their skin. The creatures were about the size and shape of men, but – just then a couple of the greenish men spotted Window approaching. There was nothing he could do except continue towards them. Fortunately, they didn't seem to be carrying any weapons.

Rather than their bodies being covered by smooth skin, the odd people-by-the-sea were covered by lightly greenish sections of skin. Their skin looked a bit like scales, but it was not. It was simply skin that seemed to fit together in sections as scales might. It was light green in color, with short silver streaks through much of it.

As best Window could tell, all of the creatures appeared to be males, each wearing nothing but brief, belted coverings about their midsections. Their necks were rather long, as were their arms and fingers. Webs of smooth skin stretched between part of their fingers and between their toes.

The creatures' facial features were human-like, but their foreheads and cheeks were angled to a slight crease towards the front of their faces. They had short, soft-looking, greenish hair on their heads, and their eyes were larger than a man's would be. As on the rest of their bodies, the skin on their faces was green with silver running through it.

The odd men had a very slight fish-like look about them. Window knew immediately that he was in for another very interesting afternoon in the unknown East.

Window took a deep breath, and walked on up to the group of men, as he thought of what to say to them. Of course, he didn't know if Raine's gift of language would work with these strange sea-men. As he grew close, he spoke to greet the curious creatures. *"Hello, men of the Middle Sea. I have come from a land far away. May I join you for a while?"* At least that is what he said in his mind. What came out of his mouth was *"Pol-sae sentae-aer fal. Rae-tu-re an-satel. Trie-sal-enti-sen."* Window was surprised to hear his own voice speaking the odd, smoothly flowing, melodic language of the sea-people.

The seven green-skinned men calmly turned to look at Window and slightly nodded their heads in his direction.

"Pol-sae tu-enmasue sae," one of the beings answered. As he spoke, his mouth moved more than a man's would, creating words

that hinted at being sung, rather than spoken. *"Tir-re-es son-tee-sem-lae sil. Or an naf-re-en Laycel-lia ree-sen dre-ae."*

For a moment, Window thought that the man was speaking in Atlandan, because in Window's mind he heard the creature's reply clearly as, *"You are welcome to join us. We have been waiting for you. Our friends, the birds, have told us of your journey to these Laycellian lands."*

So, the sea-people greeted Window cordially, and invited him to join them at their campfire that was a bit farther up the shore. They also called to Circles to come along, as well. Apparently, they had been aware of the two travelers since the day before, when an up-lands sea-bird had reported that strangers were approaching.

Circles reluctantly came from his hiding place in the bushes and joined the others. At first, he was concerned about being near the tall fish-looking men, but felt more comfortable after Window explained to Circles that the strange men could talk to birds, too. One of the men was fascinated by Circles' fur and politely rubbed his scaly-looking fingers through the bright, white fluff on Circles' head. Circles laughed at that, and rubbed his hand on the tall creature's knee in reply. Gel-Rin was the creature's name. He and Circles walked together to the men's camp.

"How did you learn to talk to birds?" Circles asked his new companion – but the creature couldn't understand the question. Circles spoke in every language he knew, but Gel-Rin could not comprehend the Woot. Circles would have to rely on Window to translate the conversations with these beings.

As they followed the men to their camp, it was clear that there would be no bed for Window to sleep in tonight, and no lemon-tea for Circles. These sea-creatures had no boats or buildings, only a single large room facing the sea, dug into the side of a hill, and reinforced with heavy tree limbs and large sea-stones. It was apparently a temporary shelter from the sun and the wind. Window felt that these creatures probably didn't need any protection from the rain.

As the group neared their shelter, seven sea-females stood from their seats by a small fire and welcomed the visitors silently. The women were smaller than the men and had slightly lighter skin. Some were thinly clad while others wore nothing at all. Their slippery looking skin and sleek bodies gave the impression of an ability to swim without effort.

Unlike the men, the women's hair was long and flowing, reaching to the middle of their backs and beyond, and an even lighter green than their bodies. They had apparently been working on treating some kind of animal skins, which were hanging from cords strung between several trees.

Window and Circles were led to a shaded area in front of the under-hill shelter-house. There they were invited to sit on one of the giant turtle shells placed around the fire. When everyone was seated, the strange men told Window the story of their lives near the sea. Most of their story was told by Lay-Ran, who seemed to be their leader.

They were called the Sea-True, and this was the southern end of their lands, Laycellia. The Sea-True loved swimming and fishing and exploring the shore-edge caves and inlets of the Middle Sea. They lived a simple life and didn't care much about houses or buildings or even boats. They were friends with many of the sea-creatures and sometimes rode on the sea-lizards and huge water-horses.

More of their kind lived in villages along the eastern edge of the Laycellian Sea – not the "Middle Sea", as Flitter had called it. Sea-True were men, but not men like Window and those who lived in the south and east.

"Do you mean that there <u>are</u> other men who live here in the east – and are there roads and cities and ships?" Window asked excitedly.

"We live at the edge of the Very East," explained Lay-Ran. We are the last of the ancient peoples here. *"There are many lands and many men, such as yourself, across the Eastern Plains and the Eastern Kingdoms, between here and the ocean."*

Occasionally we encounter men from the east, or the south, but we prefer to stay to ourselves.

"Hey, Circles," Window relayed to his friend, "I know where the ocean is."

"Where's that, Window?" Circles wanted to know.

"Far to the east."

"You are a smart man," Circles kidded him. "Did they also tell you where the sun and moon can be found? And while you are at it, ask them about the Silkie. I'd like to hear that answer."

"Have you ever met any men from the west before?" Window asked Lay-Ran.

"Many years ago, we were sometimes visited by a man who would occasionally come through Laycellia as he traveled to the east and then returned to the lands of the far-away west. It was him who told us about the Woots and other ancient Talkers in the far western world. That is why we were not surprised by your friend, Circles."

The talk of the traveler who visited the west caused thoughts of the traveler who visited his uncle at the Summer Breeze to jump into Window's head. He pulled the medallion from his pocket and showed it to the sea-creatures.

As he had done so many times, Window asked, *"Have you ever seen this before?"* To his wild surprise, he got an answer he absolutely did not expect.

"The design on the metal looks very much like one that belonged to the man from the west we just spoke of." Then Lay-Ran asked an extremely exciting question. *"Would you like to see it?"*

"See it? Is it here? Yes, I would like to see it!" Window answered almost breathlessly. He could hardly believe the Sea-True's offer. "Circles, they have something for us to see — something like the medallion!"

Window and Circles jumped to their feet and followed Lay-Ran and two other men for several minutes up a narrow dirt path to the entrance of another hill-side cave. This cave appeared to be naturally formed but had a small wooden door. Two of the Sea-

Trues went inside, and in a couple of minutes, emerged carrying a long, and very old looking, wooden box.

The box was placed on the grass and Lay-Ran slowly pulled its aged wooden top aside. The two travelers leaned over the edge of the container and peered inside.

"Window! Look at that! Who could it be?" Circles asked as their eyes fell upon a human skeleton – a skeleton still wearing ragged, rotted remains of clothes. The former owner's body had deteriorated completely to dust, but his bones and some of his clothing remained.

The white of the bones contrasted with the faded, crumbling cloth that was, a long time ago, what appeared to be a soldier's uniform. Around the midsection of the skeleton was a leather belt to which was attached the bottom part of a leather shoulder sash. In the coffin, next to the bones, there was a thin, sparkling, jewel-handled battle-sword and a metal hand-shield bearing the red outline of a heart above two horizontal bars. Lay-Ran invited Window to examine the remains.

The remaining cloth of the soldier's uniform crumbled to Window's touch but the leather of the sash was still in useable condition. Attached by rivets to the sash, was a rusted, metal insignia. It appeared to be a military medallion – a lot like Window's medallion! The three slanted blue bars were there but they were different lengths and there was not the star in the center. It was so close – it was almost the same design as the medallion!

Window reached into the coffin and unhooked the sash from the soldier's belt. He pulled the sash from around the skeleton and lifted it and closely examined the medallion. Then as Window turned the sash over to look at its backside, he received a shock so surprising that it took his breath away. Written in faded, but still readable, Atlandan letters on the back of the sash was the name of the long dead soldier – J. Revell!

The skeleton was the remains of John Revell! – the long-lost member of Grandpa's expedition – Oldsmith's partner who returned with him to the Northlands to search for the Battleplain coins and the mines in the east! It was Revell, who had disappeared in the Northlands years and years before! Somehow, Revell had found his way to the edge of the Very East – and died in Laycellia – so many, many miles and years from his home.

But the surprises were not over for Window and Circles. When Window pulled the belt from around Revell's skeleton and examined the back of it as well, he received another completely shocking surprise. As on the sash, on the back of Revell's belt was written the name of its former owner – not Revell, but W. Windowen! – Window's grandfather!

Revell must have borrowed Grandpa Windowen's belt while on the original expedition and never returned it. It was fantastic – Window found his grandfather's belt, fifty years later and halfway across the world in the land of the sea-people! Even his Uncle Breeze would have a difficult time believing this story!

Along with Revell's bones and weapons, Window found a few other things in the coffin – six silver, Freeland, crossed-swords coins, and two Freeland, silver lance coins, – they could have been from the Battleplain treasure box, Window thought.

And, still attached to Revell's boots were rusted riding spurs. Apparently, Revell was a horseman in his new life in the east.

Then Window made one other discovery. He noticed, in a corner of the coffin, mixed with the dark, dusty remains of Revell's body, the glint of a small amount of silver dust. Window couldn't be sure, but wondered if it might be trillion. Could it be that Revell had found the Battleplain coins – and a trillion mine as well? What else could this man have found in his search for treasure?

Window and Circles spent many minutes examining the objects. When Lay-Ran learned that Window knew the name of the man in the coffin, he invited Window to take Revell's sword and shield, and the belt and coins as well. Window graciously accepted.

He held the sword up in the sunlight. It was beautiful – sleek, and flashing with reflected light. The bright, many-colored, sparkling stones on its handle appeared to be very valuable. Window wondered where Revell had obtained such a small treasure.

The shield was also beautifully crafted and its colors were in perfect condition. The red heart and bars were bright against a solid white background. Circles wore the weapons as they all returned to the Sea-True camp.

At the camp, Lay-Ran invited the travelers to stay for supper and for the night. The Lacellian women had caught fish in a net down at the water's edge and several of the men were roasting the fish on sticks turning over the fire.

That evening's conversations around the fire of the Sea-True lasted long into the night. Circles sat with Gel-Rin, who was happy to keep him company as Window spoke with the others. Lay-Ran told Window the story of how the horseman's remains came to be in the Sea-True's cemetery-cave.

Over many years, Revell had made enemies of the horsemen of the eastern plains, but Lay-Ran didn't know how. Twice before, Revell had been chased by the horsemen as far as the Sea. When last he came to the Sea-True, he had been injured by arrows and did not recover from his wounds. When he died, he was placed in the burial cave as he had requested of them.

So, that was it. Revell's search for riches had taken him to the far eastern plains. Oldsmith's partner had traveled beyond the Northlands mines and the Ancient Lands to the edge of the Very East. Window had discovered at least a part of the secret life of John Revell.

The Sea-True leader spoke of the many kingdoms of men to the south and east of Laycellia. He thought that Revell's sword and shield must be from one of them.

Window dug through his pack and retrieved the shining, silver-blue key Revell had given to Oldsmith, in Calisay, more than forty years before.

"I have a key from Revell," Window explained to the Sea-True, as he held it up in the firelight. The mysterious key flashed its silver-blue reflection across the Laycellian clearing.

"Years ago, while he was being chased, Revell asked his friend, Oldsmith, to keep it safe. It must be the key to something very valuable for someone to chase Revell all the way to the Northlands.”

As Window held up Revell's key, Circles could see the heart shape of its handle-end. His thoughts connected the heart on the key to the heart on Revell's shield. Immediately, he knew what he wanted to do.
"Let's go find Revell's treasures, Window – and the rest of the Freeland coins, too. Your grandfather is counting on you. And maybe Revell hid his treasures by the Angels somewhere."

Window smiled at Circles. He loved his happy little friend. He restated Circles' wishes as a question to which he already knew the answer.

"Shall we go south, and on to the far kingdoms of the Very East? Shall we go find the ocean – and Revell's treasures – <u>and</u> the Angels?
The little Woot replied, with love in <u>his</u> heart as well. "I will go anywhere with you, Window."
"We will leave in the morning."

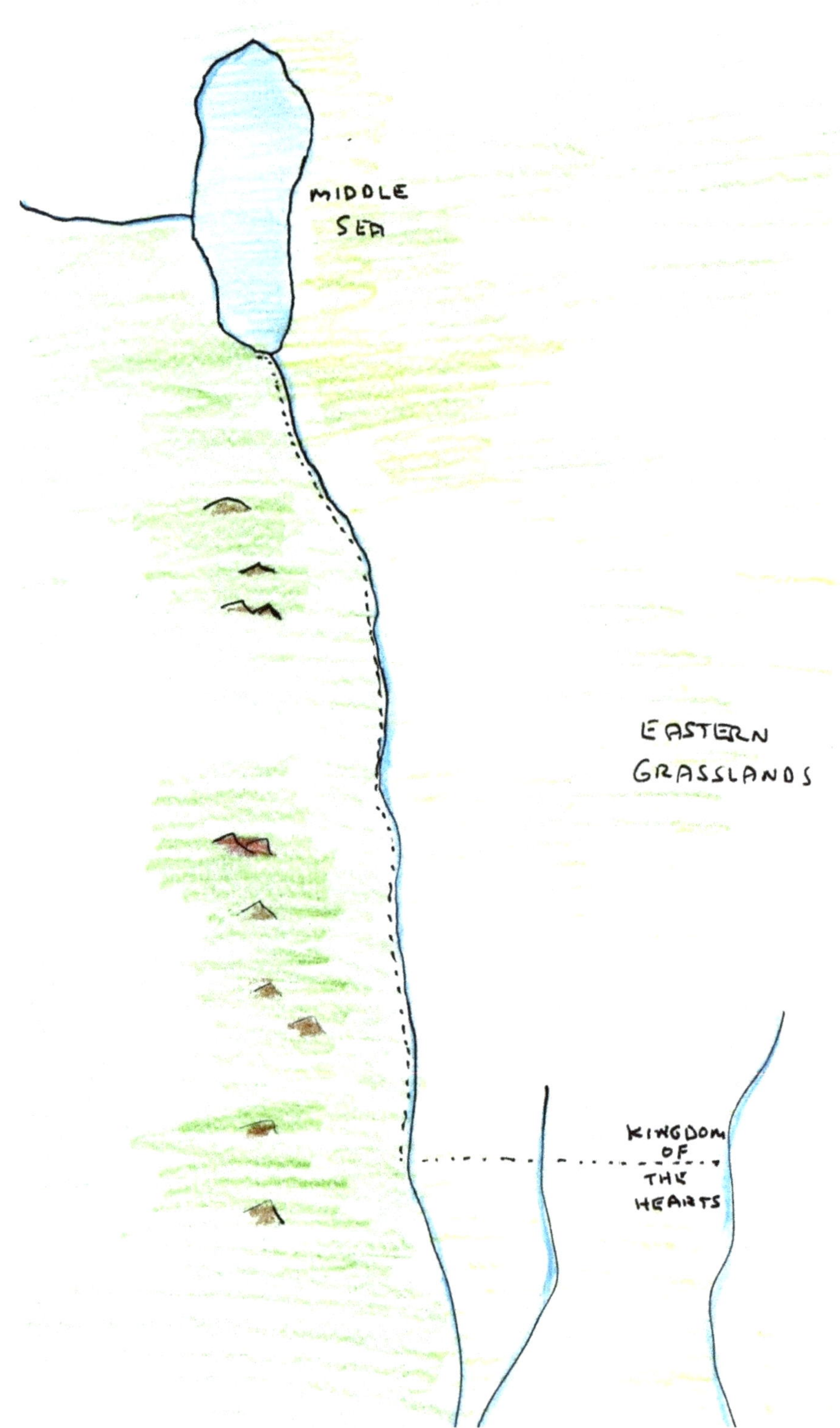

MIDDLE
SEA
EASTERN
GRASSLANDS
KINGDOM
OF
THE
HEARTS

CHAPTER TWENTY-TWO

TO THE GRASSLANDS KINGDOM

The sun was breaking over the trees on the Laycellian eastern horizon just as Circles opened his eyes. Woots don't usually dream, but last night Circles had spent most of his sleeping time finding treasures and Angels and oceans.

"Wake up, Window. We have a long way to go," he reminded his friend.

Window rolled over and looked around. Several of the Sea-True were already at their fire, turning a large, flat dal-fish slowly over the flames.

Gel-Rin came over to the travelers and spoke to Circles as he handed him some very thick and soft-looking pad-leaves. Circles thanked him and took a bite. They were delicious. Soon everyone was enjoying breakfast as Window and Lay-Ran talked a bit more.

"Ask him about the birds, Window," Circles spoke between bites. "Ask him about how they talk to the birds."

In a minute, Window relayed the answer from Lay-Ran. The Sea-True did not actually talk to the birds, but the Sea-True females had learned to listen to them very carefully and could understand the chatter of several different types – and the birds were always chattering. Circles was kind of glad to hear that Sea-True could not actually talk to birds. That was still his specialty.

As Window spoke with Lay-Ran, Circles looked out toward the seashore and the water beyond. To his surprise, he watched as two of the Sea-True men walked out of the water – not swam and then stood up when nearing the shore – but walked, upright, from under the waves and up onto the grass.

"It seems that these sea-people have talents they forgot to tell us about," Circles thought to himself. "I wonder what else they didn't mention."

Lay-Ran had given instructions to Window on traveling to the eastern lands of men. Directly to the east of Laycellia were the open lands that were home to the many tribes of plains horsemen. The horsemen lived in camps and villages cut into the edge of the lonely prairie forests and on the shores of the rivers that wound through the open grasslands. The plains riders rode to their far borders capturing wild horses and protecting their claim to their lands that stretched across far to the east. It was men from one of these tribes that had killed Revell. Lay-Ran counseled Window to keep from any encounters with the plains horsemen.

Farther to the south and east of Laycellia were the many eastern kingdoms of men. If Window and Circles were to reach the ocean, they would have to go in that direction. How far it might be, he did not know.

The first part of their journey, however, would be very easy. The Sea-True would build the travelers a raft to take them down the river that flowed to the south from the Laycellian Sea. The river should carry them far beyond the plains of the horsemen. From there, the two explorers would need to discover the way to the ocean.

Although Window and Circles still had some of their food remaining, the Sea-True females had prepared the travelers a container, made from giant sea-leaves, which held dried fish, and water-vegetables that grew nearby in the wet low-lands.

One female, whose name was Re-Enne, was particularly fascinated with Circles after the Woot had thanked her for her kindness in sea-dove chatter. As Re-Enne stood and spoke to Circles, Window realized how sleek and attractive she was, in her fish-woman sort of way. Her long arms were held easily at her sides, as her tall, slick, gently curved body flashed green in the morning sun. Her large, bright eyes looked at Circles with wonder and kindness.

The Sea-True had been so friendly to the travelers that, for a moment, Window thought perhaps these sea-people really <u>were</u> Angels from under the water. He hoped he and Circles would be able to stop and see them again on their way back to the west.

The river to the south was several miles farther along the coast from the Sea-True camp. It poured from a wide, low mouth on the south-eastern edge of the Laycellian Sea and flowed south, along the western edge of the plains.

Lay-Ran had gone on ahead with some of the men to build the raft for the travelers. As the rest of the group followed later, Gel-Rin walked with Circles and Re-Enne walked with Window.

"Go ahead, Window. Go ahead," Circles, prompted his friend.

"I will, Circles. I will," came the reply.

The woman looked curiously at Window as he asked, *"Re-Enne, do you know where the Angels live?"*

"I dream of the Angels, sometimes, Window, but I have never seen one. Our stories tell of Angels by the grand-sea – the ocean. I hope you can find the ocean, and the Angels."

"If we do, I will try to come back and tell you about them."

"I would like that, Window. I would like that."

The mid-day sun was high overhead as the travelers reached the river landing. There they found another hill-side shelter and a small wooden dock which suggested that the sea-people also spent time on the river. Window saw no boats near the dock.

As promised, the Sea-True had built Window and Circles a raft made from bundles of river reeds and covered it with a layer of thin willow branches. On the back edge of the raft, there was a simple, steering rudder that would allow the rafters to guide their craft to the shore when desired. The raft was large enough to easily hold the travelers and their packs and their weapons and two rafting-poles on their journey to the south. Their belongings were loaded on board as the two explorers said their goodbyes. Circles gave Gel-Rin and Re-Enne a hug, and Window clasped hands with Lay-Ran.

The other Sea-True stood on the shore under the shade of some tall oaks as Gel-Rin and Re-Enne pushed the raft away from the river dock. Both of the sea-people had quickly come to care for the two strangers from the west. Re-Enne called one final wish to the raft as it quickly moved away from shore.

"Re-sae-tu cel-tae-in, cu-an-ge faesa," Circles heard Re-Enne's melodic voice call to them. But what Window heard was *"Travel safely to the unknown lands of the Angels."*

Circles called back a sea-dove goodbye, *"Ca-tay, Ca-tay,"* but he was already too far away from the dock to be heard. In just another minute the current had drawn the travelers out to the middle of the wide river. They turned and waved one last time as the sea-people faded from view.

++++++++

It was a beautiful early-autumn day for a trip down the river. A clear sky was overhead as the raft sped past the trees on their right and the grassland plains on their left.

Circles had never been on any kind of boat before – and he loved it – the breeze in his face and the lands floating by. He lay down and rested his head back against his pack and relaxed as the river narrowed and the raft drifted even more quickly along the plains of the east.

But as nice as the day was, Circles missed the Sea-True and began to feel lonely. He just stared blankly at the shoreline for several minutes as they sped past.

"I wish Flitter was here," he said at last.

"Maybe you could find another bird to talk to, Circles. One that knows this river."

"I'll try, Window. I'll try to do that."

But, in this lonely part of the world, very few birds flew overhead, and any that did were too high above for Circles to call to them. He decided to search the lands with his far-scope, but found nothing but empty grasslands as far as his scope could see.

Then, as the river started to widen a bit again, ahead to their left he saw something more interesting than birds.

A group of five horsemen were in the grasslands perhaps a half mile from the river.

"Look, Window," Circles pointed towards the riders, who had noticed the raft and halted their horses.

Through his scope, Circles could clearly see a bow and quiver of arrows attached to one of the riders and the long strips of colored cloth that hung from the ends of the spears the others carried. The river travelers and the plains riders curiously watched each other as the raft drifted by.

"I would like to ride a horse someday," Circles shared with Window. But then, remembering Lay-Ran's story of Revell, quickly added, "But not one of those horses."

The river swiftly took the travelers beyond the horsemen and on farther to the south.

After several more hours, the forests on their right faded completely and soon the river was in a land of tall grass and only some occasional small trees. There were some low hills to the west, but to the east the grasslands still stretched as far as they could see.

Circles was thinking out loud. "Wow, I hope we don't have to walk all this way back home, Window. That would take us a long, long time." Then Circles had another thought. "Maybe the Angels would take us home."

"I hope so, Circles. That would be a very Angel-like thing to do."

Window gazed out across the edge of the eastern plains as they hurried by on their way to the south. He thought to himself, "Yeah, I hope that, too, Circles. We are a long, long way from home."

"Hey, look, Window," Circles spoke up several minutes later. "The river is gone!"

Window peered down the river, but about a quarter of a mile ahead of them it disappeared from view. They could follow the water just that far before all they could see, where they should see the river, was the blue of the sky.

"Circles, there must be steep rapids or a waterfall ahead! Quick, hook your arms tightly through your bow and quiver, and hang on!" called Window, as he frantically unhooked their pack straps and looped them under the thick willow branches in the floor of the raft. "If we go over steep falls, we could lose everything! Hurry!"

Window pulled Revell's shield and sword and the two rafting poles under him, and grabbed on as tightly as he could to the raft. In just another minute the two travelers were swept over the crest of the falls! – except they weren't really falls – or rapids. It was just a gentle drop in the river as they went over the edge of a hilltop. They found themselves at the top of a massive hillside. It was the start of the longest riverslide they could imagine. Far below them, they could see the river as it once again became level and continued on through flat grasslands.

The ground, and the river, dropped before them as the raft started down the side of a hill that must have gone straight, steadily, and gently downward without turn or change for at least a mile. It was a very fast ride, but a very smooth one. The travelers loosened their grips on the raft and enjoyed their delightful ride down the hillside. The wind slammed against their faces as the raft picked up more and more speed. On the riverbank, the grass and bushes raced past them in almost a blur.

"This is better than any snow slide," Circles called out laughingly to Window. The Woot held his face straight ahead, as the buffeting air flapped and fluttered his fur wildly. Window, too, was really enjoying the ride.

Then, about halfway down the sliding river, Circles yelled to his friend again, "Look, Window, Tanibears! Tanibears!"

And there they were – three small, light brown bears sitting, side by side, in a row about half way up the edge of the flat hillside that slanted down to the edge of the falling river. The bears seemed to be just sitting and watching as the raft raced by. Window couldn't believe it, but it had to be them! Window had sung the Tanibears song when he was a boy. Circles knew it, too.

"I didn't know they were real, Window." Circles called to him. "There are no Tanibears in the Deep Woods. I didn't know they were real!"

Then, at almost the same time, the two swift-rafters started to sing.

> "Two little Tanibears, sitting on the hillside
> Watching the world go by
> One says 'Go,' but the other says 'No'
> So they sit and they watch all night
>
> Three little Tanibears, sitting on the hillside
> Watching the world go by
> Two say 'Go,' but the other says 'No'
> So they sit and they watch all night
>
> Four little Tanibears, sitting..."

By the time the singers reached the sixth Tanibear, they had tired of the rhyme. "Ya know, Window, now that I think about it, the Tanibear song isn't really very good. I'll bet that no Woot made it up. Woots would have written a better rhyme than that."

Window just smiled at his friend. The raft splashed down into the wide river at the bottom of the tall, tall hill. Their exciting ride down the riverslide was over.

Below the riverslide, the river became wide and slower again. They floated on for another half hour or so, and then Window steered the raft to the shore where the travelers would camp for the night. They were so tired that they didn't even try to build a fire. They just flopped down on Window's blanket and closed their eyes. Both travelers slept soundly on their first night on their way to the distant south.

The next day on the river was rather uneventful. The west bank again held light forests and hills although the grasslands remained unchanged to the east. The main excitement of the day was that Circles was able to call a large plains-dove down to talk to him. The bird was white with two red bars on his wings. The red bars reminded Circles of the red bars on Revell's shield and so Circles thought that the dove should be able to tell him where the kingdom of the heart-shield was located.

The bird chattered with Circles for a long time as the raft continued on its way down the river. Unfortunately, the dove, whose name was Sky-swift, didn't recognize the heart design, but told Circles that he met new birds every day, some that had flown for many miles across the plains, and that he would ask every one he met if they knew of the heart kingdom. Sky-swift did know that directly to the east of where they were now, there were only tribes of horsemen, and no kingdoms large enough to have cities of men.

Circles was thrilled to have at last found a "smart bird" as he called the dove. The bird perched on Circles' pack, next to where the Woot was sitting, and joined the travelers on their way down the river. Circles and the bird talked of the river and the plains for a long time. Sky-swift even claimed to have once talked to a highlands hawk that been all the way to the far westlands. Of course, Sky-swift couldn't say how far the far westlands were.

Circles shared some of his berries with the dove as they floated along. When Sky-swift left the travelers, he promised to return to them again sometime, but he couldn't be sure when that might be.

The ride down the river to the south continued to go smoothly. As the sun started to sink below the western hills, the travelers stopped to camp for the night. They had found a forested area along the river and so there was plenty of wood for a fire. After a meal of water-vegetables and dried fish, the ocean-hunters rested as the campfire flames jumped high in the night.

The moon was out and so, as he liked to do, Window took Charm from his pocket to join them at the fire for the evening. As it turned out, this evening around the fire was to be very special indeed.

As he sat by the fire, Window listened to the comforting sound of the breeze through the leaves. He looked up at the willow trees above and behind him and watched their small branches twisting and turning as the early autumn leaves rustled in the night air. It was a very pleasant sound that changed as the wind changed.

"Let's play Rainbow Chips," Circles suggested. Charm jumped up and down, agreeing to play Circles in the first game.

Window watched on as the other two matched red chips and captured green chips and doubled orange chips until, with a very lucky move, Charm tripled his blues, winning the game.

Charm was so happy that he flew over to tease Circles and went under the fur on Circles' neck. Then the sparkling-light quickly buzzed back and forth as fast as he could, which tickled Circles. Circles started laughing and running around as he tried to get Charm out of his fur. Window noticed that, as Circles was laughing and shaking, the wind through the trees was shaking their leaves, too, causing the leaves to seem to laugh along with Circles.

Finally, Charm flew out from Circles' fur and returned to his spot on a log. Circles came and sat down next to Window, as Window still listened to the wind in the trees. The briskly moving night air filled the campsite with the sound of rustling leaves and quietly whooshing wind.

"Isn't it funny, Circles? How it sometimes sounds like the leaves are talking to us?"

Another slight breeze blew through the trees above them.

"But, Window," an astonished Circles replied. "The leaves _are_ talking to us! Listen!"

Window closed his eyes to concentrate better on the sound of the wind in the trees. Suddenly, he heard it, too. It _did_ sound like someone, or something, was speaking to them from the willow trees overhead and behind them to the west. The sounds of the leaves blowing in the wind were like words.

"Do you hear that, Window?" Circles excitedly asked. "Did you hear that?"

Then the evening breeze blew once more from off the river and through the campsite and into the trees. The leaves on the trees danced and rippled again in the moving air.

As Window and Circles listened to the leaves, the voice from the trees spoke again, but this time the travelers could understand it more clearly – and the voice was speaking to them!

"Greetings, Resting Travelers. May I join you for a while?"

On the log next to Window, Charm flashed wildly in the moonlight. He had heard the voice, too.

It was an odd, dancing voice, mixed with the ordinary sound of the leaves being rustled by the wind. But, there was no doubt – the leaves were speaking to them! The willow leaves were fluttering and moving in the breeze and blowing against each other. The sound of the leaves hitting and rubbing against each other formed the words Window heard.

As the ocean-hunters sat in stunned silence, the rustling leaves spoke again. *"I, too, am a traveler. I have been all around the world many, many times. I used to have friends among the winds, but now I am all alone – and I am lonely. Will you talk with me for a while?"*

"Are you an Angel?" Circles immediately asked of the mysterious voice from the trees.

The evening breeze again blew through the leaves. *"I am the last of the talking winds. The others are all gone. Since the world was young, the talking winds have gotten separated and scattered by sun and storms and age, and have lost their strength. Now, the winds sometimes listen, but they keep their thoughts to themselves. And, although I am very old, I am the youngest of all the winds. I can still talk – but there are no other winds to talk to."*

"Are you sure that you are not an Angel?" Circles again questioned the voice.

"No, I am not an Angel," replied the voice in the leaves. *"I am just a traveler, such as you."*

"You should travel through the Deep Woods sometimes," Circles suggested. "That is where I am from."

"I have been there once, a long time ago. Is it still a beautiful place?" the friendly wind wanted to know.

"Sometimes it is – but only sometimes," replied Circles, not caring to go into any detail about the monsters.

Looking up at the fluttering leaves, Circles continued, "Window is from the Windlands. I'll bet you have been there before."

"I was there long before the Windlands got its name."

"Wow! How old are you?" Circles went on with his questioning. Window sat quietly, holding Charm in his hand, listening in wonder to the Woot and the voice of the leaves.

"I am from before the Ice Age."

"The Ice Age that is coming from Polartica?"

"The first Ice Age – the world has changed many times since its beginning."

"Do you know where the Angels live," asked Circles, hoping for help in their search.

"No. I haven't seen Angels in a long, long time."

"But, did you really see Angels a long time ago?"

"Well, I think they were Angels – but, I cannot be sure."

Circles was disappointed by that answer. He thought a moment, then, continued his questioning. "And where do you go each day?"

"I travel where I like, or where the gentle winds take me. Sometimes I travel to the far-away lands or join with the clouds as they fly over the seas – but I have to stay away from storms. If I get caught in a big storm, I could be scattered and blown away and be lost forever."

"Would you like to travel with us for a while?" Circles offered. "Maybe you could help us find a treasure we are looking for."

"I will try to visit with you again, but beyond that, I can not be certain. Now I am only a small wind, and when other winds are nearby they sometimes blow me far away from where I wish to go."

Then the voice of the wind somehow sounded sad. *"And because of that, I regret that I must leave you after just this short visit. Another wind is coming here from across the plains – but I thank you for your kind company."*

"And be mindful of a breeze passing through the trees, or a whirlwind of dust on the ground, or the quiet song of a wind-chime. It could be me coming to visit again."

"I hope we see you soon," replied Circles, disappointed at the shortness of their conversation.

"I would like that, Kind Travelers. I will look for you, and visit when I am able."

In the trees around the camp, the branches shook and the leaves rustled one last time – and then the extraordinary wind was gone. Suddenly, the campsite became very still, and the leaves were quiet. Only the soft crackling of the fire spoke to them.

In a few minutes the leaves started to talk again – but not with words. The leaves spoke to the travelers only as they usually did – with a gentle, comforting rustling as the breeze from across the grasslands passed by. Window had always loved the gentle sound of the wind in the trees – but from now on, he would love it much more than ever!
Circles turned to Window, but still stunned by their visitor, didn't know what to say.
Window simply rubbed his hand through the fluffy fur on Circles' head. Window didn't know what to say either. Then, after another few minutes of listening to the breeze together, Window returned Charm to his pocket and simply said, "Good night, Circles."
They had been on so many fantastic adventures together they really didn't need to say too much with words. Circles just gave Window a knowing look, and a quick, "Good night to you, too, Dear Friend."
They both fell asleep that night with the song of the wind in their heads.

++++++++

The early morning brought the travelers another day on their journey to the south. The river, which had been so straight for most of the way, started to have wide twists and turns, which made their trip a bit more interesting. The grasslands remained to their east, and they saw no sights of people or villages. That soon changed.

As the raft continued to drift through the flat, grassy lowlands, they came around a wide turn and were surprised to see another group of horsemen along the eastern riverbank. These were not, wild, roughly clad horsemen on swift plains horses, like those they had passed farther to the north. These were horse soldiers in light armor and matching cloaks, riding large horses and carrying tall spears upright at their sides. They reminded Window of the soldiers of the noblehouses near Calisay.

"Well, Circles. We have found men from the South," Window announced to his friend. "I guess it is time to meet them."

"Yeah, I guess," came the reply. There was a sound of uncertainty in Circles' voice.

Window steered the raft over to the eastern shore. It was an area of thin grass and dusty ground that came right down to the water's edge. Circles helped Window pull the raft onto the low riverbank as the horsemen sat silently on their horses and watched, from several hundred feet away.

All but one of the horsemen held a long metal spear in one hand and rested its butt end on the ground next to them. These riders also had a shield and a bow that hung from the side of their saddle. They didn't seem to be aggressive, but they also were not happily greeting the new visitors to their lands.

Window pulled Revell's shield from under his pack and hooked his grandfather's belt holding Revell's sword around his waist. Circles held his bow, but did not notch an arrow.

"Well, let's go," Window quietly spoke to Circles. They shared a quick glance at each other and started up the short incline to the flatlands of the plains. Window was again counting on Raine's gift of language to allow him to speak to the men.

There were eight horsemen – seven were wearing dull, dirty-grey tunics and riding dull, dirty-brown horses. The eighth rider, who was smaller than the others, was atop a silky black stallion. This rider wore a bright, white tunic, covered with subtle silver designs, and black leggings – but held no weapon.

The riders sat motionless in their saddles as the travelers approached them. Window's boots kicked up dust from the bare spots between the patches of plains grass as he and Circles grew closer.

"Window, look!" Circles quietly spoke in surprise. Window immediately understood the reason for Circles' words.

The rider wearing the white tunic was a woman! – a young-looking woman! Her golden-brown hair was tied back with a bright red scarf, and she wore a sparkling jeweled headband across her forehead. Each of her wrists was adorned with a jeweled bracelet and a piece of short, flowing, sparkling cloth that followed her hands as she moved her arms.

The woman called out to the others, *"Horsemen, prepare your weapons!"* She was only a girl, maybe sixteen, or so, and she was in command of the horsemen!

"As you wish, Captain," answered the other riders in unison. They raised their spears and pointed them toward the approaching travelers.

There was nothing else for Window and Circles to do except to continue toward the soldiers. Circles almost reached for an arrow, but changed his mind. Window kept his right hand away from his sword but still carried Revell's shield on his left arm. Circles took another trusting look at Window. There was no turning back.

Then, as they got still closer, Window noticed it. Almost hidden among the swirling silver designs on the girl's tunic was a smaller design – on the left side of her tunic, over her chest. It was the outline of a bright red heart – with a single red bar beneath it!

Window and Circles walked bravely right to the group of spear-wielding soldiers and stopped before them. They, of course, didn't know what to expect from the riders, but they never could have guessed what did happen next.

The young commander of the riders rode forward of the others and confronted the ocean-hunters. The girl – the Captain of the Horsemen Guard – looked down from her horse at the two travelers and spoke demandingly to Window. *"Where did you get my grandfather's shield?"*

Window was shocked. Revell's shield came from the family of this young girl Captain. He must have stolen it. What other explanation could there be? But, how would she know it was the shield of her grandfather?

The young Captain of the horsemen didn't wait for an answer to her question. She immediately called out in strong military fashion, *"Guards – bind them and take their weapons!"*

"They are going to take us as prisoners," Window softly spoke to Circles. They each took a few steps backward as the horsemen, with their spears pointing directly at the travelers, moved their horses toward them.

But then, Window noticed something beyond the half circle of approaching horsemen. Off a few hundred feet in the dusty plain behind the riders something was swiftly moving. None of the riders were aware of it, but a whirlwind of grasslands dust was swirling directly towards them. Circles noticed it, too. It quickly grew in size and picked up speed. It was about twice as tall as the men and their horses, and would engulf them in just a few more seconds.

"Hey, Window," Circles calmly observed. "Looks like our leaf-talking friend is back for another visit."

Window couldn't keep a big smile from jumping to his face. Something very windy was about to happen.

And, several things <u>did</u> happen, almost at once. First, Window's arms were thrown up over his head as though he had intentionally raised them. At the same time, there was a tremendous explosion of noise like the sound of a cannon being fired. Next, seven horsemen of the Guard were picked up from their horses and thrown to the ground, landing on their backs in the grass and dust. As the horsemen hit the ground, their spears came flying down from the sky, sticking into the dirt very close to their shaken bodies. The spear shafts vibrated in the air, as the soldiers struggled to regain their breathing.

And in that same instant, the two travelers from the west gained the awe and unchallenged regard of the young Captain of the Horsemen. The soldiers under her command had been defeated by a single man – who carried an unknown power in his hands. She had studied military matters for more than a year, but nothing like this had been covered in her practice and preparation. The girl bravely dismounted from her horse and approached the two mysterious strangers.

Shaking as she spoke, she lowered her head in a sign of respect. *"I apologize for my rudeness, Welcome Travelers. Please forgive me."*

Circles couldn't understand the girl's words, but he understood their meaning. He bowed to her and replied, "I am happy to meet you, also."

The young commander of the horsemen looked to Window, waiting for his response. He could sense the uncertainty in her voice and in her eyes. Window politely addressed the girl, in a language she understood, *"My name is Window, and this is my friend, Circles."*

Her response was clear and strong. *"I am Anna Bliss, Princess of the Hearts."*

++++++++

The journey to the castle of the Hearts would take two and a half days on horseback. They would ride directly across the grasslands to the east, ford the River Resayan above the falls, and then ride on to the Kingdom Village beyond. Window and Circles had accepted Princess Anna's invitation to come with her back to the Heart castle before they continued on their way to the ocean.

Anna had taken a quick liking of the little Woot, whom she called Cirsay, which was the Heartan word for Prince. Circles rode with her, seated before her in her saddle, atop the beautiful stallion, Mystic. Circles told her that it was almost as much fun as riding a Silkie, but she didn't understand.

There <u>was</u> no actual Prince of the Hearts. There was also no King. Anna was the only child of Queen Karinne, who ruled the grasslands kingdom. Anna's father had been killed in battle a few years before, by raiders from one of the Northern Plains tribes.

But, the amazing John Revell actually <u>was</u> Princess Anna's grandfather. Anna told Window the story as he rode next to her on the Guard supply-horse across the wide grasslands on their way to the castle.

This is how it happened.

Many years before, Revell had traveled well beyond the Northlands mines to the far eastern plains searching for riches. One day, he came upon the aftermath of a fierce battle between the soldiers of Heart and the horsemen of Treelinay, a vast, wild area to the north of the Heart plains

Revell searched through the scattered weapons and the bodies of the dead, looking for anything of value. In the midst of the field of death, he saw the bright colored glint of metal or jewels coming from across the battlefield. He hoped that it would be something of value he could recover. It turned out to be the most valuable thing on the entire eastern plains. It was the seriously injured King of the Hearts.

Revell, seeing a chance for great riches, saved the king from death and eventually returned him to the Heart castle, farther to the south. There, Revell was treated as a hero, and given a house and cattle as a reward. But, a house and cattle was not enough for the treasure-hungry Revell. He continued to be celebrated by the small royal family and eventually he persuaded the King's only child, a daughter, to marry him.

Revell, and his wife, who soon became the young Queen, Kestelle, also had a daughter, Karinne, who would later become Queen. But, Revell was not satisfied even to be married to the Queen, or to have a future Queen as a daughter.   He would often leave the Kingdom for months at a time, riding the fastest and strongest horse the Captain of the Guard could provide. He would return, weeks or months later, with a few coins or jewels or other small treasures – and sometimes with injuries.

Then once, after he left the Kingdom, the months and then years went by without his return. His wife and daughter grew to live without him. Upon the death of Revell's wife, their daughter, Karinne, became queen. Queen Karinne also married a commoner, the Horsemen Officer Bliss. Now, Revell's granddaughter, Anna Bliss, was the heir to the throne of the Hearts.

John Revell was eventually thought of less and less often in the Kingdom, until eventually, he was mostly forgotten by the Hearts – except for his daughter and granddaughter.

In the Kingdom of the Hearts, the Kings and Queens wore a red heart as their royal symbol, while Royal Children wore a red heart with a red bar underneath. Others of the Royal Family wore a red heart with two bars beneath it. Anna had often been in the Royal Hall of Weapons, and had been told many times, the story of the empty hook on the Wall of Shields. She knew that her grandfather's shield was still missing and recognized it as the one Window was carrying at the river.

The journey to the Heart castle was enjoyable for the travelers. The leaves on the few plains trees they passed were turning their autumn colors, which added pleasant spots of red and orange to the otherwise empty vista. Window rode along through the sage-grass and will-flowers, listening to the gentle clop-clop of the horses and the soft jingle of the horsemen's spurs. The sky above them was wide and blue as they crossed the sea of green eastern-plains grass. Window sometimes closed his eyes, and a few times almost fell asleep as the mid-day sun kept him warm in the breeze.

Once, as Circles rode along with Princess Anna, he called a plains sky-bird down to talk to him. She was already in awe of the wind power of the man from the west, and now she became fascinated by the bird languages of the Woot as well. She decided to learn all she could about these strangers.

Anna started at once, teaching Circles some important words and phrases in the Heart language. In just a couple of days, he could already understand much of what she spoke simply to him.

By the middle of the third day of their journey with the horsemen, Window could see the Heart castle on the horizon. It was built of beautiful white stone, and rose dramatically into the sky above the flat of the grasslands. Its turrets lifted bright red tri-flags still higher before the white of the billowing clouds.

The Kingdom of the Hearts was a kingdom of fast, beautiful horses and beautiful, low stone buildings, but the castle rose high into the middle-plains sky. It stood on the northern edge of the Kingdom City that stretched away from the castle and off into the grassland to the south.

Anna had sent a rider ahead to announce their arrival. As they neared the towering castle, Window marveled at the size and beauty of such a building constructed in the middle of the grasslands. It was built of the pale, grey, stone from a quarry near the river farther to the east. Each of the castle's three towers held stairways and arched windows – each which gave a dramatic, panoramic view of the surrounding grasslands.

As they reached the Heart castle, the Horsemen of the Guard turned toward the Kingdom stables, but Princess Anna and her two visitors from afar continued to the castle's west portico. Anna's mother, Queen Karinne, sat in the shade of the elms and greeted her returning daughter and her guests.

The Queen of the Hearts was a beautiful and gentle woman. Her hair was light in color and fell far over her shoulders. She wore a long and flowing, light red robe of thin material that followed her gracefully as she walked.

Window was struck by what a pleasant and attractive woman she was. She was nothing like his idea of what a queen would look like. Of course, he had never met a queen before.

Window and Circles were made very welcome at the castle. Everyone was anxious to hear the story of the long-lost Prince Revell. Anna, Queen Karinne, and the small royal family made up of various distant aunts, uncles, and cousins soon considered the two travelers as almost a part of the family as they made themselves at home in the castle.

Circles got to have lemon-tea to drink and Window was given, not just a bed to sleep in, but an entire floor in the small, east wing of the castle. He and Circles were invited to stay for as long as they wished.

The Queen, especially, was fascinated by Window's stories of John Revell – her father whom she had never known very well,

and about whom she knew very little. She wanted to hear all
about the original Windlands Expedition and Revell's return to
the Northlands with Oldsmith, and his death with the Sea-True.
Of course, every story Window told, led to more questions and
more stories and more afternoons in the shade on the castle day-
porch.

Window asked about the Freelands coins from the Battleplain,
but the Queen told him she had never seen any coins from the far
western lands among her father possessions.

While Window spent much of his days talking with Queen
Karinne, Circles spent his time outdoors with Princess Anna. She
let him use her horse, Cameo, and she rode on Mystic. Cameo was
a smaller horse, and Circles was a smaller rider, so they matched
perfectly. As the days went by, the Princess taught Circles how to
ride Cameo, and he taught her how to listen to the morning call of
a plains field-wren. The two of them grew very fond of each other.

When Anna and Circles were not riding and listening to field-
wrens, they were busy practicing archery on the royal target field.
Circles' archery skills were a bit better than hers, but Anna's
tricks while riding were the best of anyone in the Kingdom.

Anna's golden-brown hair would fly wildly as she rode Mystic
while standing atop his saddle or jumped him across the highest
barriers on the riding field. She loved to race the members of her
Guard, and while riding on Mystic, could easily beat all of the
men. She was young, pretty, smart, talented, fearless, and
determined. Anna Bliss, Princess of the Hearts, was a treasure
herself.

The Princess felt especially caring of Circles one afternoon
when he haltingly asked her his favorite question. *Princess, do
you know where the Angels live?"*

Anna used to dream of Angels sometimes, but since she started
studying to be a Captain of the Guard, a year or so ago, and now
had serious grown-up concerns, she had dismissed such thoughts
from her mind. Until Circles asked, she hadn't thought of Angels
in a long time.

Anna saw the hope in her little friend's eyes, and answered him reluctantly, *"I wish I did, Cirsay, but there aren't any Angels around here."*

That same afternoon found Window and Queen Karinne in the open day-chamber, once again speaking of the Queen's father. Window had brought his notebook from his room because the Queen wanted to see the list of the Northlands Expedition members that included Revell's name.

Karinne read down the list of Expedition names as Window had done a hundred times before.

      R. Kensing   (Reed)
      S. Rails   (Coastown)
      John Revell   (Newtown)
      Jess Lucette   (Summerland)

"It is very odd, Window, to see my father's name here. It is from so many years ago, and so very, very far away – as though it is from another world." Then she added, *"Well, I guess that it is another world."*

The Queen closed her eyes for a moment. *"Can you tell me about Newtown, Window? Have you ever been there?"*

"I have heard that it is a beautiful city, Your Majesty – a city built almost entirely of the same peach-colored bricks. I think it has about five thousand people living there. And, it is known for having the most beautiful bridges and beautiful women in all of the Windlands. I think that you would fit right in there," Window added admiringly.

Karinne responded with a soft smile but didn't say anything.

Window continued, *"But, I don't know much else about it. I wish I could help you."*

"And, what do you know about the other names on this list?" Queen Karinne went on. *"How about Mister Lucette? What do you know about him?"*

"I know that his grandson may be the one who started me on my travels that brought me here. It may be, that because of his grandson, I am sitting here with you right now."

"Isn't it odd, Window, how little things in life can have such a big effect on everything?

The Queen again thought silently for a few moments. Then she asked, *"Where do you suppose this life-changing grandson is right now?*

"I don't know, Your Majesty – probably off on another grand adventure somewhere."

The Queen closed her eyes again in thought. Window looked out across the castle yard to the grasslands beyond.

+++++++++

[AT THE SUMMERLAND BRIDGE]

Far, far to the west, on the southern Windcoast, Mollie Lucette stood in the early morning sun. Then she leaned over the center railing of the Lighthouse River Bridge and looked down into the water. It seemed to be the same as yesterday, wet and fast moving, as it started its last half-mile to the ocean.

Mollie was nine years old, and she liked to, at least once a day, hang over the side of the bridge and think. Her curly, dark-brown hair swung beneath her and waved in the slight breeze coming in from the Atlandic. Then her dark brown eyes squinted against the sun as she stood upright again and looked back towards the mansions of Summerland.

A few minutes before, Mollie had climbed the one hundred and thirty-two steps to the top of the Lighthouse. From there, she could easily look over the trees and see the masts of the Suzie Lacane anchored in the harbor beyond. Mollie had decided to stow away on the Lacane, and sail her to Triston, or maybe Trellesenay, so she needed to plan her escape from Summerland carefully.

50

Down below the River Hill, Mollie could see the beginnings of the tree-lined drives and the wide walkways where she would soon watch the promenade of the latest gowns and evening dresses from Lanarienne, as the Summerland ladies paraded them. Mollie had waited for this day for a long, long time. She was going to be a dress-maker when she grew up – or maybe a dress maker's model-girl – or maybe an actress.

But right now she had something better to do. Yesterday she had found an old map in her secret room, and today she would follow it to find the lost treasure. Mollie would probably get her clothes pretty dirty, but her mother had become used to that by now. Finding treasure takes a lot of digging and climbing, as everyone knows.

After that, Mollie Lucette would run home for lunch. She would need plenty of nourishment, because right after lunch, she was leading a band of Caratousan natives across the New South Rangelands to rustle three thousand head of cattle. And, that could take her the rest of the afternoon. It was another very busy day in the life of a Summerland adventuress.

+++++++++

Queen Karinne opened her eyes as Window closed his notebook. A pleasant, calming breeze blew through the open walls of their meeting room.

The afternoon sun was shining on his hands as Window reached for his pocket. He was about to say, *"I have something else to show you,"* but, just as he began, Anna burst into the castle day-chamber and frantically yelled to her mother and to Window, *"The Ides are attacking! The Ides are attacking!"*

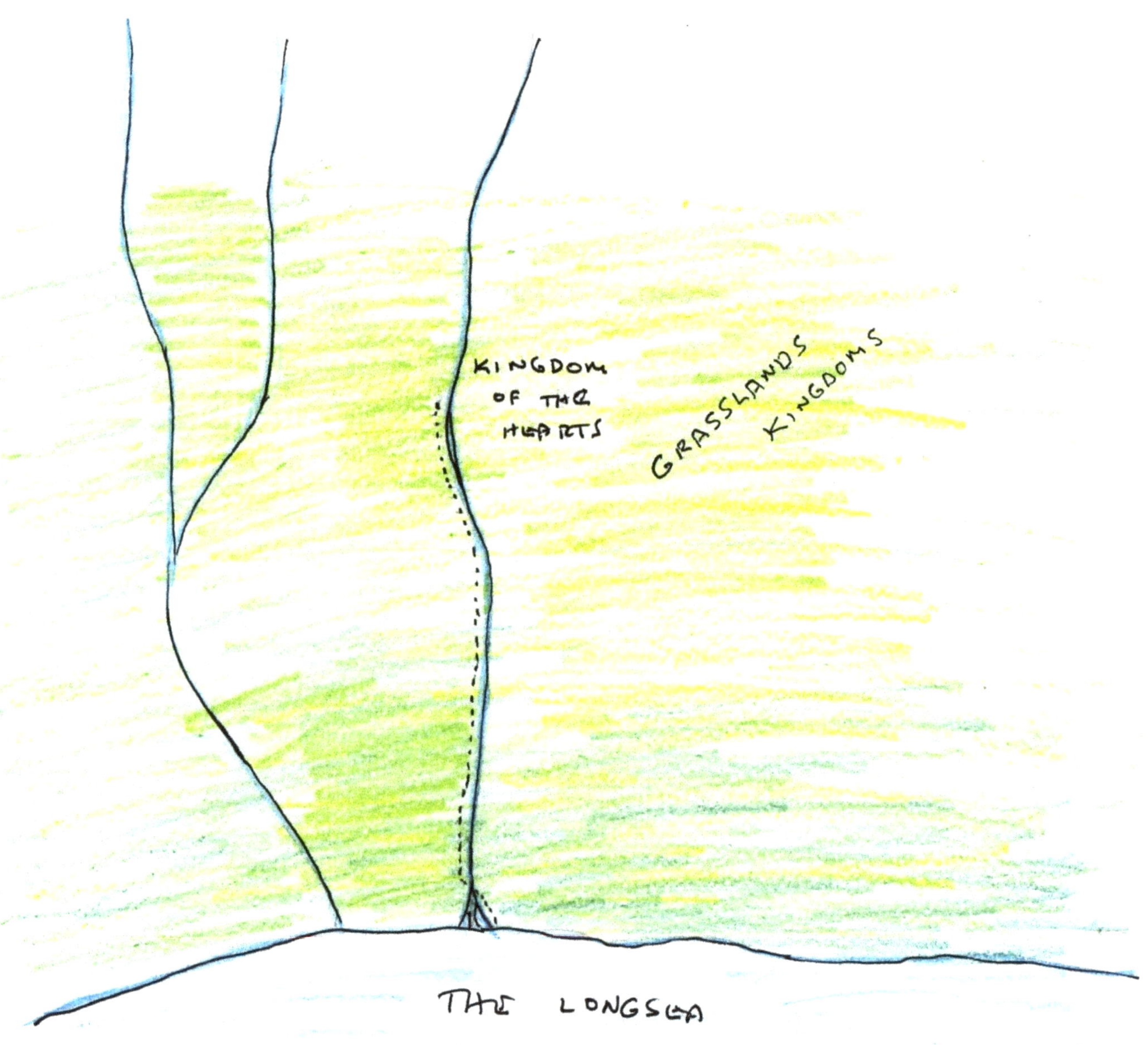

KINGDOM OF THE HEARTS
GRASSLANDS KINGDOMS
THE LONGSEA

CHAPTER TWENTY-THREE

TO THE SOUTHERN WATERS

Window raced to the north castle portico. The scene before him
was frantic. Soldiers and castle tradesmen were rushing in every
direction in their attempts to escape the attacking Ide horsemen,
or to mount their own horses for battle.

Off to the north side of the castle, sections of the palace corrals
and riding-field fences had been knocked down. Wildly shouting
Ide raiders were chasing confused palace horses through the
breaches and driving them off to more mounted Ide horsemen
waiting in the grass-fields far beyond the castle yard.

Anna was already astride Mystic and charging towards the
raiders. She held her silver battle sword high in her right hand as
she shouted orders to several members of the Guard beside her.

Window pulled his sword from the back portico hooks and
raced to the stables. He ran inside and looked for a horse, any
horse – but there were none. The stables had already been
emptied by the attacking Ides. He was too late to help! It had
happened so quickly!

On the far side of the riding-fields, scores of Ide archers were
launching their deadly arrows into the stable yard to dissuade a
counterattack or pursuit by the defending Hearts. Anna charged
on not seeming to care of the danger she faced.

She had practiced her swordwork for many months with the
Guard soldiers and she was ready. She was only a girl, but she,
too, was deadly as she rode directly into the line of archers and cut

though the leather and the wooden shields of those who stood in her way. In just a minute, she had killed two of the attackers and chased several more to retreat. To her left and right, other Guardsmen had joined her in the assault of the archers. The Ides were retreating, but at least a hundred of the Hearts' finest horses were scattered across the near plain and were already being rounded up by the Ide horsemen.

"Guard, pursue!" she screamed to those still in their saddles. Five Guard horsemen followed the girl after the withdrawing attackers.

A sixth rider chased after the young Captain of the Guard. It was Circles! He was astride Cameo and readying an arrow in his bow as he determinedly galloped out to the battle.

A Guardsman next to Anna took an Ide arrow in his chest and fell to his death. Another rider's horse fell beneath him.

Anna rode on. She would not discard her duty to her kingdom or to her family. She would fight to her own death if need be. The other Heart riders broke away from her and began to round up the many horses running free on the plain. They were soon joined by still others, who were trying to save the beautiful horses.

But Anna and Mystic continued their pursuit – and Circles was about a quarter of a mile behind her. Just then, two of the retreating Ide archers turned their horses for one final attack upon the pursuing Anna.

The Ides' great bows each sent an arrow towards the fearless Princess. Their arrows missed their mark of the young Captain, but both slammed into her beautiful stallion. Mystic fell under her as Anna was tossed wildly to the ground.

The archers, sensing the possibility of another Heart death, rode back toward where Anna had fallen. They each placed another arrow in their bow. Anna lay stunned on the ground as the mounted archers drew near.

"Princess!" screamed a small voice from across the grass. "Princess!"

She could barely raise her head in response. One archer raised his bow to send a final arrow into the nearly motionless body of the fallen girl.

But that arrow fell harmlessly to the ground, as a different arrow entered his shoulder – an arrow sent by Circles! The riders retreated again, this time without turning back.

Circles rode to where Anna lay on the ground next to Mystic. He jumped from Cameo and rushed to her side. He sat next to her and carefully lifted her head into his lap.

"Please be okay, Anna! Please be okay!" he desperately pleaded as his soft hands brushed the sweat and dirt from her face and forehead.

Anna opened her eyes and felt the safety and caring in the hands of her little Woot friend. She managed a weak smile as she spoke. *Well, Cirsay, I was wrong. I guess that there are Angels around here.*

Circles had saved the Princess of the Hearts!

The next several days were days of sadness in the Kingdom. Six horsemen of the Guard had been killed by the attacking Ides. Four of the Hearts' horses were also killed, and thirty were stolen.

Those Hearts who were killed were buried in the wide grass cemetery outside the east castle wall. The fences were repaired and the castle gardeners worked tirelessly to erase all signs of the attack from the palace grounds.

The brave Princess was badly shaken by her ordeal, but not seriously hurt. Her greatest injuries were to her spirit. Anna had killed two men, which she found very difficult to accept. During the attack, she acted according to her training and didn't have time to think about it. But afterwards, she was bothered greatly by the deaths from her sword. She knew that it was necessary, as she protected her Kingdom and her family, but it was still a difficult memory to forget. She cried unceasingly as she washed the blood of the dead men from her sword. She was seventeen years of age, but now, much, much older in experience.

Happily, Mystic would recover from his wounds. Anna spent hours each day, tending to him and keeping him company in the stable. She also would walk him, every afternoon, in the riding-field and around the castle grounds.

Cameo now belonged to Circles, as a gift from Anna. And like her, he spent much of his time with his horse, too. Anna had taught him how to brush and feed the animal, and it comforted him to do that.

And, also in appreciation for what Circles had done, Queen Karinne had a gift for him. She offered Circles a house and some cattle as his own, whenever he wished to return to the Kingdom.

Window could hardly believe it. And, he was so proud of his friend. "Circles, of all the things in the world I am sure of, there is nothing I am more sure of than that you are the only Woot in the world who owns a house and cattle! You are an amazing Woot!"

"I guess Raine's finger-rings really knew what they were talking about," Circles replied.

"And I guess that you have made some more good choices."

"Yeah, I guess," Circles answered modestly.

++++++++

Many of the travelers' evenings at the castle of the Hearts were spent quietly with the Queen and the Princess. While Circles would practice speaking the Heart language with Window, Karinne would often lie on one of the ornately cushioned settees in the evening-room and read a book from the castle library. Her hair and her scarves flowed over the cushions and pillows as she enjoyed a mystery or a romantic story of exploration.

After a hard day of riding, archery, and attending to military matters, Anna enjoyed sitting quietly and knitting. Window thought it was an odd pastime for a young woman, but Anna found it extremely relaxing. She was presently working on the knitting of a multicolored winter scarf in preparation for the cold snows that would be blowing across the grasslands in a couple of months.

Anna found the repeated pattern of wrapping the yarn and pulling it through the scarf, accompanied by the steady clicking of the needles against each other, very comforting.

In the afternoons, if her Captain's duties were complete, Anna would sometimes paint on the day-porch. She often painted pictures of forests and mountains that she had never seen, but would someday like to.

"Window, you have seen mountains and the ocean," the Princess once spoke to him. Her eyes were sad and tired. The duties of the Captain of the Guard were difficult for anyone, but especially for a young woman, such as her. *"I so want to see them someday. I feel I will be missing a part of me until I do. My life here sometimes seems to be as flat as the grasslands."*

"They are beautiful, Anna. Maybe you could come with Circles and me to look for the eastern ocean."

If only I could, Window. If only my duties would allow." The young Princess turned so Window would not see her cry.

There was only one thing that Window had not yet spoken to the Queen about regarding her father. Window had waited to tell her of the key that John Revell had given to Oldsmith – the key with the heart-shaped handle.

As he looked at it once more, Window was, again, struck by its beauty. It was in perfect condition – brilliantly shining, as if it was made only yesterday. "Certainly it was made of a special metal, but not gold or silver," he thought. "Since it shines in two colors, perhaps it was made of vermillion."

It was late one night in the evening-room when Window took the key from his pocket. It reflected silver-blue in the light of the wall lamp.

"I have something to show you, Your Majesty. It belonged to your father many years ago. He gave it to his friend Oldsmith in the Northlands to keep for him. Circles and I think that it might be the key to a treasure somewhere."

The Queen took the key from Window and quietly stared at it for a moment. Then she gently slid her fingers along the shaft of the key and started to softly cry.

"I know this key, Window. This is my Pixie Key!"

Window looked on in surprise. Karinne held the shining key to her breast and repeated quietly to herself, *"Oh, Window. This is my Pixie Key."*

Then with tears glistening in her blue eyes, the Queen took a deep breath and sighed. She quietly told Window the story of Revell's blue-silver key.

"When I was a little girl, and my father would return to the Kingdom from one of his long absences, he would always tell me a story about where he had been. Usually he told of traveling to some far-away land I had never heard of. I used to get the feeling that much of what he told me was not true – but only that he wished it <u>was</u> true. But, I never questioned him about that."

"One story he told me many times was that when he was a young man, before he came to the eastern plains, he searched for riches in abandoned mines of the far, far west."

"He said that while searching for gold and silver and jewels, he had found a special key that was made by the Pixies."

"He told me that the key was magic and would open any door. I was so young that I believed his story of a magic key. But, he said the key was lost, and that he would someday return to the far west and find it. Many times, he promised to bring this key back to me – the Pixie Key."

The Queen spoke more and more softly as she went on with her story. Window had to move in closer to her to hear her voice.

"So, each time my father was absent from the castle, I would wait for him to return with the key, but he always returned without it. Then, he would promise the key again, but he never did bring it to me. Each time I was terribly disappointed. When I grew older, I accepted the idea that the key had never really existed."

Window was sure of what he should do. *"My Dear Queen Karinne, I would like you to have the key, to keep as your own. I am certain that Revell's partner, Oldsmith, would agree. Thirty years is long enough to wait for this gift from your father."*

The Queen began to cry again. *"He once asked me if I ever dreamed of treasures and riches. I told him that I was already a Princess and didn't need any more treasures or riches."*

The Queen looked down, away from Window's eyes. *"I think that he was disappointed by my answer."*

Then, with another sigh, the Queen's spirits lifted. Karinne looked back again at Window. *"Thank you, Window. This key is so very important to me. And, <u>you</u> are very important to me. You have come from so far away to give me what no one else possibly could. I am grateful beyond words. I will treasure this key always. And, I will treasure our friendship. You and Circles have certainly been joys to us here. We can never repay you."*

Then the grateful Queen kissed Window's cheek as she softly spoke. *"You are a treasure to me."*

Window slept well that night.

The next morning, as the kitchen-servant, Tillia, brought them breakfast, and before Anna and Circles went out to the stables, Karinne told them of her father's key.

"How did you know that this key was the Pixie Key?" Circles asked of the Queen.

"My father told me that his key was made by the Heart Pixies – not the Moon Pixies."

"I didn't know there were different kinds of Pixies."

"That's why I am the Queen and you are not," kidded Karinne.

"Well, that's one reason, maybe," replied Circles, unsure of how to respond to the jokes of a Queen.

Princess Anna looked on, smiling, as her little friend continued his questions.

"And did you try to open any locked doors with your Pixie Key, Your Queenness?" Circles mistakenly addressed Karinne.

"I tried it on an old, rusted lock in the cow barn this morning, but it didn't fit. And, last night, I tried to open the door to my private-room, but that didn't work either. I think that maybe a key from the Heart Pixies only opens doors to people's hearts like it did mine when Window gave it to me."

"Do you really think that it is a key from Pixies, Ma-Ma?" Anna
asked.

*"I don't know, Darling Daughter. But, Window thinks that it
may be made of vermillion, which is Pixie dust."*

"Vermillion," repeated Anna. *"I love that name."*

So apparently, Revell's key wasn't a key to the kind of treasure
that Window expected. But as Circles said to him later, "Some
treasures are better than others, and the Queen and Princess of
Hearts are the best kind."

During that same conversation, Circles agreed with Window
that it wasn't necessary to tell the Queen that Revell had probably
stolen the key – either from the Pixies or from someone else. "We
will be secret-keepers," Circles confided.

There were more surprises for the two west-lands travelers as
they stayed in the Kingdom of the Hearts. One night in the castle
evening-room, Window noticed a deck of playing cards on a shelf
with the Queen's books.

"Do you play cards here at the castle?" he asked Anna, as she
lay on the floor in her evening-skirt doing nothing in particular,
flopped across the beautiful woven carpet that filled the room.

"I love to play," the Princess answered with enthusiasm. *"But
it has been a long time."*

"Would you like to play something now?"

"Yes. Let's do!" she immediately answered. *"I'll get Ma-Ma!"*
The girl jumped up and hurried into the common-room to look for
her mother.

"Get Circles, too," Window yelled after her.

It suddenly struck Window how Queens and Princesses were
just ordinary people in special positions. Before meeting Karinne
and Anna, he never would have thought that Royalty would do
common things just like everyone else. But, Anna enjoyed doing
many ordinary things like riding and painting and singing and
knitting, and now, he discovered, playing cards.

"Senning, would you please set up the table for us?" Karinne happily called to the evening-servant, as the Queen made her way into the room. *"And please bring drinks for everyone – including yourself."*

Karinne and Anna hadn't played cards in months – since well before Anna had become a Princess. And even before then, they often had only each other to play with. The other Royal Family members usually weren't interested.

"What will we play?" asked Circles, in pretty good Heartan, as he followed Anna back from the kitchen. He had been there trying to get the house-servant, Sevy, to share the fruit-bread she was having as her late evening meal. *"I only know how to play one game – Northdraw."*

"Let's check the cards, Circles," Window suggested. "They are probably different from the Windlands deck we played with in the Northlands."

Window spread the deck of cards before him, across the shinning wood of the evening-room table. His eyes were met by an attractive array of color and shapes. It only took him, and Circles, a few seconds of silent amazement to discover that this deck of cards was much more interesting than they could have imagined. There were so many things to notice that they could hardly comment on one thing before they saw another.

"Look, Window, the Eastenne Star!" Circles exclaimed.

As in the Windlands playing card deck, there were four different Kingdom sets – red diamonds, red hearts, grey stars, and grey moons. The cards of the Star Kingdom set were each marked with a star, as in the Windlands deck, – but not an ordinary five-pointed star. They were stars made from four crossed bars – the same as the stars that marked the King's Treasure in the Eastenne Province – the stars that Circles called the Stars Of The Angels!

"And, look at this symbol on the armor of this soldier card," Circles pointed out to Window. "It's the same as the one that was on Revell's sash at the Sea-True's – the three uneven blue bars!"

"Are these cards of real soldiers from real Kingdoms?" Window excitedly asked the Queen. *"These are the blue bars your father was wearing on his sash when he died."*

"Those bars represent the water of the River Kingdoms far to our south. I guess he must have been there during one of his absences from our castle – and somehow joined the soldiers there."

Circles noticed something else, *"Hey, there are <u>two</u> diagonal red bars on this soldier's armor,"*

"Those represent the wing-bars of the plains-dove and honor the grasslands kingdoms," Anna explained.

"I have a friend with those bars," Circles bragged, referring to Sky-Swift.

"Let me show you the whole deck, Window," Karinne offered.

Window slid all of the cards back together and handed the deck to the Queen. She took the cards and turned them face-up one at a time, arranging them into Kingdom sets on the table in front of her. Each set contained four Royal cards, ten Soldier cards, plus an Arrow card. The Queen explained each card as it was revealed.

"The Star Kingdom set honors the Kingdoms of the Oceanlands, which first brought people to the Very East... The two green leaves on this armor represent the many kingdoms of the eastern forest... This card is the only soldier with no armor..."

Then Window noticed, in the pictures on the Royal Family cards, each was holding something.

"The King is holding a sword," Window observed.

"Signifying strength," the Queen explained.

"The Queen is holding a key."

"Signifying wisdom."

"The Captain is holding a banner."

"Signifying courage."

"And the Princess is holding a flower."

"Signifying beauty."

Picking up the Queen of Hearts card and looking at it more closely, Circles spoke to Karinne. *"You look a lot prettier than the Queen of Hearts on this card."*

Karinne smiled her response to the comment.

Then Circles noticed something else. "Look, Window. The key that the Queen of Hearts is holding in her hand – it's Revell's key!"

It was true. In the Queen's hand on the card was a key just like Revell's heart-handled key Window had given to Karinne.

"I don't remember that the key the Queen was holding was a heart key," Karinne puzzled.

"It must have been, Ma-Ma. How could it have changed?"

"Yeah, how could the Pixies manage that?" Circles spoke up.

The Queen looked at him, but had no answer.

She went on, turning the cards one at a time.

"And look at the flower the Heart Princess is holding," Circles pointed out to Window. It's a sky-flower, like the ones near the mines in the Eastenne Province – the ones on the springcookie board!"

"Do flowers like these grow here in the East?" Window asked the Queen.

"No, I have never seen a flower like that, Window. But old Kingdom stories tell that they are Angel Flowers and grow where the Angels live."

Then, and most surprising of all, the Queen turned over the final card. It was a single special card – and it <u>was</u> an Angel card! *"... to watch over all of the Kingdoms,"* the Queen explained.

It was a beautiful Angel picture – a winged-women dressed in flowing material wrapped around her – with beautiful curved and angled letters across the bottom of her dress.

"She is why this deck is called the Angel Deck. There are stories, from our earliest days, that Angels used to watch over all of the kingdoms." Then, while nodding towards Anna, the Queen added, *"but now, only a few Princesses believe that those stories of Angels might be true."*

Anna smiled, and shook her head and shoulders as though she were just a silly girl to believe such things.

"But, Queenie," Circle addressed Karinne, with unintended disrespect. *"On her dress – those are <u>real</u> Angel letters! We have*

seen them before, in the West!" Then, he added, *"Well, we think they are Angel letters."*

Circles thought on, trying to come up with a way of connecting all of the cards and symbols together. "Hey, Window, do Angels play cards?"

"I don't know much about Angels, Circles. I guess that they do whatever they want."

Then Circles thought he had something figured out. "I'll bet that playing card games gives the Pixies and the Angels something to do, when they don't have anything to do."

"When would that be?" Window pressed him.

"Oh, like on rainy days or something," Circles explained.

"Where did the designs on these cards come from, Your Majesty?" Window wondered aloud.

"These are the designs that the Eastern Lands have used since our earliest days."

Suddenly, another idea sprang into Circles' head – his best idea yet. His eyes lit up as he jumped to his feet. "It's another map, Window, like the springcookie board! I'll bet that the playing cards are a map to another treasure! – the lost treasure of the East!"

"What lost treasure of the East? Where did you hear about that?"

"Well, I don't know, but let's go find it!"

"We don't need any more treasure, Circles. We have plenty of treasure back home."

"But what about finding <u>Revell's</u> lost coins and all of <u>his</u> other treasures?"

"Well, we found Revell's family, instead."

"I know, but we are such good treasure hunters that we should just keep finding them."

"Yeah, Circles. It seems that way. But, maybe, it is sometimes better to have undiscovered treasures to look for than to find them all."

Circles pressed on with his idea. *"Are there any lost treasures around here?"* he asked the Queen.

"Well, there is one – the treasure of the White Bridge," Anna answered for her.

"Where is the White Bridge?" Circles immediately wanted to know.

"Somewhere by the Southern Waters – far to the south of here."

"How can it be lost, if you know where it is?"

"Well, the bridge is not lost – the treasure is lost," Anna explained. *"It was once hidden at the bridge, but it was stolen."*

"I'll bet Revell took it," Circles immediately suggested.

Then Circles realized that he shouldn't have said that. The Queen gave him a little pat on the shoulder to let him know it was okay.

Anna continued, *"There was even a rhyme about it when I was little."*

> *"Treasure lies across the bridge*
> *Dressed in white from west to east*
> *Sun above and wind below*
> *Double towers at your feet"*

"That's sure not much of a rhyme," Circles complained. *"I'll bet it wasn't much of a treasure either."*

"I have heard that it <u>is</u> a very beautiful bridge," Queen Karinne offered. *"It was built by the first of the River Kingdoms."*

"And," Anna added, *"you will be able to see it for yourself, Cirsay. If you go to the Southern Waters on your way to the ocean, you will pass the White Bridge."*

"Let's go that way, Window. Maybe there is still some treasure around there someplace."

"Okay, Circles. We will go past the White Bridge on our way to the ocean."

"What color is the White Bridge?" Circles asked the Queen. She gave him an odd look, and a smile.

"Just checking," he sheepishly explained. *"Just checking."*

It took a long time that evening before the card playing actually began. But finally, it did. Senning continued to bring bread snacks and drinks as the new Royal Family played Triple Arrow, a game that was remarkably like Northdraw. Anna explained the game to Circles and Window and, before long, everyone was having fun – matching symbols, stealing soldiers, and otherwise doing their best to win the castle from the King.

As they played, the Princess and the Queen seemed happier than the two treasure hunters had ever seen them. Karinne's voice was joyous and Anna's eyes were bright. Their delight made Window enjoy the games all the more. The laughter continued long into the night.

++++++++

Early the next afternoon, as Window looked down from the turret of his sleeping-room to the castle yard below, he watched three armed horsemen ride away toward the eastern grasslands. He didn't recognize the curved orange lines of their armor symbols.

"I wonder where they are from," he thought. "I'll ask Karinne."

The Queen was on the covered day-porch when Window joined her. Before he could ask her about the horsemen, she spoke to him.

"Window, I have news that I wish to share with you. Riders came from the far eastern kingdoms this morning. The Hearts have been invited by the Kingdoms of the Very East to attend a Meeting of the Flags. The meeting will take place in Oceienne, which is a city at the Far Ocean.

"It will be attended by representatives of the many countries and kingdoms of the Very East and the surrounding Oceanlands. Royalty and special envoys of the many lands also will attend. As a courtesy, the Kingdoms of the plains have been invited to send representatives as well. But it is a very far distance from here, and Heart does not have pressing issues with the Very East, so it is not

imperative that we attend. But, still we wish to honor the invitation and send someone to represent us."

Window listened with anticipation of what the Queen was about to say.

"It seems to me, Window, that if you will consent, you and Circles would be the perfect representatives for the Hearts – especially since you know so many languages, and you already wish to travel to the ocean."

The Queen easily read the answer in Window's eyes and smile. She reached over to the porch side-table and pulled one of the knitting needles from Anna's unfinished scarf that was resting there. Holding it like a Royal scepter, she touched Window on the shoulder.

"Window, would you honor us and be my personal lieutenant at the Meeting of the Flags?"

Window was pleased beyond almost any speech. He and Circles would travel to Oceienne – and the Oceanlands of the Very East – just where they wanted to go. It was perfect for them.

"Certainly, Your Majesty. Your wish will be reality," Window replied as he bowed to his Royal friend. *"I'll go tell Circles right away."*

Karinne nodded her consent and Window rushed to find his ocean-hunting friend.

++++++++

Window and Circles would leave for the eastern sea in three days. They would travel to the Southern Waters, first by small boat down the river that flowed just to the east of the Heart Kingdom City. Once reaching the Southern Waters they would travel by foot along the coast until reaching the Eastway, the road that would lead them directly east to Oceienne and the Far Ocean.

Anna had one last request of Circles, before he left. He had told her about the Kites of Calisay, and, although Heart children in the city flew kites, the Princess had never flown a kite herself. So, she asked Circles to help her build a kite and fly it.

The two of them spent one afternoon working in the castle yard-shop, building a beautiful pink kite – Anna chose the color – and the next afternoon in the grassland fields beyond the north fences. The kite flew flawlessly in the steady breeze coming off of the plains.

Circles had given Anna the long, multicolored kite tail that had belonged to Locker and Frazzle, the Owts. He had brought the tail with him through the many months and over all of the uncountable miles from the Deep Woods. He had kept it in his pack because it was so important to him, but now he said he finally found a good home for it. Anna was thrilled to have such a gift.

"It's wonderful, Cirsay," the Princess almost squealed as the kite fluttered high above them. *"I want to go to Calisay with you someday. May I please?"*

"That is an excellent idea, Annie," the happy Woot replied. *"An excellent idea."*

The tail's colors flapped beautifully in the wind as her kite climbed almost out of sight. Circles was proud that something from his part of the world was now a part of the far eastern lands.

After several hours of successful kite flying in the grasslands, the two young flyers needed some new challenges. So, first, Circles pulled the kite behind him as he rode across the riding-field on Cameo. That actually worked pretty well. Anna's hair flew in the wind as she tried to ride behind Cameo on Mystic and catch the colorful kite tail with her hand.

Next, they took the kite to the east tower turret and tried to fly it from there. That was not very successful. What was successful, however, was the time the two friends spent together. Both Anna and Circles immensely enjoyed the kite flying and the memories of fun they would never forget.

"You are the best friend I have ever had," Anna confessed to Circles, as she hung the kite on its new hook in the yard-shop.

"You are the sweetest and best Princess in the history of the world," came his reply.

The two friends held hands as they walked from the yard-shop to the castle. There were tears in their eyes.

++++++++

It was a sad time of parting for the travelers and the Queen and Princess of the Hearts.

Circles had decided to leave Cameo at the castle. *"I love him, but he will be better off here with you and his friends, Anna, than with me dragging him halfway across the world,"* Circles declared. Anna promised to keep him safe and healthy until Circles returned.

Karinne offered Window his pick of the Kingdom horses as a gift but he declined. *"Since you will not accept one of the Royal horses, Window, what may I give you as my symbol of our friendship?"*

Window quickly had his answer. *"I have two requests, Your Majesty. I will, of course, return your father's shield to the Kingdom, but I would like to keep Revell's sword as my own."*

"It is yours," answered the Queen.

"And, instead of a horse as a gift from you, I would like to have a pair of spurs from the Royal Horsemen. When I was a boy, I used to imagine growing up to become a cattle driver of the New South Rangelands in my homelands. If you agree, and, should that ever happen, I will already have my spurs."

"You shall have them, Window, along with my thanks for all you have done for us." The Queens eyes again showed her caring for the young traveler from so far away.

On the evening before the travelers would be leaving, Karinne and Window went for a walk around the castle grounds for the last time. He and Circles had stayed with the Hearts for several weeks and now the colorful leaves of autumn covered the few tall trees of the castle-yard. It was a pleasant walk as the two friends talked quietly for a long time. As the sun was setting in the west, Window noticed dark clouds were coming across the eastern plains towards them. Rain was on the way.

The travelers' last night in the Kingdom of the Hearts was spent on the open-porch high on the eastern side of the main castle tower. The sky-watchers looked off to the east where the storm had begun. The sun had set completely so the sky was black before them. Then lightning began flashing on the distant horizon, giving a fantastic show of light and sound to the Queen and the others.

As the storm move closer, the crash of the thunder became so loud and frequent that conversation was almost impossible. So, everyone just sat quietly and watched and listened as the sky flashed and sparked and roared before them. There was not much anyone could think of saying anyway, so they just shared the night each in their own thoughts.

As the rain splashed across the eastern castle river, Circles asked his friend, "What do you think, Window? How much longer until the rain gets here?"

"Looks like about five minutes to me."

Then suddenly the wind changed direction and pushed the storm away from them towards the south. Soon the lightning and thunder were, once again, in the far distance.

"I rode all night in the rain once," Anna started the story telling. *"My friend, Princess Tresette, and I were returning from her kingdom, far to the east of the river..."*

They stayed up late into the night, with the breeze blowing across their faces, speaking of storms and friends and rivers. It was a beautiful night in the Kingdom of the Hearts.

+++++++++

[BEYOND THE SENESTELLE GATE]

On the other side of the stars, Raene Dejjreonne opened his eyes. Above, and to his right, the main viewer-window was expanding. Through the long, rectangular semi-glass,

*the bright white reflection from the Calysasian Moon shone
across his face.*

*Raine stretched his arms and sat up. As he looked out at
the beautiful white surface of the moon before him, his mind
jumped. Something was wrong. It was not the Calysasian
Moon!*

*There should be at least three other moons in his screen.
Somehow, the Star Journey must have reformed on the other
side of the Lorrisian System – or anywhere! A quick scan of
the light-dials confirmed his fear. Someone, or something,
had interfered with his jump. He was seven hundred trillion
miles from Tessimaysan!*

*The Senestelle-Talavenne Stargate was behind him, but
he couldn't locate it on his board. It seemed to have
disappeared along with half of the stars on his map.*

*Since the storm at Fantessian Resenne that had sent him
so far outside that system, his ship had been repaired, his
rings had been repaired – he had been repaired. It should
have been an easy trip home. Someone else had another
idea.*

*A brief flash of the board-lights caught his attention. A
crisp voice entered his head. "Captain, there has been an
attempt by the Vendasti to disrupt the S-Gate. We advise
that you postpone your traverse until security has been
confirmed."*

*"Well," the starman spoke to himself, "It's a bit too late for
that. Maybe I can re-mast and sail by wave until I reach the
Center. It's in that direction – I think."*

*As the ship started to move, the unknown sun on his port
side shot out its tongues of fire across a million miles of
nothingness. They licked at the edge of the Star Journey as
it sped past.*

*Soon the giant lightwood craft sails reached to their limit.
The wind from the angry sun caught them and threw the*

ship across another million miles. Three minutes later, the system was lost behind him.

The starman settled in for the long flight. He was used to the hours and days of being alone, but still they were difficult to endure. Especially since he had been away so very long.

After fifteen quiet hours his goal was almost in sight. He looked out through the semi-glass as Trecellia formed before him. The blue of the world almost perfectly matched the blue of his skin.

Then, Raine glanced towards his desk-shelf. The tiny containers of trillion and vermillion sat there silently, not realizing how important they were about to become. He might just have time to reach the Xellian Kingdom outpost before the attack.

Once again, his thoughts turned to her. "I miss you, Darling Nikee. I'll be back as soon as I can," he sighed to himself. "I need you as the leaves need the wind."

Suddenly, the z-meters started to jump. The fore-sail numbers dropped almost to zero. The signal-board lights all flashed at once. His finger-rings buzzed for attention. It was another lonely and dangerous day for Star-messenger Raine, somewhere in the T-Laycelle System.

+++++++++

The early morning light found the travelers ready to depart from the Grasslands Kingdom. They would ride their horses the few miles to the eastern river, then load their supplies into a small rivercraft for the journey down to the Southern Waters. From there, since their boat would not be big enough to navigate the waters beyond the river, they would travel by foot to the ocean in the Very East.

On the journey, Window and Circles would carry their regular packs and supplies, plus food from the Royal kitchen, specially chosen and packed by Tillia. And the Queen had given them a large Heart Kingdom flag for the ceremony at Oceienne, to be flown with those of all attending. The travelers also would carry the letter of invitation from the Horsemen of the Very East to assure safe passage through the many kingdoms on their way.

Anna would ride with the ocean-hunters to the river and assure that they were successfully on their way. Then she would follow, on Mystic, along the riverbank as their boat drifted to the south.
     Anna explained, *"I will escort you to the boundary of the Kingdom. It is my duty as Captain of the Guard to secure its borders at all times – and my honor to accompany you that far on your journey."*

Queen Karinne hugged both travelers and kissed them on the cheek. Her only words were, *"Be safe – and return when you can."* Once again, her blue eyes were clouded with tears.

Window hung their packs and weapons on the horses and they were off. Anna rode between Window and Circles out the east castle gate. About a quarter mile outside of the gate, the road passed by the gravestones of the Kingdom Cemetery. Anna spoke quietly, *"Window, could we stop for just a moment? My father lies here. I would like him to meet you two."*
     The three riders dismounted and walked to a simple grave, marked with the same white stone as that used to build the castle.
     Beneath the two-barred Heart symbol, the inscription on the stone read,

Prince Ranning Bliss
House of the Hearts
Captain of the Guard
E.Y. 201

Then, just as Window liked to do, the young Princess leaned over and ran her finger through the letters of her father's name.

Anna was about to say something to her father, but she changed her mind. Without a word, Anna returned to her horse and the others followed.

At the river the boat was waiting. It was made of plains-wood and had a pointed bow and two oars for rowing, when necessary. The travelers loaded their packs and weapons aboard and stood to say goodbye to the Princess.

Anna pushed her golden-brown hair from in front of her golden-brown eyes and hugged Window. Then as she kissed Circles near where she thought his cheek would be, Anna spoke in perfect Atlandan, "Circles, you are my friend forever. I will keep Cameo until you and I can ride together again."

"You have been practicing!" Circles replied in surprise. He hugged her about the waist and kissed her hand. She bowed in return. Some of her hair fell in his face and tickled his nose. Circles smiled his response.

"Goodbye, Dear Princess," he quietly spoke to her.

"Goodbye, Cirsay," came her quiet answer.

In another minute, the two ocean-hunters were again traveling to the south. As the boat took them downstream, Anna and Mystic followed along the bank, keeping them company. It struck Window how regal she appeared – proud and confident, and capable. She was a beautiful Princess of the Hearts.

The Princess stayed with the travelers for about an hour. Then she stopped and stood up from her saddle and waved. The ocean-hunters returned her wave and disappeared from her sight around a bend in the river.

++++++++

The trip to the Southern Waters would only take a few days. The boat ride was smooth and easy as the current carried them silently along. The travelers quickly returned to their old ways of making camp and sitting around the fire in the evenings.

On their second night of camping, the moon was overhead so
Window brought Charm out to join them. It took a few minutes in
the moonlight to wake him up. He hadn't been out of Window's
pocket in weeks. He didn't seem too happy, but cheered up with
some quick flying over the river and a game of Rainbow Chips.

As the travelers drifted farther and farther south, the river
widened and slowed. It separated into many delta channels and
seemed to change from being one river to being scores of small
rivers. Several times they drifted into large wetlands of reeds and
cattails and had to work hard with the oars to get free of the
tangled growth.

In one place, they encountered hundreds of butterflies that flew
along with them or rode along on their packs. Another time they
passed a spot with scores of holes dug into the side of the
riverbank.

"What lives in there, Window?"

"Riverbank holediggers, I think."

"Oh."

By the middle of their third day on the river, the travelers
could see its end up ahead. They worked their way to the eastern
side of the delta waters and drifted to the bank. Soon they were
standing at the edge of another great body of water, sparkling out
before them.

"Is this the ocean, Window?"

"No, it is called the Longsea. The ocean is still far from here"

"It sure looks like the ocean," Circles assured his friend. "It
sure looks like the ocean."

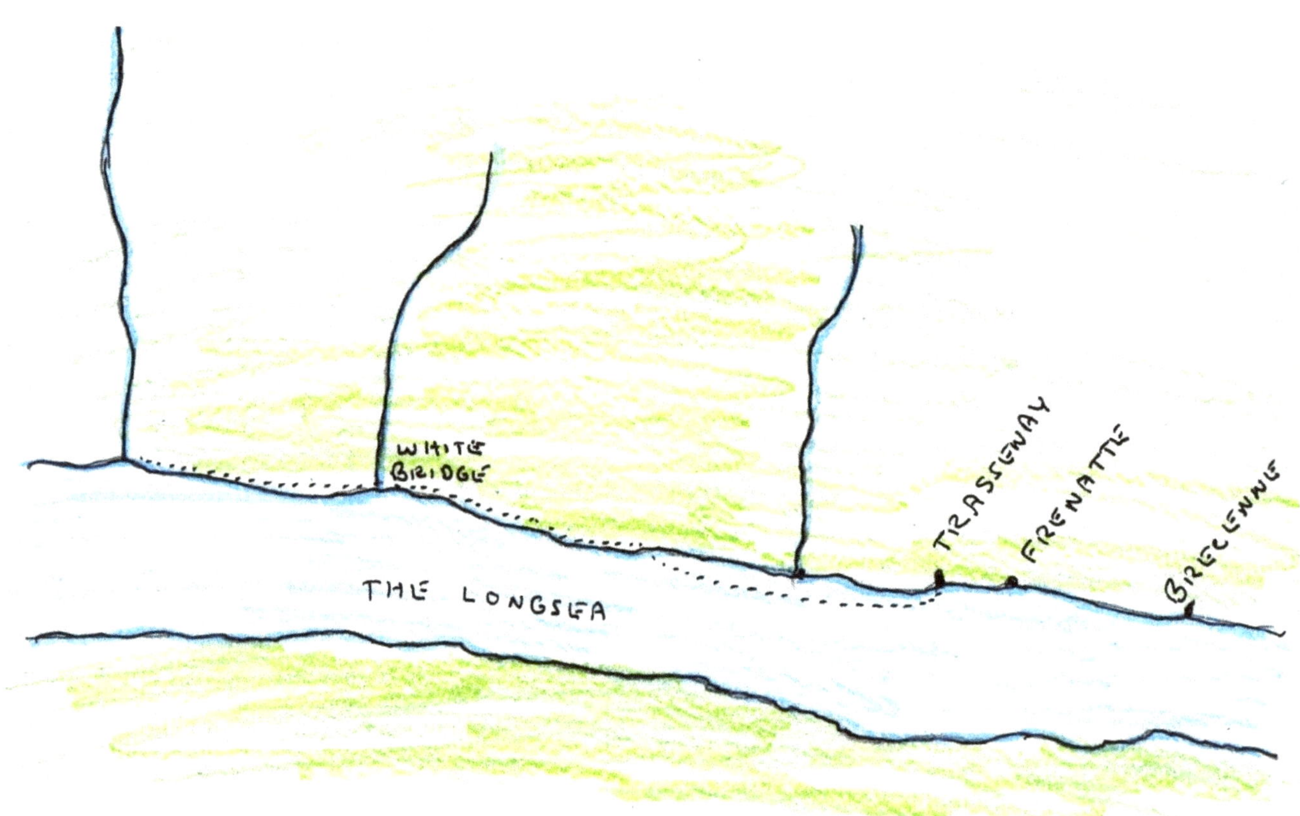

WHITE
BRIDGE
THE LONGSEA
TRASIGNAY
FRENATTE
BRIECLENNE

"Try one of these," Circles said to Window as he handed his ocean-hunting friend a long cane-like plant he had just pulled from the lowland marsh along the sea. Window took the tan-colored stick and easily broke it into sections. He raised it to his mouth – it tasted sweet – and pretty good for something growing wild along the shore.

The two travelers were on their second day of following the Longsea shoreline. It was a long, thin sea that stretched far to the east where it eventually reached the ocean. On their first day in the land of the River Kingdoms they had to work their way through tall seagrass and tangled seapads, but this morning they reached the end – or you could say the beginning – of the road that would follow the coast all the way to the Far Ocean. The road would stop at the city of Oceienne, the seaport several hundred miles to the east.

So now the journey was much easier. All the travelers had to do was stay on the road and avoid trouble. Window carried the letter from the Queen of the Hearts that should allow them passage through any of the River and Forest Kingdoms on their way.

As it continued on to the east, the road began to pass beneath stands of tall trees and was joined along the way by many other roads, and small rivers, meeting it from the north. Up each of the roads was one of the River Kingdoms, and the boundary of each kingdom was marked by a small tower.

Circles said they passed twenty towers before he stopped counting. Each tower bore the kingdom symbol at its base. Window and Circles recognized several symbols that were on soldiers' armor in the Eastlands Kingdoms card deck.

Apparently, the River Kingdoms people didn't care for the sea too much, because only twice did the travelers pass anyone on the road. Those people they did pass didn't say anything more than a brief greeting. Maybe they were not used to seeing a man carrying a sword and a Woot armed with a bow.

On their first night of camping along the sea, Circles called a grey gull down from a tree to talk for a while. The bird didn't have anything interesting to say but it did have the loudest whistle Circles had ever heard.

On their second day along the coast road, some dark, quickly-moving clouds showered them with a gentle rain. The days were still pleasant but the nights were beginning to get rather cold.

"Sometimes I wish I had brought Cameo along, Window," Circles shared as he rested on a big rock, and looked out across the blue water to their south. "Riding him is sure easier than walking."

"Sometimes I wish I had brought Tillia along," joked Window, as he remembered her delicious morning-cakes at the Heart Castle.

"Sometimes I wish I had brought Panni and Rings along," Circles added with a sadness in his voice. After a moment, he spoke again.

"Window, that's the part of having an adventure I don't like – having to leave someone I really care about. I wish that didn't have to happen."

Window had no good answer for his friend. Circles was deep in thought.

"I wonder if Angels ever get sad."

Again, Window couldn't think of anything to say.

After another minute, Circles had another question. "Do you think we will ever find an Angel?"

"Well, we found the Silkie."

Another quiet minute went by. "Let's ask the Pixie dust."

"Okay, which kind do you want to try?"

"Let's ask the trillion this time."

Window took the trillion tin from his pack and put a pinch of the dust on Circles' hand. Circles gently tossed the dust into the air.

"It's working, Window! It's working!"

The trillion left a path of silver sparkles as it floated off to the east. Circles was thrilled.

"Looks like we are headed in the right direction. I wonder what the Angels are doing so far away from the Ancient Lands."

"Maybe someday we will be able to ask them."

"I would like that, Window."

The next day on their way along the coast brought the travelers to a wide river flowing across their path. As they got closer, Window recognized the description Karinne had given him.

"Hey, Circles. It's the White Bridge."

"It's not very white."

"It's pretty old. I guess that the paint lost its color and wore off."

Before them on the road was a large wooden bridge spanning perhaps a hundred feet above a low, wide river that emptied into the sea to their right. It was about two hundred feet from where they stood to the other side of the river. The bridge was made from hundreds of square, wooden beams of many different lengths. On each side of the river, there were two tall wooden bridge towers to support its entire weight. The tower beams crossed each other again and again as the towers reached high into the air. Between these end-towers, was a long arch of beams that reached to the matching tower on the other side of the river. Hanging from the arches were more crossed beams that reached down and held up the sides of the bridge. Between these sides stretched the wide bridge floor.

Approaching the bridge on the road gave the effect of entering a forest of trees. From its side, the bridge appeared as a repeating pattern of triangles and arcs.

"Queen Karinne was right, Window. It is a beautiful bridge. I wonder where the treasure was hidden."

Circles repeated Anna's rhyme.

"Treasure lies across the bridge
Dressed in white from west to east
Sun above and wind below
Double towers at your feet."

"The first two lines must mean as you walk across the White Bridge traveling east," Circles suggested. "That's the way we are already going. I'll bet the treasure was on the east side of the river."

Circles continued his analysis. "The sun would be above the bridge and the wind could blow below the bridge, I guess. That doesn't help much. There are two towers at each end. Maybe the treasure was hidden in those towers."

They started across the bridge and stopped in the middle.

"Let's have lunch first, Circles decided. "I'm not in any hurry to not find some treasure."

As the travelers opened their food packs, Circles was still thinking. "This really is a nice looking bridge, Window. Do you know what would make it look even better?"

"What's that?"

"Some angel letters carved into the beams here – or one of the Cat-eyes' designs."

"Why don't you carve something, Circles, so that the next Angel hunter who comes along here will have something to look at?"

"Like what?"

"Do you have a favorite design or symbol?"

"I like the Angel letters."

"Do you remember how any of them are made?"

"Not exactly. I guess I'll have to make up my own Angel
letters."

"Anna thinks you are an Angel, so I guess maybe you can make
your own letters."

Circles sat down on the wide cross-beam that served as the
railing on the south side of the bridge. Window took his boot knife
from its sheath and handed it to Circles.

The little Woot-angel chose a spot on one of the diagonal bridge
beams and scratched a design into the ancient wood. It was a
combination of two curved lines joined by a short bar.

Then, following his scratches, Circles used Window's knife to
carefully dig into the beam. In just a couple of minutes, he was
finished.

Circles stood back from his design and admired it. "Thanks for
letting me use your knife, Window."

"Hey, that's pretty good, Circles. Where did you learn to make
Angel letters?"

"At Angel school."

Then Circles wondered, "Do Angels have to go to school,
Window?"

"Only if they want to."

The treasure hunters rested on the bridge for a while and had
lunch. Tillia's cakes were delicious and there was still some
lemon-tea, which they finished.

"Okay, Circles, let's find where the treasure was hidden."

They crossed to the east side of the bridge and searched around
at the base of the support towers. Each of the towers was made of
eight huge beams with one end buried in the ground and the other
end rising high above them to meet the arch across the water.
The bases of the towers were totally overgrown with bushes and
weeds and even small trees. It was obvious that no one had
disturbed the wood of those bases for a long time.

Circles worked his way between and under the bushes to
examine the wood of one of the tower bases. He disappeared into
the underbrush and called out his observations.

"Hey, Window. There used to be thinner boards around these beams that would have made an enclosed room-like place. Most of the boards have been torn off. I'll bet that this is where the treasure was hidden."

Circles emerged from the weeds and bushes and declared, "I want to check the other tower."

He went to the tower on the north side of the bridge and dug his way into the underbrush on that side.

"Window! Window! The base of this tower still has most of the wood around it. There is just one small hole in the side-wood. And just above the ground there is a little square door, about a foot across. And the door has a keyhole!"

"Wow, Circles," Window called into the bushes. "Too bad we don't have Revell's heart key. We could sure use it now."

"Window, the lock is broken – the door will open!"

Window waited as Circles opened the door to the White Bridge treasure. At first, all Window heard was some rustling in the bushes. Then there was more rustling of the bushes as Circles pushed his way out into the open again.

"Well?" Window asked his friend. "Was there any treasure inside the tower door?"

"We have found the White Bridge treasure, Window – two chipsquirrels, some twigs, and a large pile of acorns."

A huge smile came across Window's face. "Looks as if Anna was all wrong about the treasure being stolen. It has been here waiting for us the whole time."

Circles continued on about the Princess. "She will be very surprised when we tell her about it. The Hearts will probably make up a new rhyme so that a hundred years from now, the little Heart children will still be singing about the brave Window and Circles who found the fabulous treasure of the White Bridge."

Then Window had an idea. "Let's add to the treasure, Circles. Let's put something inside the tower so that if someone else ever looks for it, they will find even more than we did."

"I know," Circles, excitedly replied, " – a Freeland coin – one of Revell's Freeland coins! It really would be a treasure to someone around here. They would have no idea where it came from, or how it got here."

Window didn't answer right away. He was lost in thought about what happened to him because he found the unknown medallion on the Town Road in the Windlands.

"You know, Circles. That is an excellent idea. Wouldn't it be something if someday someone found the coin and it started <u>them</u> on a grand adventure – maybe even one that took them all the way to the Windlands? Your idea is wonderful."

"Hey, and we are in the River Kingdoms. Their symbol on the playing cards is the one with the three blue bars – almost like the ones on your medallion."

Window dug into his pack and retrieved one of Revell's silver, Freeland, crossed-swords coins. It shone brilliantly in the sun as he handed it to Circles.

Circles held the coin high over his head and declared, "Here is the new treasure of the White Bridge. When we got here, there was no silver or gold. But there is now!"

The Woot worked his way back into the bushes and laid the coin inside the little treasure room.

"Here, I'll trade you," Circles spoke, as if the squirrels were still there. He picked up one of the acorns and popped it into his mouth. "Hey, not bad," he said aloud to himself, as he closed the tower room door.

After some more bush-rustling, Circles again emerged into the sunlight. "I love treasure hunting," he announced to Window.

+++++++++

[BENEATH THE CAIRISTON TOWER]

Far across the River Kingdoms, the Eastern Grasslands, and on beyond the distant mountains and Outlands to the west, Rook Ceediney was running through the shadows between the buildings of Calisay. It was the middle of the night. The soldiers were chasing him.

Rook's troubles had started earlier that evening. Every one of the Atters – the Calisay band of street children who had learned Atlandan so they could speak secretly to each other – had a job to do. Four of them were to start by throwing rocks at the tower guards at the gate to the base-building of the middle tower – Cairiston's tower – the tower named for the King Alezan's eldest son.

The plan was simple – well, not really simple. The Atters were to get the tower outer-gate guards to leave their post long enough for Rook and his cousin, Mellie, to sneak inside.

Rook's grandfather's friend, Denard, at the Matenne Palace horse-stables, had been inside the Cairiston tower a few years before. The soldiers there knew of an escape tunnel that was built for the King during the time when Calisay was under siege by the Atlandan Army. According to Denard, the brick-lined tunnel went from inside the tower base-building and exited somewhere outside the wall of the tower yard.

The plan was Mellie's plan. Months before, the dark haired, dark eyed, dream-filled girl from Laveselle, had promised herself to become a treasure hunter. She had come to Calisay determined to find the hidden third treasure of King Alezan.

Yes, the plan was simple – if you call having some eight and nine and ten-year-old kids being chased by the hated guards of Prince Martellan, while Rook and his seventeen year old cousin sneaked inside the tower building that held the Guards headquarters, simple. The rest of the simple plan was for Rook and Mellie to avoid anyone inside, to find the tunnel access that Denard thought was on the west side of the base building, follow it to its end, figure out a way to open the metal re-enforced door that was probably there, and leave the tower grounds with that door now unlocked and unbarred. Returning to the tower at another time to make off with the King's treasure was a part of the plan that had not yet been devised.

*Actually, there <u>were</u> a few problems with the plan –
well, about three dozen problems – in the form of soldiers of
the Prince.*

*The first part of the plan worked flawlessly. Four of the
Atters – Ace, Lixy, and her two brothers, climbed the low
tower-yard wall, and pelted the two outer guards with some
carefully-chosen rocks. The guards left their posts as they
chased the kids into the streets beyond the yard.*

*But then, things became increasingly dangerous. The
guards quickly gave up the chase and returned to the tower-
yard gate. By then, Rook and Mellie were already inside the
tower building, where they hoped that the rest of the soldiers
would be asleep. It <u>was</u> the middle of the night.*

*The outer chamber-room was larger than Rook expected,
but was empty of soldiers. It held several weapons cabinets,
three tables, chairs, and a lot of boots, all lined up in a row.*

*Unfortunately the trespassers ran into a guard who
wasn't very sleepy that night. Rook asked the surprised man
where the King's treasures were kept, and as he ordered the
boy to approach him, Mellie stepped out from behind a
cabinet and sort of hit him over the head with a small brick
she had brought along in her cloth shoulder-bag, "just in
case."*

*Also in Mellie's bag was a light chain holding forty-six
keys the Atters had collected, just in case she had to open
something that needed help being opened.*

*Mellie had never hit anyone with a brick before, but she
was assertive and fairly calm as she did so for the first time.
The soldier fell to the floor, unconscious. She and Rook
dragged him behind the cabinet.*

*The young trespassers quickly left the room and entered
the hallway to their left. If Denard was correct, the tunnel
door would be somewhere along the outer wall on that side of
the building – but it would probably be hidden. As they
quietly moved down the outer hallway, they passed, on their*

right, doors opening into the kitchen, the laundry, and the soldiers' sleeping quarters. They could hear snoring coming from inside one of the rooms.

The long hallway came to an end at a wall holding a door. Rook tried the handle – it was unlocked! They opened the door and stepped through into a closet – a very deep closet, crowded with brooms, cleaning materials, containers of paint, tools, and even racks of soldier's uniforms.

Mellie pulled the door shut behind them. Rook reached a match from his pocket and struck it. It only took a minute for him to find what they were looking for. In the outer, side-wall of the closet, behind several racks of soldier's raincoats, was another, smaller door – a locked door. There was an external lock securely mounted to its frame, with a locking bar buried deep into the doorframe. Denard was right. The passageway was there. They had found the hidden tunnel!

Suddenly, they could hear loud, angry voices in the hallway. The soldiers had been alerted that someone was in the tower-house!

Quickly, Mellie dug in her bag for her chain of keys. Her heart was pounding, her mind was rushing – but her hands were steady. By the light of another match, she quickly picked the four keys from her chain that she thought might be the right size for the lock's rather large keyhole.

She tried the first key – it didn't turn in the keyhole. She tried the second key – it didn't turn in the keyhole. She tried the third key – it started to turn, but then stopped – the lock was too rusted.

"Come on. Come on!" Rook hurried her.

Mellie twisted the key to remove it from the lock. It was stuck. It wouldn't turn! She couldn't get it out!

They heard more soldiers' voices. The voices were getting closer.

"What are we going to do?" Rook frantically asked. "We are trapped in here!"

Mellie calmly unhooked the chain that held the stuck key to the others. She would have to leave that one key but she

*wasn't going to lose all of her keys. The Atters would be
needing them for other "projects" around the city.*

"Mellie! They are coming. I can hear them!"

*The girl had dreamed for months of finding the King's
Treasure. She wasn't going to let an old rusted lock stop her
now. She threw the keys back into her bag and reached for
the brick she had used to convince the guard to leave them
alone.*

*She smashed the brick against the rusted lock with all of
her strength. The brick convinced the lock to break loose of
its mountings. Rook tugged on the door and it opened as
well. They stepped through the door.*

*The two, young, would-be burglars found themselves
inside a narrow, musty, brick-lined passageway. Rook
pulled the door to the closet closed behind them. Now,
unless they could escape from the other end of the tunnel,
they were trapped for sure.*

*Voices and noises came from the other side of the closed
door. The tower intruders scrambled down the tunnel as
Rook lit another of his quickly dwindling match supply to
light the way. The air was old and stale. The matches kept
going out.*

*The tunnel was about two hundred feet long. Mellie was
breathing heavily as they made their way along, stumbling
on the rough bricks of the floor.*

*Rook had only two matches left. He struck one of them.
There it was! Cut into the side of the King's escape tunnel
was another door! It was wooden and reinforced with thick
metal bands. This door had no handle or hinge or lock
showing. It was a door that could certainly not easily be
opened. A door that could not be opened must be a door that
is protecting something very valuable on the other side of it –
something like a King's treasure, perhaps!*

*The cousins stared at the door and glanced knowingly at
each other. They were smiling as the match burned out.*

With their hands feeling along the brick passage wall, Rook and Mellie worked their way on in the total darkness. Finally, without warning, they bumped up against the tunnel's end.

"Should I light the last match?" Rook asked his older, and perhaps, wiser, cousin.

"Not yet, Rooky," Mellie instructed. "We may need that when we come back in here for the treasure," she explained jokingly, with undefeatable confidence.

"Oh yeah, I forgot," came his less than enthusiastic reply.

Mellie ran her fingertips lightly down the wall at the end of the passage. There was a small door, but she could feel no lock. The door was secured by a heavy metal bar resting in metal brackets on the door and the wall beside it.

"There is a cross-bar, Rook. Help me lift it," she instructed him.

They each grabbed on to an end of the heavy bar and lifted. It wouldn't move. It was stuck – wedged into its supporting brackets.

Mellie again reached into her bag and grabbed her trusted brick. In the darkness, she measured the distance from where she stood to the crossbar. The passageway echoed with the sound of stone on metal as she swung the brick upward and slammed it against the bottom edge of the invisible barrier.

Rook pulled up on the bar. It moved! It lifted free of its mountings.

Mellie pushed against the door with her shoulder. It opened slightly. Outside, there were bushes and weeds grown right up against the door. The door moved just enough for her and Rook to slide through. They pushed through the doorway and into the night. The door was part of a wall and was almost undetectable from the outside. They carefully pushed the door closed again.

Outside, it was still dark, except for the light of the moon. But there <u>was</u> one more major problem – they were not *outside the tower grounds as they had expected. They were still within the outer wall!*

"I'm tired of sneaking, Mellie," Rook declared. "Let's just run for it."

Mellie couldn't think of any better idea. "Okay, Rooky. Lead the way."

They hurried towards the front gate but then stopped as it came into view. The guards that had chased Ace and Lixy, and her brothers – Mellie never could remember their names – had returned to their post. They stood leaning against the stone gate-posts, looking out into the city for any more attacks by the band of city children. And, the two original guards had been joined by four others.

"Ready," Rook warned his partner in crime – Mellie took a deep breath. "Go!"

Rook and Mellie started running as fast as they could. They crossed the tower yard grass without slowing. The guards heard them coming, but not in time. Just as the guards turned, the cousins ran past them and out into the street. Five of the soldiers took off after the fleeing kids.

Suddenly, those guards had a bit more to do than chase two trespassers. Out of the shadows – from behind rain-barrels and porches and buildings – came running twenty-five of Calisay's finest street children – yelling and throwing rocks and sticks.

The soldiers had to choose – which ruffian would they chase? It didn't make much difference. The children knew the streets much better than the soldiers did.

The small army of Atters ran through alleys and behind sheds and into barns, and soon they had all disappeared into the shadows of the Calisay night.

Mellie jumped onto a porch and dived off its other side into some bushes. She was hidden and safe. But Mellie's cousin was not so lucky. Two soldiers were right behind him.

Rook Ceediney was running through the shadows between the buildings of Calisay. It was the middle of the night. The soldiers were chasing him.

+++++++++

The treasure finders left the White Bridge behind them as they continued east along the seacoast. They were entering the lands of the Forest Kingdoms. The trees were bigger and the forests thicker. But the road remained easy as they made their way to the ocean.

Occasionally, they passed some docks on the water and small villages. Easterners they encountered on the road were pleasant to them and it seemed as though the journey to the Very East was going to go very smoothly.

Circles talked with several sea-birds along the way, all of which were very friendly, and two of which had seen other groups of travelers who seemed to also be going to the Meeting of the Flags at Oceienne.

As Window spoke with people they passed on the road, he was surprised to learn that most of the Eastern Kingdoms spoke languages very similar to the Heartan language of Queen Karinne. Apparently, all of the Kingdoms were settled in their earliest days by ships bringing people from the same lands – probably farther to the east.

Window had wondered, when he was at the Heart Kingdom, if there was any ancient connection between that Kingdom and the Old Country of Hearte, to which his father sometimes sailed. The lands had almost the same name, but their languages were not similar.

As the days and miles went on, the travelers noticed that more and more of the easterners they passed on the road were armed. They carried swords and rods and seemed less friendly to the strangers.

Circles asked a bright red-finch about it, and the bird said that there had been raids on several of the Longsea port villages by pirates from the far-away Oceania.

The pirates were ruthless raiders who came ashore and violently took whatever they wanted – sometimes even kidnapping young men and boys and enslaving them on board their ships. All along the coast, the people were afraid that the pirates might strike them next.

One afternoon the travelers came upon a cemetery on a high piece of ground overlooking the sea. They stopped for lunch and rested by the gravestones as they had done before.

As they ate and looked out to the sea before them, Window spoke. "I'm not sure why, Circles, but I always find cemeteries somehow comforting and relaxing – maybe it is because they are so peaceful."

"What happens to people when they die, Window. It seems sad when they are gone."

"I don't know, Circles. Maybe we could ask the Angels. They might know."

Then Circles' voice seemed sad and tired – and his shoulders drooped. "We have been looking a long time, Window. What if we can't find the Angels?"

"Maybe they can find us."

That comment raised Circles' spirits quite a bit. "Hey, yeah," he replied with a smile. "Why should we have to do all of the work around here?"

On their fifth day beyond the White Bridge, as the travelers reached the base of a steep rise in the road, Circles stopped to adjust his pack strap. Window walked on ahead and followed the road up the hill. At the top of the rise, he stopped and looked down ahead of them to where the sea pushed into the shore.

Anchored in the shallow inlet water was a ship – a small, open, sea-skimmer with only three sails. On the sand of the shore near the boat stood a dozen of the ship's crew. They were rough looking men with long straggly, partially braided hair and wearing heavy clothes and boots. Each man carried a side-sword.

At the top of the ship's main mast, flapping in the breeze, was the triangle-shaped flag of the hated Pik Kingdom. In white cloth, sewn onto the black of the flag, was the Kingdom's symbol – a circle with two diagonal bars crossing through it. It was a coastal raiding ship of the Pik pirates!

The Piks had seen Window and immediately started to walk towards him. He would not be able to escape. He was sure to be captured by the advancing pirates. Circles was coming up the steep hill behind Window but had not yet reached the top of the rise, so the raiders had not yet seen him.
Circles was only a few steps from coming into the view of the pirates. Window had to do <u>something</u> to keep the Piks from seeing his friend. Window turned and walked slightly down the back side of the hill where he was partially hidden from the Piks' view. He quickly slipped off his pack and threw it to the side of the road, halfway down the hill into an area of many bushes and tall weeds.
As Circles almost reached the top of the hill, he started to ask, "Hey, Window. Why did you..."
Window took another step towards Circles and pushed his friend as hard as he could backwards, off the road and down the hill! Circles and his pack and bow went tumbling down the incline behind them. He rolled past bushes and through some tall grass. He finally caught himself as he rolled against some prickly berry bushes, but Window had already turned and walked towards the approaching men. They would capture him, but they had not seen Circles.

Window glanced out into the sea beyond the approaching raiders. There was no whirlwind of water coming from behind them. The travelers' leaf-talking wind friend would not be rescuing them this time.
As a last thought, Window reached into his pocket and pulled Charm from the bottom. Then he quickly raised his foot and dropped the crystal-light into his boot. He felt Charm as the sleeping spark slid down the side of his ankle.

The Pik raiders were not interested in any conversation. Two
of them roughly grabbed Window while another pulled Revell's
sword from its scabbard. A fourth pulled the knife from Window's
boot-sheath.

"Fen dahk pehk. Den seht!" the Pik captain growled at his
crew. The language was very rough sounding. It contained no
rhythmic patterns or pleasant-sounding words. It was harsh and
ugly.

The Piks made no attempt to talk to Window. It seemed that
the Piks knew that no one in the Very East Kingdoms would be
able to understand them.

However, Window was no ordinary traveler from the Very East
Kingdoms. Window once had a far-away friend with science-rings.
He could understand everything the pirates said.

"I think I'll just keep that secret to myself." he thought.

The Piks bound Window's hands with rough cord behind his
back and pushed him into their boat.

As Window looked back towards the shore, he saw one of the
pirates standing at the hilltop where he had been with Circles.
The pirate looked down into the bushes and tall weeds on the
other side of the hill for a moment. Then he turned back towards
the ship. He had decided not to look for Window's pack, or
anything else, in the underbrush. Circles was safe!

The crew unfurled the sails against the wind and the Pik ship
moved back into the sea. Window was pushed to one side of the
boat with coils of heavy rope and stacks of folded flax cloth used to
repair damaged sails. He sat against a coil of the rope and
thought. The ship tossed him back and forth as it buffeted the
Longsea waves.

"Well, it looks like I may never get the chance to write that
book of my adventures after all," Window admitted to himself. "I
wonder what Bill and the guys would say about this."

Window caught a bit of conversation as the ship was turned
and sailed to the east along the shore. This ship was to join with a
large Pik frigate later in the evening. Window would be joining

the crew of that ship before it sailed back to Pik waters far to the east and south.

"Take us to the Dredden," the Pik ship-master commanded his first mate. *"The Captain wants to set for the Oceienne waters tonight."*

Window knew he was in a very tough spot, but his concern for himself was overtaken by his concern for Circles.

"I hope I didn't push him too hard. I hope he didn't get hurt. I hope he is not too frightened."

Window thought of his little friend, alone, and certainly afraid. It broke his heart to think of it. It would be very difficult for Circles. "At least he has the Pixie dust to help him get back home."

Then Window realized – Circles would never go back home without him. He would search for years to find him. But the pirates were going to take Window back to the Pik Kingdom in far south Oceania. Circles could never find him there. No one could ever find him there. It would be hopeless to think of it.

Window gazed out across the beautiful water of the Longsea. The sun was warm but the breeze was cold. His wrists burned from the rough cord wound tightly around them. His mind was jumbled.

Window's thoughts turned to his father. "I always thought that my first time aboard a sailing ship would be with him – maybe sailing to Triston or somewhere. Now..." He tried to make himself think of something else. He could think of nothing else!

A majestic grey sea-gull flew over the ship and landed on the sail-bars for a rest. "If only I could talk to one of those birds, I could maybe tell Circles where I was," Window's mind raced on. "If only I hadn't gone on this stupid adventure. If only I had been more careful. If only I hadn't...." Window's mind was reeling. "I'm sorry, Circles. I'm sorry, Mary. I'm sorry, everybody." He fell into a terrible sleep as the ship took him farther to the east.

++++++++

"Get up!" a Pik sailor yelled at Window. He accompanied his command with a painful jab of his boot into Window's side. *"The Captain wants to see you."*

Window tried to shake his head clear. He stood as best he could and was pushed to the edge of the boat. He looked up. His small ship was tied against the side of the massive Pik frigate, Dredden. Its cannon-ports were open but its seventeen sails were furled. The ship was anchored for the night at the edge of the Forest Kingdom harbor at Trassenay. The sun was almost down and the lamps had been lit in the crew quarters on board the ship.

A rope was hooked to Window's belt and he was hoisted up the rough lumber of the ship's hull. Once aboard he was marched across the deck and up a few steps to the Captain's office. The door was opened and Window was shoved inside. The Captain was not there but someone else was.

Sitting on the floor and leaning against the sidewall, beneath a long, ornate window was another prisoner. Like Window, his hands had been tied behind his back, but then, another rope tied him to a metal ring on the wall. He appeared to have been there for a long time.

The prisoner was a man of about thirty years old. His clothes were torn and his dark hair and beard were ragged. Mixed with his beard was blood from cuts on his face that had dried and been left there. He had, obviously, been beaten by the Piks.

The man looked up as Window was thrown into the room. His tired eyes met with Window's.

"Who are you?" Window curiously asked the man.

"I am the Captain of the fools who let themselves be captured by the Piks," the man spoke, with contempt and anger in his voice. *"And who are you?"*

"I am your new lieutenant," Window replied.

The man smiled at Window's response. He hadn't smiled in a long time.

"And what brings you to take a cruise with the Piks this fine autumn eve, Master Lieutenant?"

"I have heard that the company on board this ship was the finest in all the land."

"*You heard correctly, stranger. By what name shall I call for you at dinner time?*"

"*You may call me Window. And please make sure that the potatoes are hot and served with butter.*"

The man smiled again

"*And how shall I address you?*" Window asked of his fellow prisoner.

"*Well, I am the Captain of the Seaflyer, which is a wind cruiser. But I am also the quartermaster, deckhand, gunner, carpenter, cook, and pilot.*"

"*Well, Captain Pilot, it sounds as if your crew is a bit undermanned.*"

"*I'm taking a few weeks off from my duties. My ship lies at anchor in harbor to the east of here, waiting for my return.*"

"*What brings you to the pleasant waters of the east?*" the man continued.

"*I'm looking for treasure. Would you know where any might be?*"

"*If I see any, I will send a prompt report.*"

"*I can see that this is going to be a very enjoyable voyage.*"

The man nodded his head towards the empty spot next to where he was sitting. Window flopped down on the floor and joined him, leaning against the wall.

The man's name was Reed Cardette. He had been chasing Pik pirates for months, trying to avenge the death of his parents at their hands. But he had tried one time too many and had been captured two weeks earlier in the harbor at Frenatte, which was farther to the east. Now he and Window were both to be taken to the Pik Kingdom and sold as crewmen aboard one of the many Pik ships.

Window looked around the Captain's office. Towards the middle of the room was a large chart table. He could see several yellowed charts open and partially covering each other. On the parts of the charts hanging off the edge of the table, Window could see the designations of countries and sea-lanes. Behind the table, to Window's right, was the Captain's large desk. It held a large flagon, a pistol, several writing pens, and Window's sword and knife.

Mounted on the wall behind the desk was a large, rectangular, framed, wooden board that held a collection of patches and medals and medallions. It was not a neatly arranged collection like the one at Oldsmith's house in Calisay. These items were stuck to the board in random fashion.

Captain Cardette noticed that Window had seen the charts on the table.

"If I could get a look of those maps, I could do a lot of damage to the Piks. This is the Pik Kingdom-ship. Captain Sarrenne is the commander of all of the Piks in the Very East. He and his lieutenant make their plans here, around these charts"

The man continued, *"If I had them, I would know all of the Pik safe harbors, all of their sea-lanes to Oceania, all of their storage-strongholds – and maybe even where they took my horses."*

Window listened as Pilot Cardette told him of the Pik raid when his parents were killed and their horses were stolen.

"The Captain and his lieutenant have spent an hour here every night looking over those charts. If only I could understand what they are saying. Sarrenne knows that no one from the Eastern Kingdoms can understand the Pik language. So they can discuss whatever they wish without worry that we will learn anything from them."

"What time do they usually do that?"

"Right after their evening meal. Probably in about an hour."

Window closed his eyes and tried to rest. He wanted to be alert when the Pik officers arrived.

It was dark outside before Captain Sarrenne and his Lieutenant, Lasedde, entered the ship's office. A small wall-lamp was burning and casting flickering shadows across the room.

"Lieutenant, search the new prisoner."

The Lieutenant pulled Window to his feet.

Window's knife and sword had already been taken from him. There was only one thing he still carried in his pocket. Lasedde felt it through the material of Window's pants, dug in his pocket, and pulled out the medallion.

"Here, Captain – another souvenir for your wall." He tossed the medallion onto the Captain's desk. It gave a small clank as it bounced across the hard wood. It gave Window a sickening feeling in his stomach to see his cherished medallion bring handled by the disgusting Piks.

The Captain looked at the medallion carelessly. *"Where is this from?"* he asked towards Window, but didn't expect an answer. He didn't get one.

Sarrenne flipped the medallion over in his hand and turned around towards his collection. Some of his captured medallions and patches were nailed or pinned to the soft wood of the wallboard. Some were stuck under the thin strip of wood that framed the board. Sarrenne took Window's medallion and shoved a corner of it under the framing strip. Window's faded medallion, that had been his companion since the very beginning, was now just one of a hundred nailed or mounted on the Captain's wall on board the Pik frigate Dredden. Window's spirits fell even lower than they had been.

"Tie him," Sarrenne commanded. The officer pushed Window to the floor and secured his already roped hands to the wall.

Cardette and Window sat quietly as the officers discussed their military plans. Cardette drifted off to sleep, but Window listened carefully, trying to remember as much of what they said as he could. After about twenty minutes the officers finished their discussion and left the room. Window sat and thought.

After about another twenty minutes the full moon passed from behind some clouds and its light streamed in through the window behind the prisoners. The moonlight beams struck the floor about the middle of the room. Window silently watched as the minutes slowly passed and the moon rose higher in the sky. With each passing minute, the moonlight moved closer across the floor towards the two prisoners.

Window had an idea – a very important idea.

"Cardette. Cardette," Window whispered to his fellow prisoner. *"Wake up."*

The man opened his eyes

"I need you to pull my boot off."

"What's the matter? Does your foot itch?" Cardette asked gruffly.

"Just do it!" ordered Window, in a very uncharacteristic manner.

The two men twisted around so that Cardette could get a hold of Window's boot. It took a few minutes but they were successful. The boot came off. Window was able to pick it up behind his back.

Window turned the boot upside down and gave it a shake. Something small and blue rolled out of the boot and onto the floor.

"What's that?" asked the windflyer captain.

Without responding, Window gave Charm a kick that sent him rolling into the moonlight near the middle of the room. Charm started to flash, and just a few seconds he was flying around and around the room passing through the moonbeam and becoming more and more awake.

Captain Cardette watched with great interest, and a great smile on his face.

"Charm, I have a request. I am tied to the wall. Can you burn through my ropes so I can be free of them?"

The crystal-light jumped up and down in the air, then immediately flew behind Window and landed on the rope binding him. Charm buzzed furiously back and forth across a section of the rope, over and over again. Twice he flew again into the moonbeam to regain his strength, and then again attacked the rope.

Window's heart was pumping rapidly – his mind jumping and hoping. He could feel the heat of the quickly moving light on his wrists. Window frantically pulled and twisted the rope as Charm continued to slowly cut through its fibers.

It took only one more desperate minute. The last of the rope strands broke apart! Charm had freed Window!

Window pulled the rope from his hands as he stood up. He grabbed his boot knife from the desk and in another minute had cut the rope holding Cardette. Both men were free! Cardette rushed to the chart table and hurriedly rolled up all of the charts and maps and stuck them under his arm. Window returned his knife to his boot-sheath, shoved Charm into his pocket, and grabbed his sword.

Cardette could not pass the chance to destroy the Pik ship. He tore the wall lamp from its mountings and threw it against the curtains around the window. As the glass of the lamp shattered, the oil splattered everywhere – the curtains and wall burst wildly into flames!

"Come on!" he yelled at Window, and grabbed his arm. *"Let's go!"*

Window turned to retrieve his medallion from the wall, but Cardette pulled him again, toward the door.

"Come on. It's going to get very hot in here!"

Window glanced back across the room. Flames had climbed to the ceiling and were creeping across the floor towards the Captain's desk. He could hear the shouts of the Pik crewmen who had seen the fire through the window and were rushing to the scene.

Window took one last look at his treasured medallion, still stuck to the wall of the now-flaming Pik ship. His heart broke. There was no time! He would have to leave it! Cardette gave another pull on Window's arm and they burst from the room just as the ship's crewmembers were arriving.

Cardette smashed his elbow into one sailor and pushed him into two others as he pointed Window towards the nearest side of the ship. The two of them scrambled over some wooden crates and a low railing. And then, in just a few more seconds, Captain Cardette and his young lieutenant were in the cold, cold water of the harbor at Trassenay.

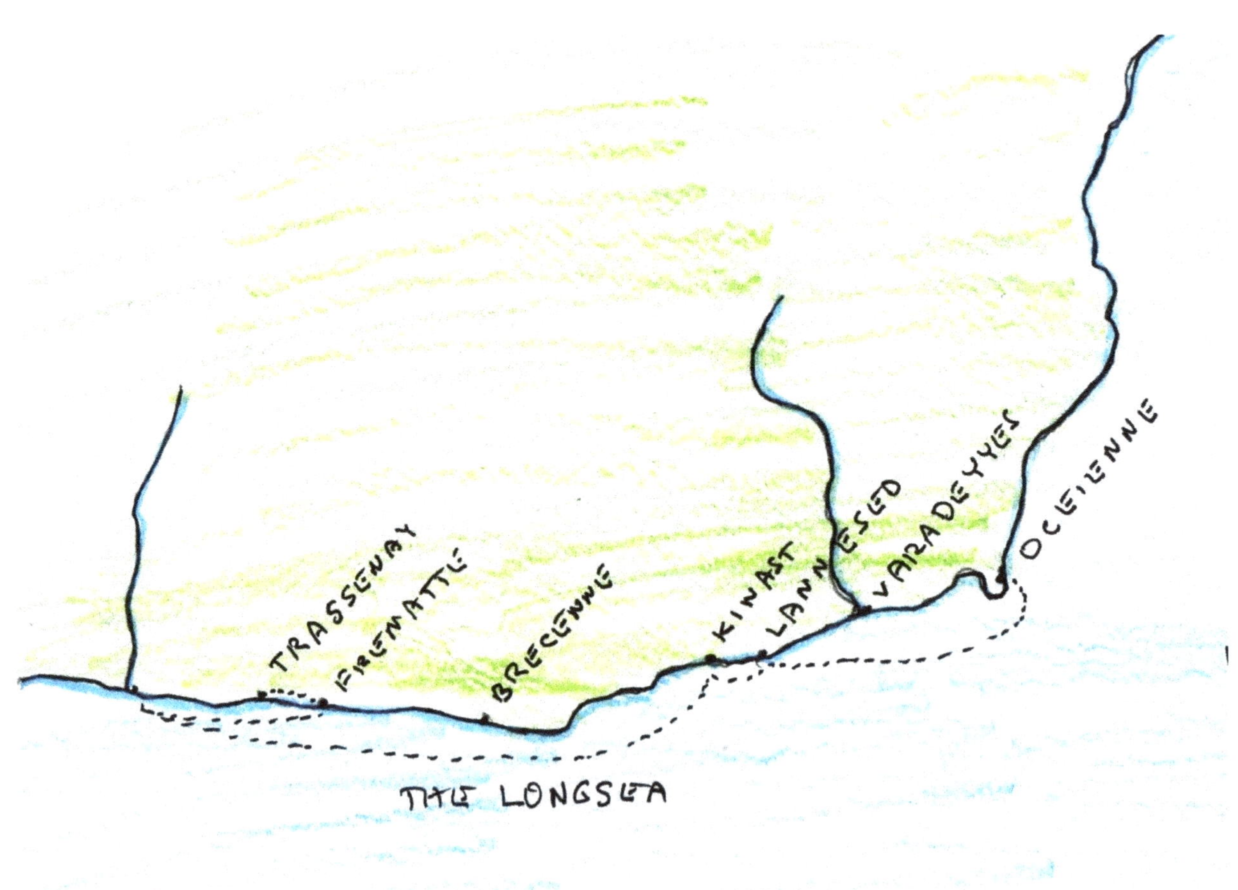

TRASSENAY
FIRENATTU
BRECIENNE
KINAST
LANNESED
VARADEYYES
OCEIENNE
THE LONGSEA

CHAPTER TWENTY-FIVE

TO THE SEA CITY

Cardette and Window struggled through the water towards the Trasennay Harbor dock. Window still had his sword in his hand and the Captain Pilot held an armload of maps. Window finally got his sword returned to its scabbard and then could more easily make his way to the shore.

The Longsea water was chilling. High above them, on the deck of the Dredden, sailors were frantically working to douse the fire in the Captain's office. Cardette watched hopefully as flames broke through the window and caught one of the side-sails on fire. He swore in disgust as the fire was put out by crewmen throwing buckets of water quickly drawn up from the harbor.

The two escaped prisoners worked their way to a low docking area and climbed out of the water. Cardette cursed again as, by the light of the moon, he quickly scanned the charts he had stolen. They were useless! All of the pirate Captain Sarenne's notations and lines and markings were now just smears of ink. He angrily crumpled up the papers and threw them into the harbor.

Window sat on the pier and looked up at the moon. Charm had saved him! He was lost from Circles, but Window's spirits had risen. Sitting at the edge of the water and gazing at the moon was a lot better than being sold into slavery. At least now he was free to go looking for Circles.

As he and Cardette rested for a minute, Window thought back to the Summer Breeze and his Uncle Bill. Bill surely was right about looking for adventure – and sometimes it even comes looking for you. Then Window felt for the medallion in his pocket, as he had a thousand times. It wasn't there – his spirits fell again.

Across the harbor on the Dredden, the Captain's room was dark. The hated ship once again sat quietly in the waters of Trasennay.

Cardette and Window hadn't spoken since their escape. The Captain turned to Window and simply said, *"Well?"*

Window responded carelessly, *"Well, I'm hungry. Let's go find something to eat."*

The Captain responded in kind. *"Okay, Master Lieutenant, you are hereby assigned kitchen duty."*

"And where, Good Sir, would be the location of the kitchen?"

"Do you know the wharf area here in Trasennay?"

"No, Captain. This is my first visit to your fine community."

"Well then, I suggest we start at the Lucky Gander. It is only a few streets in that direction."

"What's so lucky about it?"

"<u>You</u> are lucky if you get anything to eat – when you don't have any money."

Captain Cardette continued, *"Master Lieutenant, do you happen to have a penny or two about your person?"*

"Unfortunately, my coin purse was left in the custody of a friend of mine, who is not presently in the near vicinity."

Window pushed thoughts of Circles from his mind, and, although he had already been told while on board the Dredden the answer to his question, continued their conversation. *"And Captain, where is your ship anchored this fine evening?"*

"It awaits my return in the harbor at Frenatte.

"I have heard that the community of Frenatte is very pleasant this time of year."

"Not for me, it wasn't, Master Lieutenant. Not for me."

The two cold, wet, tired men climbed up the side of a grassy hill and soon found themselves on the crooked, dirty streets of Trasennay. The shops were all closed but the taverns were brightly lit. In each establishment, loud sailors, and louder dockmen, pushed against each other as they fought their way to the bar. Cardette led Window past four or five such places – to the Lucky Gander.

"We should be alright here – if Yerring is around. The Gander is his place."

Cardette and his lieutenant walked up the steps to the attached, wooden side-walk and pushed through the wide, open door. The night air was cold outside, but inside the crowd of men and the many burning lamps heated the air.

Several rough looking sailors turned to look at the arriving men. One pointed out to his friend the sword that Window was wearing on his belt. Others in the tavern carried swords or knives, but none were anything like the jewel-handled sword that Window carried. It sparkled brightly and caught the attention of everyone who saw it. It looked completely out of place hanging from the belt of a wet and dirty traveler.

"Where's Yerring?" the escaped Seaflyer captain demanded of the bartender.

"Who's your friend, Cardette – a lost prince of the Kingdoms?"

"He has signed on to my crew to kill Piks. Stay out of our way or you may be his first victim."

The man let out a hardy laugh. Window wished his new companion would keep his Pik killing ideas to himself.

Cardette led them to a table at the side of the room. While the noise and conversation of the crowded tavern filled the air, the two men ate a meal of fish and potatoes. Cardette's friend, Yerring, found them in a few minutes. He was large and bearded and deep voiced.

"I hear that you can't pay for the fish, Cardette."

"I set fire to the Captain's office on the Dredden tonight."

"Well then, the fish is happily yours! Next time, set fire to the sails."

"I'll remember your kind advice, Yerring. You are always so helpful."

"Who's your sword-carrying friend?"

"He rescued me from the Dredden, so I thought I would repay him with one of your fine meals."

"One of my meals for your life? You are overpaying him, Captain. Perhaps I should demand the return of one of my potatoes."

"Perhaps you should, Master Proprietor. Perhaps you should."

Yerring left the two men and returned to his duties. Window and the Captain finished their meal, and talked until the last sailor had been chased from the tavern.

Cardette was very impressed with the young man from the Grasslands Kingdom who had a jeweled sword on his belt – and a magic light in his pocket. Window didn't tell Cardette any more about himself than he thought he needed to. He just explained that he was traveling from the Grasslands to the Meeting of the Flags in Oceienne, and that his friend had been lost on the coast road. He also warned Cardette that Circles was from the very-far west and was, well, not like anyone around here.

Cardette had always sailed alone, but he liked the young traveler, and wanted to know him better. *"Would you and your lost friend care to join me hunting the Piks?"*

"I appreciate your generous offer, Captain. Let's find my friend and ask him of his wishes."

After being escorted from the tavern, the two men walked the streets of the village for a while and ended up sitting on some crates on the dock. They watched the sun come up as they made their plans. Cardette was very appreciative of Window's rescue of him, and would repay him by helping him find Circles, and then taking them to the Meeting of the Flags. Window loved the idea. He had found someone to help him look for Circles – and a ship ride to Oceienne.

They would first follow the road to the east where Cardette's ship was at anchor, and then return along the coast, searching for Circles.

By mid-morning of the next day, the two hungry Woot hunters were standing on the *Frenatte* harbor dock. Cardette's ship, the Seaflyer, was a beautiful ship – small, sleek, and fast. He told Window it could outrun any other ship on the sea. Window hoped that Cardette would not have to prove that was true. And, although it wasn't his father's ship, at least, this time, Window would not be sailing while being tied to a wall.

Cardette gave Window some simple instructions and the men readied the craft. Before long, the open-bodied flyer was sailing over the gentle waves of the Longsea. The sun was overhead but the wind was cold. Cardette gave Window a jacket to wear on top of his overshirt. Window wondered if he would ever again see his pack that he had tossed to the bottom of the hill past Circles. He wondered if he would ever see Circles again. He had to find him.

The voyage back past the harbor at Trassenay was quick and smooth. Cardette was an expert sailor and knew his ship well. Window sat against some boxes and enjoyed the trip. For the man who could have still been a prisoner in the hold of a Pik ship, it was a beautiful day.

Along the coast, the flyer passed two merchant vessels and then the Dredden, which was sailing back to the Oceanlands in the east.

"It's a good thing Sarrenne doesn't know that this is my ship. Otherwise we would be running from twenty-pound cannonballs right now."

"Yeah, good thing," agreed Window, enthusiastically.

Cardette looked longingly at the hated Pik ship as they passed it, wanting so badly to send it to the bottom of the sea. Window looked longingly at it for an entirely different reason.

"Where do you think that your far-western friend will be, Window," Cardette wanted to know. *"Sitting on a big rock along the shore?"*

"Well, he would be, if he knew we were looking for him, but probably he is hiding, afraid that he will be captured, too. I am so worried about him. He is from so very far away."

"And," Window added, *"he is so small, it would be really easy to miss him, even if he is on the road."*

Cardette kept the craft as close to shore as he could as the Seaflyer searched along the coast road. The miles and hours drifted by. Window hoped and hoped that he would just look towards the shore and see his little, white friend strolling along the road.

But it was not to be. At dusk, Cardette guided his ship to a shallow inlet for the night. *"We'll start early,"* he told Window as they furled the sails and tied them.

The next morning brought a light shower and more searching of the coast road. Window fixed his eyes on the shore and rarely turned away, even for a moment. He was becoming very discouraged. Circles could be anywhere. Then Window remembered – Circles was smart. His spirits rose a little.

Late in the afternoon, the trees of a little village appeared on the horizon. The town was on the coast road, built at the spot where a small river flowed into the Longsea. It turned out to be Window's favorite little village in all of the Eastlands.

At the western edge of the town, Window could see a bridge that crossed over the river. It was a pleasant looking bridge, surrounded by pleasant looking trees. On the edge of the bridge was a long thick wooden railing. High above the railing, flapping in the afternoon breeze, was a bright red kite. Sitting on the railing, holding the kite string, was Window's favorite Woot in all the world – Circles!

"There he is! Cardette, there he is! Quickly, there he is!"

Cardette was not used to taking orders but he joined in Window's happiness at discovering his lost friend. Cardette's heart, hardened so greatly by the killing of his parents, had become a bit more loving as he had listened to Window speak of Circles. Now his heart softened even more as he watched Window's joy at finding his friend.

The little Woot, of course, didn't know why the wind-flyer was coming toward the bridge. He never would have thought that Window would be on such a ship.

Cardette steered the wind-flyer directly up to the bridge.
"Circles! Circles! Circles!" Window called again and again.
The Woot couldn't believe it. His loving Window was on the ship. It jumped through his mind, "It's Window! It's Window!"

Circles hooked the end of the kite string between two boards of the bridge and stood up shouting. Even before the boat touched the shore, Window had jumped to the grass. Circles scurried down the embankment to greet him. Their reunion was sweet and exciting and joyful. Window and Circles squeezed each other as they never had before. Tears were in their eyes. They didn't want to let go.
Cardette had thrown all caring from his life and his heart, but watching the two best friends reunite, he, too, started to cry. He hadn't even cried when he found his parents dead. It was so painful for him he buried the feelings deep inside himself. Now, some of them were breaking free. He was glad that the others were too busy to see his tears.
The reunion between the two friends was joyous. Circles thanked Cardette twenty times for bringing Window to him. Cardette thanked Circles once for being so easy to find.

"Where did you get the kite, Circles?" Window wondered.
"I made it yesterday."
"And where did you get the kite-making materials?"
"I borrowed them from a work-shed in the village. A very nice lady yelled at me, but I didn't have any trouble slipping away from her when she grabbed me."
"So, you might say she was very helpful," Window offered.
"Well, she was a bit unhappy when I scared her chickens."

"Don't you like this paper? "Circles went on. "I knew if you came along here, you would be able to see it."
"You are a smart Woot, Circles," Window replied.

"That's what my Mama always said." Circles hadn't thought of home in a long time.

The two friends sat quietly, thinking, and looking out across the water. Then Circles told Window of his being alone.

"At first I was confused and a little angry that you shoved me down the hill. When I stopped rolling, I had my breath knocked out of me, so I couldn't call to you. That was a good thing, because when I looked out from between the bushes, I saw a pirate standing at the top of the hill. I figured that you had hidden somewhere nearby, too."

"After the man left the hill, I waited a few minutes, then carefully climbed up to see if he had gone. I was happy to see that his ship was sailing away from shore."

"I called and called your name, but you didn't answer. Then I searched the hillside for you. I thought that maybe you fell and were hurt. All I found was your pack. I looked and looked for you Window. I couldn't find you. I looked and looked for you." Tears returned to Circles eyes.

"I didn't know what to do, Window. I sat on my pack at the top of the hill and tried to find the ship. It was gone, Window. You were gone!"

Circles voice got very quiet. "I was afraid, Window. I was afraid you were hurt, and I was afraid for me. I sat on the hill for a long time, just feeling sorry for myself. Then I remembered that Raine said I was a special Woot. So I made a plan."

"My plan was to wait around here for a couple of days, in case you came back, and then continue to the Meeting of the Flags. I thought maybe someone there would help me find you. If no one would help me, I was going to get captured by the Piks, too – so I could be with you."

Tears again poured from Window's eyes.

"I was really scared, Window. I was really scared without you." Circles eyes grew sad as he thought of it.

Window squeezed his friend's hand tightly and let out a deep sigh. "Me, too, Circles. Me, too."

The three hungry friends sat on the bridge of the Seaflyer and ate some lunch. Window repaid Cardette for the meal he had provided for him with some dried meat and an apple.

"I've been dragging your pack with me the whole way, Window. That's why I wasn't farther up the coast."

"Thanks, Circles, for keeping it safe."

"I did eat some of your sugar-strips without asking. I hope you don't mind."

"I don't mind, Circles. You can have <u>all</u> of my sugar-strips if you want."

"I already did, Window," replied the very happy Woot.

Two boys from the village were walking towards the bridge, kicking dirt before them on the road as they approached.

"Let's leave the kite for them, Window. They can play with it, now."

"They will never know how special it is," Window answered his reunited friend.

As the travelers got aboard the Seaflyer, the boys ran onto the bridge and waved to the ship. They had no idea what the fluffy white creature was that returned their waves.

+++++++++

[OUTSIDE THE TRAEPELLE CASTLE YARD]

Across the Eastern Kingdoms, the far mountains, and past the Ancient lands, Pantine Tresette was tired. And she hoped that today wouldn't be as cold as yesterday. It was the beginning of winter and the Northlands would soon be covered in snow. She and Rings were on the last part of their journey home. In just a few more days, they would be back at Dawson's Inn in Laveselle.

Panni reached up and tugged on the fur of her huge Brarrie friend.

"'Only a few more miles, Rings. We can camp in the forest right by the castle. I can't wait to see it again."

Rings purred his agreement.

Their trek back to the Northlands from the unknown east had not been without difficulty. It had taken much longer than expected – weeks longer. Rings' injuries had slowed them down. They were more bothersome than he thought they would be.

They also had some trouble with the nettle-flies as they passed south of the grasslands. Rings had accidentally bumped into one of their nests. Panni was in such pain they had to stop traveling for several days. Her arms and legs still ached from their stings.

And, they lost still another day searching for a way through the mountains. At last, they had reached the southeastern corner of Traepelle Province.

They pushed on across the countryside backlands for the rest of the day. The sun had long been down when the two finally reached the hiding place they had chosen for the night.

"There it is, Rings – the Traepelle Castle."

Panni stood looking out from the trees of the Traepelle Province forest. Before her, across the wide, castle side-yard, was the home she had hated so much. By the light of the moon, she looked again on her former prison.

It was a dreary time of the year. There were no flowers in the gardens. There were no chairs on the lawn. The castle walls looked cold and grey. But Panni knew that, inside, the fires in the sleeping rooms were warm. The sheets were smooth and the pillows were soft. She scanned the towers and porches, but could see no one.

"There is the dancers' day-room," she explained as she pointed out several large windows to Rings. "I wonder who is Katice's new partner?"

Panni looked across to the castle again. "I remember one warm spring day when Collette and I flew a kite from that high porch. I do miss the fun of my friends. I hope it won't be too long until I can see them again."

Panni's dreams went on. "Rings, I wish we had a kite to fly. I can't wait until the spring. Will you go to Calisay with me? We could fly our own kite this time."

She closed her eyes. "Seeing a kite flying always makes me feel free."

Then, Panni thought of someone else. "I hope Window and Circles are having a good time finding oceans. I miss them so."

Rings smiled fondly at his friend. Her eyes were bright but her hair was wrapped around her face under her scarf to keep the wind from her cheeks.

And, Panni was shivering. She pushed against him and tried to get warm. "Let's build a fire. Could you help me find some branches, please?"

In just a few minutes, the fire was blazing. Panni and Rings, once again, sat and rested and talked as they had so many times.

"I am sorry it is too dangerous for you to see your friends at the Castle, Panni. Maybe in a few months you will be able to."

"I think that we should celebrate our return, anyway."

"How will we do that?"

"Let's see if the trillion or vermillion will help us. I'll get it from my pack."

Rings didn't know what the young woman had in mind. On their trip back from the Moonlands, they had used the dust to help them find their way through the mountains, but, other than that, they had left it undisturbed.

The Brarrie sat by the fire and waited as Panni retrieved the treasured dust. It was wrapped in paper from Window's notebook and stored inside an oil-skin food pouch from Dawson's. The dust was dry, and brilliant as ever.

"Okay, Rings, here we go."
Panni took a pinch of the silver trillion and threw it into the blazing fire. As soon as the dust hit the flames, it exploded into a flash of hot, white light that lit up their camp and the trees. It was as though it was suddenly the middle of the day. The magic dust floated about the clearing, flashing and glowing, as it slowly drifted away. Then, as a breeze blew through the campsite, the clearing was again lit only by the fire.

Rings had what was as close as he could come to a big smile on his face. "Hey, that was pretty good, Panni."
Some of the glowing dust had settled on his fur. His cheeks were sparkling and his legs were glowing.
"Try the vermillion," he urged her.
Panni took a pinch of dust from the other folded paper and threw it into the flames.

This time the reaction was even more dramatic. The multicolored dust came alive, and with a loud whooshing sound, shot high into the air above the campfire. It jumped above the treetops and then three or four times as high. In the sky, the magic dust sparkled and spun and whizzed about in every direction. It was as though a thousand matches had been lit and thrown into the air, each a different color, and each rushing to put itself out. The lights flashed across the top of the forest, and high into the night sky.
"Well, if anyone at the castle is looking out the window, they certainly will wonder what that was," Rings happily observed.

114

"I hope Feather and April saw it. They love bright things."

Panni was hopeful. "Maybe my mother and my sister, Lucy, were out on the porch at home in the village tonight. They might have seen it, too."

Then Panni thought, "Or, maybe no one noticed. It is pretty late. Maybe everyone is already sleeping."

She put the dust back into her pack and sat down on the ground against Rings.

"Oh, well, maybe no one saw it," she sighed to herself.

The fire was fading, but Panni was warm against her furry friend. Rings had already fallen asleep. Just as she closed her eyes to join him, two small visitors flew out from the trees and towards the fire.

"Come on, Pinkie. They are over here," one of them called to her sparkling friend.

"Ssshh! Don't wake them, Kisses. Don't wake them."

"Where do you think they got the sparking-dust?"

"Who cares? Let's just dump out all of the stuff from their packs and go."

"You take that one."

In just a minute, Panni's clothes and food and personal items were spread across the grass.

"Nice work, Pinkie. I like how evenly you spaced her things."

"Thanks, Kiss. Now let's get going. I want to get back and do some reading before I go to sleep."

The two satisfied intruders flipped over in the air a few times as bright specks of light flew everywhere.

Near the fire, Rings was dreaming. He gave a big sleeping snort and shook his giant body. Panni woke up. She opened her eyes just in time to see a silver Pixie and a pink Pixie flying into the trees. They left trails of colored sparkles behind them as they went.

+++++++++

Circles looked up at the moon. It had drifted far to the west.

"I'll bet it's over the Deep Woods by now," he thought. "I wonder if my Mama can see it."

He glanced over at Window, again. His friend was still sleeping against his pack on the deck of the Seaflyer as he had been the last twelve times Circles had checked. "He'd better still be there in the morning," the Woot said worriedly to himself.

Window woke up briefly, opened his eyes, and looked around for a moment. "Circles, go to sleep."

Circles glanced at Window one last time to make sure he was there. Then the tired Woot finally closed his eyes. Before long, he was dreaming about flying a kite from the top of the highest mast of a giant ship.

++++++++

The Seaflyer was anchored for the night along the shore just west of Trasennay. The two far-west travelers had joined with the orphaned ship Captain to sail to the Meeting of the Flags and hunt Pik pirates on their way. Cardette could tell that there was much more to the stories of his new companions than they were revealing to him, but he didn't mind. He could also tell that these two travelers were unlike any he had ever seen. He liked the idea of keeping them close to him for a while. They might come in very handy.

The next day, the new wind-flyer passengers sat comfortably on board in the sun as the craft smoothly sailed on to the east. Cardette stayed close to the shore except when they hurried past Breceene. He didn't want to encounter any Pik ships at the moment.

Like the River and Forest Kingdoms, the Very East was also a land of kingdoms. These kingdoms extended east from where their ship was now, to the ocean, then north, up along the ocean

coast as well. The city of Oceienne was in the Kingdom of
Voxania. The Vox were the most advanced and wealthiest of all
the peoples in the Very East.

Beyond the Very East were the Oceanlands, called Oceania,
which included the many Island Kingdoms in the Far Ocean. The
Pik Kingdom was in the very south of Oceania.

Cardette knew about the Meeting of the Flags. Five years
before, the last time the kingdoms all met together, he had carried
representatives from one of the far islands to the gathering.

As they made their way to the ocean, Circles decided that he
wanted to become a sailor. He had Cardette teach him all about
raising the sails, tying the special knots, and handling the rudder.
His padded hands never slipped on a rope and his padded feet
never slipped on the wet deck.

"You are a natural sailor, Circles," Cardette called to him when
Circles easily climbed up the mast pole to free the corner of a sail
that was caught between some ropes. And, Circles was thrilled to
be allowed to be the Captain for a time, when Cardette let him
steer the swift craft.

"I'll bet that I am the best sea-captain in all of the Deep Woods,
Window." Circles bragged to his friend.

"I'll bet you are, Circles. No doubt about it."

Circles smiled broadly and turned his face into the wind. The
sea spray splashed across his silky white fir. Circles was really
enjoying his time as a Woot of the sea.

"I'll bet you are," Window repeated to himself. He was sharing
Circles' great joy with him.

As the golden sun dropped below the western horizon, the
Seaflyer sailed silently into the harbor at Kinast. It was a busy
port and there were ships of all sizes and kingdoms anchored
there for the night.

"Do you know any tavern owners in Kinast?" Window wanted to
know.

*"I use to, but I got into a little trouble with the sheriff one night
so now I just ...."* Cardette stopped talking. He had been looking

over the ships in the harbor and saw something. It was a small
single-sailed boat, tied to the dock.

Without any further explanation, he said, *That's Denagan's
skiff."*

Cardette guided the Seaflyer between several larger ships to
get closer to the dock.

*"Yerring found out that Denagan sells information to the Piks.
I am happy to announce that Master Denagan may have to swim
home to Luxania tomorrow."*

Captain Cardette pulled his wind-flyer up next to the smaller
craft.

*"Circles, take the rudder. Window, open that storage box by
your feet and hand me the drill brace and largest bit you can find."*

Both travelers did as they were instructed.

Cardette took the drill from Window and hopped from his ship
down into the skiff.

Window had never been involved in anything like this before.
Cardette was quick and smooth as he spun the shining drill bit
into the hard wood of the boat. Curls of freshly cut skiff-deck rose
from the ever-deepening hole at the tip of the drill. In just a few
seconds, a spout of seawater was shooting two feet into the air
above the deck of the skiff.

"Okay, let's go," Cardette calmly ordered as he climbed up into
the flyer. Then he took a quick look back, grabbed a wrench from
a hook on the inside wall of Denagan's boat and threw it into his
own toolbox.

Window could hardly believe it. Cardette was so smooth and
cool and matter of fact. The skiff was already sinking into the
Kinast water.

*"Let's go on to the harbor at Lannesed tonight. I don't want to
be here when Denagan can't find his boat. He might not want to
thank me in a way I would find pleasant."*

Circles and Window looked at each other. They couldn't think
of anything to say.

The travelers went farther east up the coast. Their night in the
Harbor at Lannesed was quiet and restful. They didn't happen

upon any more Lux spies, so they went to sleep without sinking any more boats.

The Meeting of the Flags was to take place in three days. The Seaflyer continued to the east, with a happy crew.

On the afternoon of the second day, Cardette yelled to his first-mate, *"Stand on the bow-bar, Circles, so you can be first to the ocean."*

"Are we there, Captain? Are we really there?" asked the happy sailor.

"As soon as we pass those cliffs to the north, we will no longer be in the Longsea. We will be in the Far Ocean."

"Window, we are there! We have made it to the ocean at last!"

The Deep Woods ocean-hunter climbed to the very front point of the ship, held on to the fore-line, and hung out over the water in front of the ship.

"Five – four – three – two – one," Window yelled to his friend.

"Woo-hoo!" yelled Circles, into the wind. "We made it!" He swung back and forth on the fore-line and sang some little Woot celebration song.

Circles climbed back inside the ship and hugged Window. "Thank you, Dear Friend. Because of you, I have seen the kites of Calisay, the Silkie, and two oceans. You are the best friend, ever."

"You make it easy, Circles. Very easy."

Circles looked out again into the sparkling water. "Window, the ocean looks a lot like the Longsea."

Circles was just a little disappointed that the ocean didn't look special somehow. "It looks a <u>lot</u> like it."

Then Circles looked out still farther to the east and squinted to see to the edge of the horizon. "What do you think is out there, Window?"

Window looked into his friend's happy eyes, but didn't say anything. Window just smiled.

++++++++

The port at Oceienne was large and very busy. There were huge Royal ships that brought Kings and Queens, and smaller ships that carried lesser representatives. The harbor was so full that many of the visitors to the city had to drop anchor along the shore. Because Cardette's ship was small, he worked his way between the larger vessels and had no difficulty finding a spot to tie up at a dock near the shore.

The two ocean-hunting travelers from the west were about to visit the largest city in all of the Very East. They stepped from the Seaflyer into another world.

On the docks and on the streets of Oceienne, Window and Circles saw visitors from near and far – from the River and Forest Kingdoms – from the middle and far kingdoms of the Very East – from the Oceanlands and Islands – all arriving for the Meeting of the Flags.

They saw fancy wagons and fancier carriages. There were soldiers and guards and servants of every description. The Royalty wore their richest clothes and their most colorful scarves. Their carriages and horses were cloaked in their brightest kingdom colors.

On the streets of the city, the townspeople dressed in their finest clothes as well, and welcomed the travelers from the far-away kingdoms with food and entertainment. The merchants did their best to interest Kings and Queens, and their lessors, with jewelry and pottery and prizes of every description.

As the day went on, more great ships joined those already crowded at the harbor. There were more ships from the Oceanlands, and the Very East Kingdoms of the Northern Coast. Covered wagons arrived from the Grasslands and joined those already filling the streets.

Window and Circles walked with Cardette as they pushed through the crowds on the streets and in the shops of Oceienne. It was exciting to be among the fanciest clothes and most powerful people in that whole part of the world.

Window was so impressed by all of the official visitors he saw, that he had forgotten something important. "Oh, yeah. We are official visitors, too," he suddenly remembered.

As they pressed on through the crowds of color and motion, Window noticed that a few people <u>were</u> looking at him and Circles. But that was not because they were so magnificent and impressive looking. It was because they looked so out of place among the royalty and other officials. Although a few men noticed his sword, no one was impressed by Window's worn, dirty, traveler's clothes. Many people, though, did stare at Circles for a long time.

The Meeting of the Flags was to take place at the Palace of the Vox Kingdom. There would be days of meetings and conferences attended by the kingdom representatives. The assembly would begin with a ceremony of the raising of the flags.

Neither Cardette nor Window had any nice clothes for Window to wear to the assembly, or money to buy any. Window was worried. "I am not sure that it will honor the Kingdom of the Hearts if I attend the Assembly looking like I just walked in from the Grasslands – which I sort of did."

"Circles, would you like to present the Heart flag at the ceremony?"

Circles didn't say anything. He just brushed his always-shiny, always-clean, fur with his hand, as though he were preparing it for the occasion.

Cardette decided to not attend the Flag Ceremony. "I'll wait for you at the ship. I don't want to leave it unguarded for too long. There may be some Pik spies around here and I am on their list of enemies. I'll wait for you important people here at my ship.

Window put on his cleanest shirt – which wasn't very clean – and walked with Circles. Circles carried the Heart flag, rolled up under his arm.

The Vox Palace was on the high ground just to the north of the harbor. The two unlikely Heart Kingdom representatives showed their official invitation to the guards at the gate. They were welcomed, and, from there, they were led to a large, open pavilion overlooking the ocean. It was a beautiful sight.

Royalty and dignitaries were everywhere. There were kings
from the Middle Kingdoms and the Queen from Aselle. There was
a prince from Tenia and a princess from Luxania. There were
Captains from Pennessa and Oceania. The Kyees were there and
the Varennes. Only the King of Pikaia had not been invited.

+++++++++

In an open expanse at the top of the hillside overlooking the
water there were thirty-five flagpoles in a line from north to
south. One at a time, a representative of each kingdom would
come forward and present their flag to the Vox officials. As the
crowd of people in the grass and on the walkways cheered, the
flags would be raised one at a time.

The ceremony began as the Voxanian Palace orchestra played
from an area to the side of the grounds. The sky was beautifully
blue and white as the flags were brought forward and raised.

Soldiers saluted and courtiers bowed and the orchestra played
as each colorful flag was sent flapping in the ocean breeze. There
were flags of every color and design – birds and swords and
crowns and trees and swirls and angles. One by one, the flagpoles
were filled, starting at the north end of the line of poles and
proceeding to the south.

Heart was the first of the Grasslands Kingdoms to be
recognized. Window waited back in the standing crowd as Circles
carried the white flag with the red heart across the stone-paved
yard to the base of the poles. Window was so proud of his friend
as Circles walked with his best Woot posture and grace. Window
thought of Queen Karinne and Anna. They would have been
proud of Circles, too. Window was happy that he was part of
honoring the Hearts.

The crowd of royal and official onlookers let out a muffled gasp
and a lot of muffled chatter as the little Woot brought the flag
forward. The attendant took the flag and slowly raised it to the
top of the pole. Circles saluted as the orchestra played the Heart
Kingdom anthem. Window had heard it played before, at the
funerals of those Hearts killed by the Ides.

Circles returned and stood by Window. It was a wonderfully colorful sight before them. Beautiful flags all framed by a beautiful sky.

"Pretty impressive, Circles," Window shared with him.

"Yes, I am," answered the little Woot as he winked at his friend.

The ceremony went on for quite a while. The last flags raised were those of the Oceanlands – the islands in the Far Ocean to the east. Window watched as two representatives from one of the Kingdoms approached the flag line.

The flag carriers seemed extremely old and frail. They were men – very tall and wrapped in beautifully shining robes. They walked carefully and deliberately as they came forward. Their flag was white with a silver design of some sort. Window couldn't see it very well as it flapped in the breeze blowing in from the ocean.

As the flag was raised, the Voxanian orchestra played the music of the Kingdom. Window was puzzled. He seemed to recognize the melody of the piece from somewhere. Where could it be? He thought back to his school days but couldn't place the music.

"Hey, Window," Circles interrupted Window's thoughts. "It sounds like they're playing Moonbow's music!"

That was it! The melody of the music of the ocean kingdom reminded Window of one of the melodies played by the Moonwood plants in the Underland! But it wasn't exactly the same, he didn't think. How could it be?

"Circles, you are right! It does ..."

Just then, two soldiers pushed roughly against Window. One of the men had drawn his side-sword and held its tip against Window's stomach.

"Where did you get a jeweled sword of the Farhill Kingdom?" the man demanded to know.

"Stole it, no doubt," the other man answered for him.

Window's thoughts were no longer of music. The men recognized the pattern of jewels on his sword. It must have come from their kingdom. Window was sure that the soldiers wouldn't be interested in the story of Revell's many exploits, so he said nothing.

"Come with us!" one of the men demanded.

The demanding soldiers were not paying any attention to Circles who was standing next to Window. Window glanced at Circles. They had been through so much together by now that a glance was enough to say a lot.

Window turned to leave with the soldiers. He started to walk from the crowd of officials. The men were following right behind him. Circles followed the soldiers.

Suddenly, Window stopped and turned around. Circles dropped to his hands and knees behind the men. Before the soldiers could react, Window gave them each a quick shove. They both tumbled over backwards across the kneeling Woot.

However, Circles wasn't kneeling for long. He sprang to his feet and raced alongside Window as they ran across the courtyard, through the Palace gate, and down the wide walkway towards the harbor. Window looked back. The Farhill Kingdom soldiers were right behind them.

At the bottom of the Palace walkway, the runners tore across the busy loading street towards the crowded docks. The Seaflyer was tied at one of the nearest dock poles on the north side of the harbor.

"Cardette! Cardette!" Circles squealed. "Cardette!"

The lounging Captain was surprised to see the two Kingdom-honored members of his crew being chased by soldiers, but quickly assessed the situation. By the time his fleeing friends reached the ship, he had already cast off the line and was hoisting the mainsail up the mast.

Without slowing his pace, Window jumped from the dock and barely made it into the boat. Circles jumped also, but didn't make it! He splashed into the water and bobbed up and down next to the ship as the soldiers arrived.

Cardette and Window both drew their swords. The pursuing soldiers became less enthusiastic about their chase as they were confronted, across the harbor waters, by two men brandishing swords in their direction. The men stood silently as Window quickly retrieved Circles from the water. As the Seaflyer moved steadily out into the harbor, the soldiers watched for a minute, then turned and walked back towards the Palace grounds.

"So, how was the ceremony?" Cardette asked with a smile.

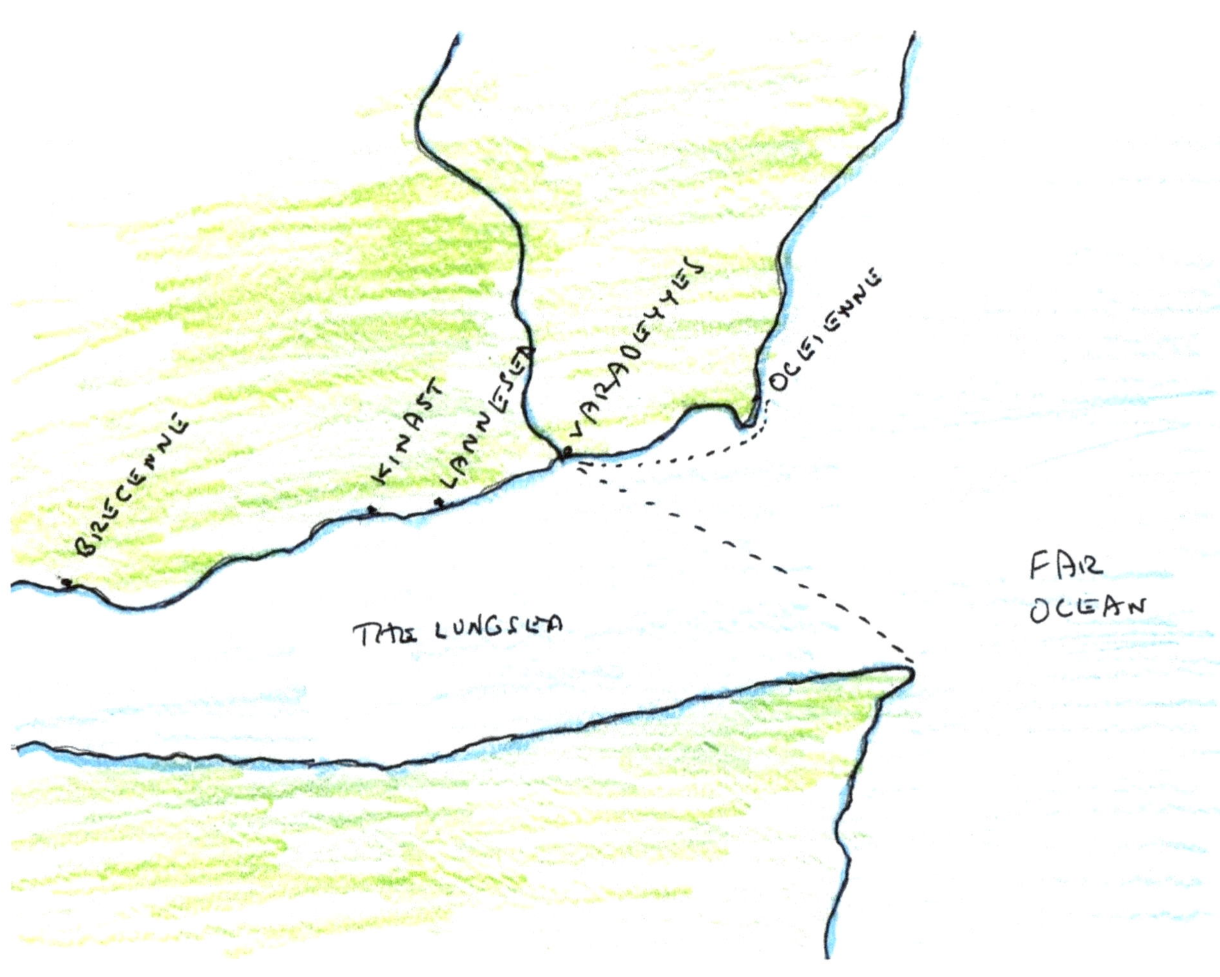

BRECEPNE
KINAST
LONNESER
VARADGYYES
OCLEIENNE
THE LUNGSEA
FAR OCEAN

CHAPTER TWENTY-SIX

TO THE FAR OCEAN POINT

"Hey, Cardette. Can you do this?"

Circles was balancing on one foot as he wound a piece of rope into a loop and tied it with a fancy line-knot.

"I don't want to do that."

"Oh."

The three outcasts from the Kingdom of the Vox were enjoying the sun as they rested aboard the Seaflyer. Window realized that he and Circles could not return to the Meeting of the Flags assembly. Cardette had decided that he should probably stay away from the Very East Kingdoms for a while – at least until things quieted down a bit. So, the sailors were relaxing in the warm ocean breeze.

The Captain thought it was pretty funny that the official representatives of the Kingdom of the Hearts were chased from the flag ceremony by soldiers.

"I am proud of you," he told his new friends. *"I always admire someone who can get into trouble by doing nothing. It's so much easier than the way I do it."*

"Where will you sail to now, Captain?" Window wondered. *"The wind seems agreeable."*

"I am still angry that I couldn't read the Dredden charts. They would have been a great help."

Window looked up at the billowing white clouds overhead. *"How long will you hunt the Piks, Cardette? Will you ever return to your home?"*

"My sister lives there again, but I promised myself that I would not return home without my family's horses."

The Captain went on, *"I know that my <u>parents</u> can never be returned, but I am sure that the Piks have not destroyed our horses. They are too valuable. So I will keep searching until I find them."*

But, his voice sounded tired. *"I have heard that the Piks have taken them to an island somewhere in the waters off the Oceania coast to the south – but there are hundreds and hundreds of islands. I could never search them all.*

Window spoke softly to the discouraged Captain. *"I know where your horses are, Cardette."*

"What do you know about horses, Window? You have only been in this part of the world for a few days."

"I heard Sarrenne and his lieutenant discussing the horses in the Captain's office on board the Dredden."

"But no one from the Very East can understand..." – then Cardette stopped himself. He had seen enough to realize that his new friends from the far-west were like no one else he would ever meet.

"Do you really know? Why didn't you tell me?" the Captain excitedly demanded.

"I wanted a nice ship ride to Oceienne. I knew that if I told you, you would immediately leave to retrieve your horses, and Circles and I would be walking again."

"I commend you on your analytical skills, Master Lieutenant. Please go on." Cardette tried to remain calm.

Window explained what he knew. *"The Piks steal many horses from the Very East Kingdoms. They keep them together on an island until they can transport them to Pikaia. Recently a Pik ship was sent there and took the stolen horses back to the far south."*

Cardette's spirits fell. He could never get his horses back from the Pik kingdom.

But Window was not yet finished. *"All of the horses except yours, that is."*

"What do you mean?"

"It seems that Captain Sarrenne and his lieutenant steal from the Piks as well as from everybody else. They particularly liked your family's Valdress horses and decided to keep them for themselves, rather than present them to their King, or share them with their crew."

"Your horses, Captain Cardette, still await you on an island off the southern ocean coast. And I know where it is," continued Window with a smile.

Cardette did his best to keep from sounding as thrilled as he was.

"I can see, Master Window, that contrary to my previous feelings on the matter, I was very fortunate to have been captured by the Piks – at least in your fine company."

Then Cardette asked the next important question. *"Will you be sharing your information with your favorite ship captain?"*

Window's thoughts flew to the other side of the world. *"No, my father, Captain Breesian, is not here – but I will share it with you."*

The Captain of the Seaflyer only heard the last part of Window's answer. But that was enough. He turned to his First-mate, *"Master Circles, take the bar."*

The happy sailor jumped up and grabbed the long rudder handle. He immediately had to lean against it to keep the craft on course.

The excited Seaflyer Captain hurriedly opened the long wooden chest Circles had been sitting on and pulled out a large, tattered, sea-chart.

"If you would be so kind as to show me where we might find the horses, Master Window, we could turn our sails without delay."

Cardette waited for Window to reply, almost without breathing. He didn't want to be breathing too loudly and cover Window's answer.

Window didn't bother to look at the map. He didn't know where any islands were located anyway.

"Sarrenne used the phrase 'southeast, between the Edge and the Point.' Do you know what that means?"

"Yes! Yes! Yes!" exclaimed an excited Cardette as he turned the map and revealed the spot. *"I know exactly where that is. There are only seven islands in that part of the ocean."*

The Captain pointed to the islands on his chart. *"It will be easy to find. Did they say which island?"*

"They spoke of keeping the horses 'behind the trees' until the transport ship arrived."

"Behind the trees?" Cardette thought furiously. *"Several of those islands are rocky and hilly. A couple of them are flatter and more forest covered."*

He moved his finger between two little dots on the map. *"The horses must be either here or here, hidden from the sight of any passing ships."*

Cardette was thrilled but still acting cool about it. *"Thank you. Thank you, Kind Sir. I appreciate your generous assistance in this regard."*

Then the Captain Pilot paused a moment and looked out across the water to the southeast. After so many months of searching, he now had a chance to regain his beloved horses. His mind was racing. There was something else he needed. He turned again to Window and quietly asked, *"Will you come with me?"*

Window glanced towards Circles who, of course, had been listening. Circles gave Window a look his friend had seen before.

Window gave their answer to the awaiting Cardette. *"When do we sail, Captain?"*

Captain Cardette gave Circles new headings for the Seaflyer. Circles turned the craft smoothly to the south – well, not really very smoothly. The Captain had to help him to keep the ship from almost overturning in the mid-day waves of the Far Sea. Circles didn't mind. He was having a grand time.

"Isn't there a Captain's hat or something I should be wearing?" he asked Cardette.

The former commander of the Seaflyer pulled a bright red signal flag from the side-chest and tied it into a loop. He dropped it over Circles' head where it rested on his shoulders.

"Now you are a real sailor, Circles," Window called to him, as the little Captain pretended to whistle a sea-tune. He had to pretend, because Circles didn't know any sea-tunes.

As the Seaflyer moved to the south, back towards the Longsea, Cardette explained to his crew where they would soon be sailing.

"The Edge is a small lonely mountain on an island called Presara, three days sail from here. The side of the mountain near the sea broke away and fell into the water. That flat side of the mountain is called the Edge."

"And where is the Point?" Window wanted to know.

"The Point is on the southern mainland. It is the very end of a tongue of land that sticks out into the ocean. Both are landmarks well known to sailors and merchants."

Then he added, *"And somewhere between are my horses."*

Window felt sorry for the man who had lost his parents and his beloved horses. *"How many horses did the Piks steal from your family, Cardette?"*

"Ten Valdress – they are very large, sleek horses. I used to love to ride them in our corral-fields and up the northern coast by our home. My father had raised Valdress for many years."

"And, how will we rescue them from the island? Your ship will probably only hold two or three."

"I am going to ask a friend of mine in Varadeyyes to help us."

"I hope he is big and strong," offered Circles. *"The horses are sure to be guarded by the Piks."*

"You will be surprised, Circles. You will be surprised." Then after thinking for a moment, he added, *"We will reach there tomorrow night."*

Window had still one more secret to reveal to his Captain friend. As they shared a lunch of dried meat and stale bread, Window tugged on the bread with his teeth and tried to tear off a piece. Finally, he was successful.

"Cardette, I sort of forgot to tell you one other thing I heard Sarrenne speak of with his lieutenant."

Cardette stuck his sharply pointed bread knife into the small table-board and cautiously waited for the details.

"Besides the horses, I know where Captain Serrenne's personal treasure stash is located, as well. It seems he and his lieutenant, Lasedde, don't return all of their stolen coins and gold chains to their King as they are supposed to. They have kept the most valuable prizes in a hiding place along the coast to Pikaia."

"And where might that hiding place be?" the extremely interested Captain asked.

"There is a chest of Pik treasures buried at The Point – by a rock at the treeline."

Captain Cardette smiled, his dark eyes glittering in the sun.

Circles jumped into the conversation. "Window, you said we have enough treasure back home."

"We do, Circles. But maybe some of the people of the Very East might like to have their stolen property returned."

"Yeah, I guess," came his unenthusiastic reply.

Cardette was much more positive in his response. *"Thank you for your fine story, Lieutenant. It just happens that the Seaflyer is already scheduled for a brief outing in that direction. Perhaps we will have time to stop by the Point for a visit to the Captain's secret hoard. It seems like that would be the polite thing to do."*

"It would seem so, Captain," Window replied. *"And I am sure you would like to repay Sarrenne for taking you on that cruise where I met you last week."*

"Yes, I would, Lieutenant. That would please me very much."

The polite owner of the Seaflyer took over the rudder from Circles so the Woot could have something to eat. In just a minute, Cardette was looking out across the water to the northeast, towards The Point, and singing to himself.

The Seaflyer skimmed across the Longsea to the southwest. The waning moon was high in the east. The cold night air chilled Circles, who was sitting next to Window by their packs.

"I miss our campfire, Window." He pushed closer to his friend.

"I guess I am getting a bit tired of the ocean, already. It just goes on and on and on. I used my far-scope today and all I could see was more water."

Window patted him on the arm. Circles went on. "It would be really hard to find anybody out here, if you were looking for them."

Clouds drifted across the moon. "Window, I wonder if the Angels live out here someplace. If <u>I</u> were an Angel, I think I would live in the mountains or the forest."

Circles continued to let his mind wander. Window listened silently as his friend went on.

"I wonder if Angels can live wherever they want."

"I wonder if we will ever see one."

"My friend, Powder, in the Deep Woods, used to dream about Angels. I wonder if she is still with her family."

"If I ever see an Angel, I will tell her about it when I get home."

"I wonder if it has snowed there yet."

"I wonder if Mama is worried about me."

Circles went to sleep thinking of home. He hadn't thought much about the Deep Woods in a long time.

+++++++++

[ON THE QUIET NIGHT HILLSIDE]

Far across the Longsea and the mountains, and beyond Riverhold and the deep forest edge, Powder was dreaming. Woots don't usually dream, but Powder was no ordinary Woot. She was a special Woot.

In her dream, Powder was leading her friends down the forest path. They were going on an adventure to see the Angels at the top of the big hill. Powder had heard that from the top of the hill you could see out of the forest and into the land beyond. Powder loved to dream about adventure, whether she was awake or not. Most Woots never even think about adventure.

Powder used to have a friend who dreamed of adventure but she hadn't seen him for a long time. She heard that he had gone to see the kites at Calisay but she didn't know what the kites at Calisay were. She only knew that they were on the other side of the Angel City, but she didn't know where that was, either.
Powder liked to dream about Angels. In her dreams, they would fly her away to magic places like the mountains or the ocean. Powder wanted to see the ocean someday. Her Mama said it was big and wet and beautiful and, while you were there, you got to eat sea-berries! Powder didn't know what sea-berries were, either, but she was determined to find out some day.

Sometimes Powder would sit on a rock or a log or a hillside and wonder about far-away places. A few weeks before, she was sitting on a big rock on the forest path and talked to an Owt who was walking up the trail. He was from the south and was going to visit a friend of his in the far north. His friend was a shepherd. Powder didn't know what a shepherd was, either. Maybe the Angels would take her there someday.
The Owt taught Powder a new song about the huge Silkie who lived on the Northern Plains. They sounded beautiful.
"I want to ride on one someday," she told the Owt.
The Owt told her that only Angels can ride on the Silkie. Powder didn't believe him.

She woke from her dream. It was cold outside her hole but she was covered with leaves and was quite comfortable. It was also dark outside. Powder decided to plan her day.
Yesterday, she and Kee and Jat and Jam and Quix and Rooh and Kan and Kix all went to the lake to see if it was frozen enough yet to slide on. It wasn't.

Well, today, first, she would try singing again. All Woots like to sing, but Powder wasn't very good at it. She was good at whistling.

Then, maybe she would ask her Mama about her fur again. Powder's fur hadn't changed yet. She was just a little worried. All of her friends had changed months ago but Powder was still bright white.

"You just have to wait, Darling," her mother had told her.

"But, I don't want to wait, Mama. I am tired of waiting."

"You just have to wait."

"Oh, well, maybe tomorrow," she had told herself.

Powder wasn't sleepy any more. She climbed out of her hole and sat on the side of the hill. The cold winter moon was climbing above the trees. The breeze fluttered her fur. She whistled a little melody to herself and listened to it sail across the quiet of the valley.

Powder stretched her arms as the moon drifted through the sky and high above the trees on the other side of the open space. Then she saw something standing in the moonlight.

"There's that shadow again. I wonder why he won't ever talk to me."

"Shadow, why won't you ever talk to me?" she called over to the misty figure. "Come keep me company. I'll tell you a story."

The shape stood silently, just drifting a bit with the breeze.

"I'll share my fen-grass with you," the friendly Woot-girl offered.

Just then, the moon went behind a cloud and the shadow disappeared. Powder sighed and shrugged her shoulders. "Oh, well, maybe tomorrow."

Powder the Woot closed her eyes and whistled another melody as she sat on the hillside. "I wonder if I will ever see Circles again," she thought to herself. "I hope so. I bet he could get that shadow to talk. I bet he could."

++++++++

The harbor at Varadeyyes was small and filled with ships as the Seaflyer sailed into port. Most of the ships were small fishing boats and medium sized transports. There was only one large merchant ship at anchor as the Seaflyer tied up at the dock. The lights of the town burned brightly in the windows along the wharf. Cardette led his crew directly to a restaurant-bar across the street from the harbor.

Inside, the restaurant was crowded with sailors and townspeople looking for an evening meal. Only a few people paid any attention to the Captain and his friends. Cardette choose a table for them near the wall.

"How will we pay for a meal this time, Cardette?" Window asked. *"Are you friends with the owner here, too?"*

"No. In fact, he chases me out whenever he sees me."

"Maybe you'd better slump down a little. You may be harder to see."

As soon as they sat down, a woman got up from her seat at the bar and come over to the travelers. She was, maybe, about Cardette's age, and, maybe, an attractive woman, but was covered by so much dirt it was impossible to be sure about either. She wore torn, canvass deck-pants and a loose, stained blouse that may have been white years before. Her curly dark hair fell in straggly strips in front of her face. She obviously was acquainted with the good Captain Cardette.

The women stuck her face down towards the Captain. She spoke with the unsophisticated style of someone who hadn't spent too many years in school.

"Where ya been, Reedy? I haven't seen ya in a while."

"Get out of here, Crossy, and leave me alone."

"That's Miss Cross to you sailor. And I don't have time to be teaching you good manners."

136

"I guess that you are too busy to be talkin' to me then. See ya around."

"Hey, wait a minute. What are you doin' in Varadeyyes?"

"Mindin' my own business. Why don't you try it sometime?"

"Because I am always thinking of helping those less talented than me – such as yourself, for example."

"You are too kind, Crossy. Don't bother. I am getting along just fine without you."

"You always were the modest kind. That's what I like about you."

"Do you know what I like about you?"

"We don't have that much time, Reedy. I want to be back to the docks by sunup."

"Why don't you stay and have a drink with us. I am sure you could tell my friends and me some entertaining stories of your latest exploits."

"I could if I knew what 'exploits' were, Reedy. Why don't you learn to talk right?"

"I'll try, Crossy. I'll try."

Window and Circles glanced at each other. They didn't say anything. They had no idea of what to say.

Crossy sat in the fourth chair and joined them in ordering a meal of chicken and biscuits. Circles passed on the chicken but asked for an apple instead.

The bartender brought drinks for everyone and Cardette introduced the far-west travelers to Miss Cross. She owned a small fleet of small boats by the *Varadeyyes* docks that she rented out to fishermen and merchants and anyone.

"This is the friend I was telling you about, Window. Crossy, here, will be helping us bring back the horses."

"Oh," replied a very surprised Window. He still couldn't think of anything else to say.

The chicken came and the horse-rescuers talked as they ate. Cardette explained his plan to his three dinner partners.

Miss Cross would find her friend, Mister Quarteir, who would
captain the Sunrise, a five-sailed supply ship that could easily
carry Cardette's ten horses.

Cardette, Window, and Circles would sail the Seaflyer to The
Point and retrieve the Dredden treasure. Then they would sail to
the northwest along the line of islands and go ashore on the two
where Cardette thought his horses might be hidden. After they
discovered which island held the horses, the Seaflyer would return
to Varadeyyes.

Cardette would use some of the Dredden treasure coins to pay
Quarteir and his crew to sail to the island to retrieve the horses.
Cardette hoped that only a few men would be guarding them.
Maybe he could buy the cooperation of those holding the horses
and get them back without Quarteir's crew having to use any force
at all. Anyway, that was his hopeful plan.

Window thought that it, actually, wasn't too bad of a plan.

The chicken and hot biscuits were delicious. The conversation
turned to questions of Crossy's family and her repair of one of her
boats. Window and Circles warmed to the woman and joined in.

She was, at first, reluctant to talk to Circles, but she quickly
found him fascinating and entertaining. He told her a funny story
about chasing a ground-rat across a frozen river that really got
her laughing. Her voice seemed to change after that.

"Someday, Master Circles, I would like to sail to your homeland
and *visit you there. Perhaps we could go fishing together."*

"I would like that, Miss Cross," answered Circles, without
mentioning a few of the difficulties that would involve. *"You
would be welcome anytime."*

Circles decided that he liked the woman.

The conversations continued. Then, as more minutes passed,
Window saw something very unexpected. As Cardette and Crossy
talked, she dropped her arm down by her side and he reached over
and touched her hand. The rough talking woman put her hand
around the Captain's hand and held it in hers. It seemed that
Window and Circles were not the only secret-keepers at the table.

Then, as it got near the time to go, Crossy's voice hardened again.

"It's always a pleasure to see you, Crossy," Cardette announced to his friend.

"Yeah, especially when you don't have any money," she replied.

"Yes, especially then. And thank you for your generosity."

"Don't get used to it," came her sharp response.

When all of the food and conversation had been finished, Crossy paid for the meals and the four conspirators left for Crossy's harbor-office room. As they turned into the street, another man got up from his table and walked to the door.

"Where ya going, Den?" someone called to him from the bar.

"I got somethin' to do," came his gruff reply. He pulled his collar over his neck and stepped into the night.

Crossy's place was warm and pleasant. She lived near the docks in a small room attached to the barn that held equipment and parts for the boats she rented. She invited her guests to sit down at a small table as she lit an oil lamp and placed it in front of them. As they talked, Cardette explained a few things to Window and Circles.

Cardette and Crossy had met by chance one day on the docks in Varadeyyes. For months, she had secretly allowed Cardette to store his clothes and other personal things, as well as supplies for the Seaflyer, in the back of her building. She also supplied him with food for his ship. Window thanked her for all of the food that he and Circles had eaten thinking it was Cardette's.

Crossy answered his thanks, *"The Good Captain does not make friends easily. You must be very important to him."*

Window replied with a similar observation. *"It seems you must be very important to him as well."*

Cardette's Varadeyyes confidante brushed the hair from her face. She expressed her agreement with Window's comment with a sigh and a smile.

+++++++++

The next morning found the crew of the Seaflyer back on the Longsea, as they sailed to the northern waters of Oceania. The air was cold on their faces as Cardette warned them, *"Winter is coming."*

"The ocean winds keep the Very East Kingdoms much warmer than the River and Forest Kingdoms, but still it gets very cold. Even on the coast, the snows sometimes are chilling. I hope to have my horses safely back in their stables at home before the worst weather is upon us."

Then, thinking of his home and speaking only to himself, he added, *"I miss my sister."*

The voyage to The Point would take them three days. Circles took out his far-scope so he could be the first one to see the land when they got near to it. Unfortunately for him, he started looking about a day early so he didn't have any success, although he did find three Varadeyyes fishing skiffs.

During the afternoon of the second day, Window asked Cardette about the odd representatives at the Meeting of the Flags. He wondered if the Captain knew which of the Oceanlands Kingdoms were represented by the frail-looking men in the long robes. Cardette thought that he did.

"They are from an island which is far beyond most of the Oceanlands. It originally had a different name, but now it is known as Everland. That is because the people there live such a long time. There are stories that everybody there lives to be well over a hundred years old."

The Captain went on. *"I don't know if that is true, but a couple of years ago, I was hired by the Varennes to bring several of the Evers to their kingdom. The men I took on my ship were old and weak. They seemed sad."*

"At the Flag Ceremony, I thought I recognized the Everland Kingdom music. Are you familiar with it?"

"No, I have never heard it," the Captain answered.

Window tried to remember the melody, but he couldn't.

Window was also wondering something else. *"Cardette, do you know when the first people came to the Eastlands – or where they came from?"*

"Most people believe these lands were first settled by people who came in ships from far over the sea – but no one is sure. The ancient Eastlands legends start with a poem about the first man and women in our lands. It is a long story of their love – and their life. I only know how it begins."

> *"Merrihart and Merrihawk*
> *Sailed on a golden ship*
> *Each was love and each was fire*
> *Searching ever o'er the sea*
> *Each was lost and each was found*
> *In the lands across the East"*

Window fell asleep that night thinking of sailing on a golden ship – to someplace warmer than where he was.

The next day the Seaflyer reached the lands on the southern side of the Longsea. Circles got out his far-scope and searched the horizon for The Point.

"I see the trees!" he excitedly announced. "I see the beach!"

Cardette set their course directly toward where Circles was looking.

In another half-hour, the Seaflyer was at anchor off the white sand of The Point. In all of the Very East, sailors knew The Point because it was the eastern-most point of land in all of the southern Oceanian mainland and marked the end of the Longsea and the beginning of the Far Ocean. It was a sand-covered tongue of land about two hundred feet wide and sticking out into the ocean from the treeline about twice that far.

The sun was high overhead as Cardette secured the rudder. Then he picked up a shovel from the tool chest and dropped over the side of the ship into the water. Window and Circles followed him into the water and up onto the sand. Circles had decided to take his bow and arrows with him, just in case. Cardette wore a knife. Window wore his sword.

"Well there is the treeline."
The treasure hunters walked across the sand towards the trees. Circles was talking to himself.
"If it wasn't so cold, this would be a great place to swim."
Circles walked on another few steps then spoke to Cardette. *"All we have to do is look for a big rock by the trees. This is going to be the easiest treasure we have ever found."*
"Do you mean you have found treasures before?" the Captain asked in surprise.
Circles looked at Window. Window looked at Circles. They didn't have to say anything.

The forest treeline stretched across The Point for just a couple hundred feet or so. Circles ran to the south end of the line and then raced along the sand next to the trees. In about a minute he had found two interesting things – a large rock, and a small boat hidden in the trees.
The boat was about fifteen feet long and had a small mast and sail. Someone had dragged it into the trees and taken down the mast pole. Then the boat was overturned, and the pole, with the sail and riggings wrapped around it, was placed under the craft, along with a box of tools. It looked as though the boat was undamaged and only needed to be reassembled to be seaworthy. It seemed that someone was preparing for a private trip on the water.

"Captain Sarrenne may be planning to retire from the pirate business," guessed Cardette. *"He could just dig up his chest, put it in this boat, and sail away."*
"Maybe it wasn't him," offered Circles. *"Maybe it was his Lieutenant, Lasedde."*
"Yeah, maybe."
"Maybe one of their crew," offered Window.

"Whoever it was, they are going to be disappointed," added Circles.

"Too bad," Cardette concluded with not much sincerity in his voice. He was smiling again.

The rock was just a big rock under the trees right at the edge of the sand. It was about half as tall as Circles and didn't have any markings on it. The treasure hunters looked all around the rock to see where it was most likely a small chest of coins and chains was most likely to be buried. Circles figured that the most likely place was the flat spot that had hardly any grass growing on it – the spot that looked like it had been disturbed sometime in the past few months.

"You are a master treasure hunter, Captain Circles," Window honored his friend. "I believe that you may be right."

Cardette placed the blade of his shovel against the ground at the spot Circles picked and put his boot on the shoulder of the shovel. He put his weight on the shovel and its blade sunk into the ground about six inches. It stopped with a dull clunk as it struck something hard.

Just as Cardette placed his foot on the shovel for another try, the treasure hunters' ears were met with a tremendous boom echoing across the sand from the ocean. They turned to see a piece of the shallow ocean floor next to the Seaflyer fly into the air surrounded by a huge spout of water.

Before they could react, there was another tremendous roar from the northwest. Another explosion of water and shallow sea bottom shot up from near the shore.

"The Dredden!" yelled Cardette. *"The Dredden! Come on!"* He threw down his shovel and started towards the shore as fast as he could run. Wood and metal flew into the air as a third cannonball ripped the railing from the south side of the Seaflyer, an instant before it impacted the water just beyond.

Window and Circles stood, shocked, for a moment, then they chased after Cardette. He had quickly gotten far ahead of them.

As Cardette ran, he pulled his knife from his belt. He raced over the sand, and splashing into the water, frantically cut the ship from its anchor.

As they ran after Cardette to the water, Window looked off to his left. The huge Pik ship and its huge sails were closing fast. A flash of fire and a plume of dark smoke shot out from one of the mighty ship's gunports. The cannonshot blasted into the beach right where Cardette had just been a moment before. Circles stopped – frozen still with fear. He was too afraid to go on. Window stopped with him.

There was another boom and another cannonball. This one hit on the sand only twenty feet in front of the standing Window and Circles. The impact of the shot and the violent spray of the sand knocked them both down backwards. The Seaflyer was already moving away from shore. Cardette was desperately working the sails to save his ship. Still another cannonball hit into the water just beyond the ship. The Seaflyer rocked violently.

Window tried to get up from the sand. Circles was pulling on his jacket to help him.

"What can we do, Window? Cardette is leaving us!"

Window stood up and looked out at the Seaflyer. For a brief moment, he saw Cardette look their direction, then quickly turn back to the task of saving his ship.

Off to their left, the massive guns of the Frigate Dredden were still firing. But the Seaflyer was fast and mobile. It was swiftly moving out into the ocean. More shots from the Dredden hit the water, but each was farther from Cardette's ship. The Seaflyer mainsail caught the Far Ocean wind and shot the craft across the waves toward safety. The Dredden turned sail in pursuit.

The Pik ship continued to fire as it chased the smaller ship. Gradually, the sound of the cannons faded as the great ship moved farther and farther from shore.

The two abandoned travelers stood silently and watched as the sails of the ships grew smaller and smaller. First the sails of the

Seaflyer, and then those of the Dredden, disappeared completely below the far horizon.

Circles was worried for their friend. "I hope Cardette is okay. I hope the Seaflyer is okay."

"Me, too, Circles. Me, too."

"I wonder if he thought of us when he realized he would have to leave."

"I'm sure he did, Circles."

"Well, Window," Circles assessed their situation. "We have nothing. We are on the wrong side of the world, and we have lost everything. Now what should we do?"

Then Circles thought for a moment and reached up and took Window's hand. "Well, we have each other." A slight smile returned to his face. "So I guess we will be alright."

The two abandoned travelers walked towards the edge of the water. Circles saw them first – two large lumps of something next to the cannonball craters in the sand a few feet from the water's edge.

Circles wiped some tears from his eyes and then his face. "Hey Window, it's our packs!"

Cardette had thrown them from the ship when he realized that to save the Seaflyer he would have to abandon his friends.

"I guess he <u>was</u> thinking of us, Window."

A very delighted and relieved Window very happily agreed, "I'm sure he was, Circles. I'm sure he was."

The two ocean-hunters sat down on top of their packs and looked out to sea towards the spot where Cardette had disappeared.

Tears returned to Circles' eyes. He raised his hand and waved it towards the empty spot on the horizon. The ocean breeze fluttered the fur on his hand and his arms and his face.

Circles' heart was aching. He knew he would probably never see the Captain again.

"Goodbye, Cardette," was all he could say.

"Goodbye, Captain," Window spoke quietly. "Farewell."

The two friends sat there on the sand for a long time. Clouds drifted by and sea birds flew overhead. One gull alighted near the travelers and squawked at Circles but Circles didn't feel like talking. The big bird lifted his head and jumped back into the air. Window watched as it disappeared over the water.

Finally, Window took a deep breath and spoke to his treasure-finding friend.
"Well, shall we go dig up those coins and things? I am sure that Sarrenne's chest is right by the rock where we thought."
"Let's just leave it there, Window. You said we don't need it, and, whatever it is, I surely am not going to drag it back to the Deep Woods with us. Maybe Cardette can come back for it."
Window put his arm around Circles' shoulder. Circles looked out into the deep blue water of the Far Ocean. The sun sparkled off the waves and the clouds billowed high above them. Circles' toes dug into the sand, warmed by the sun. A cold breeze blew across his face.
"This is a beautiful place, Window."
"Yes it is, Circles. Yes it is."

The sun flashed bright white on Circles' fur. He felt its warmth and let out a deep sigh.
"I'm tired of finding treasure, Window. Let's go home."
"Okay, Circles. Let's go home."

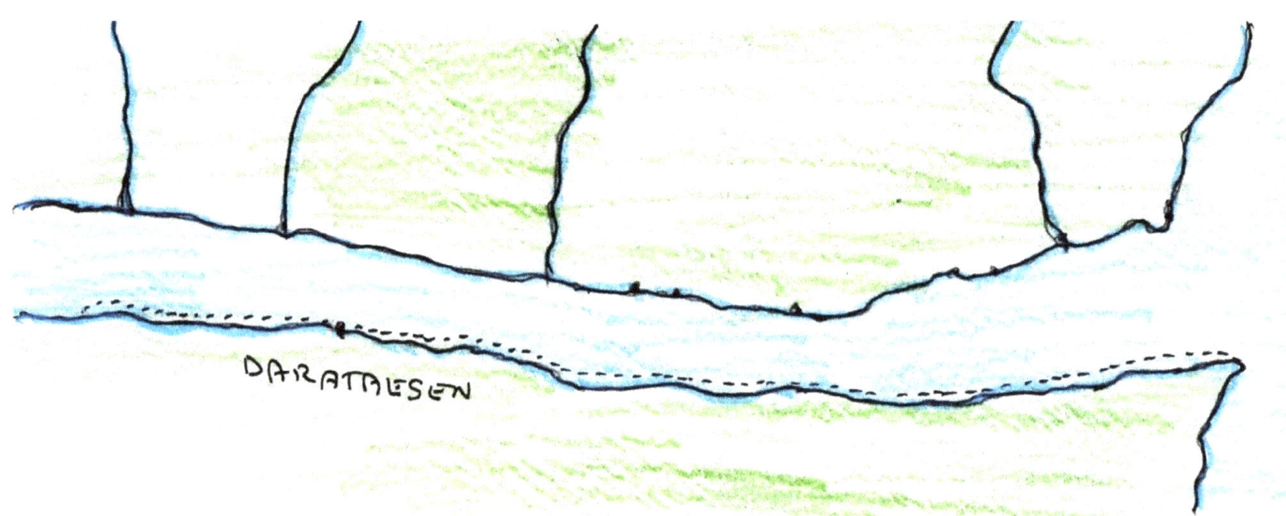

DARATHLSEN

CHAPTER TWENTY-SEVEN

ALONG THE SOUTHERN COAST

Circles and Window carried their packs back to the treeline
and dropped them in the sand near the overturned boat. Window
ran his hand over the hard, smooth wood along the bottom of the
craft. "Well, let's see if we can get the mast and sail mounted. If
we can't, we will never get home."

They flipped the boat upright and dragged it to the north shore
of The Point. It was very difficult for one man and one Woot to
pull the heavy craft through the sand so it took them quite a
while. After they finally got it to the edge of the water, they
returned for the mast and sail. Lastly, Window retrieved the
toolbox. Circles checked inside the box, and besides tools, found
matches, signal flags, and a fishing line.

"This boat is too small for us to try to sail across the Longsea,
and back to the coast road, Circles. Let's just follow along the
coast to the west on this side of the sea. That's the direction we
need to go anyway, to get home. If we stay close to the shore, we
should be alright.

"Are there any roads or cities along this side of the Longsea,
Window?"

"I don't know, Circles. I never asked Cardette because I didn't
expect us to be going home this way. But, that <u>is</u> the way home,

so let's just sail as far as we can. We will have to start walking
soon enough. And it is a very long way back to the Windlands."

"It looks like I will get my wish to see the Windlands, after all,
Window, but coming from the other direction."

"I guess that sometimes adventures have a way of getting
turned around."

The two travelers worked for about an hour to reattach the
mast and run all of the riggings. It was a good thing that they
had learned how to handle Cardette's boat or it would have been
impossible for them to make this one seaworthy.

When the boat had been reassembled and all of the lines run
they checked their packs to see how much food they had. There
was not much. Circles could always find some roots or leaves to
eat, but Window would need something more suitable for him.

Fortunately, Circles had recently borrowed a couple of apples
from the Seaflyer store-bin and a couple of packs of crackers. So
at least they would have something to eat for a day or so.

"How are we going to find something else for you, Window?
Most of the berries are gone until the spring. Only the really sour
ones remain – the ones that even the birds won't eat."

"I guess we will just have to sail along the coast and see what
we find."

"We should be pretty good at that by now, Window. We have
come a long way without always knowing where we were going.
And, we have done pretty well. We found the oceans and we found
lots of treasure."

"We didn't find the Angels, though, Circles. I am sorry about
that. Maybe they are farther out in the ocean somewhere."

Then Window had an idea. "Hey, would you like to use the
Pixie dust and ask it in which direction the Angels live?"

Circles thought it over a long time. They he answered, "No,
let's don't. If the dust tells us that the Angels are out in the ocean
someplace, we still can't go there. I think that the Angels will just
have to find us. It will be easy for them because we will be
traveling pretty slowly."

"Well then, Circles, here we are at the end of our travels to the east. We have made it a long way from home."

"I am proud of us, Window. We are very good travelers."

"We certainly made it farther than the kites of Calisay."

"Let's mark the spot. I'll carve another Angel letter into a tree so if the Angels see it they will know we were here looking for them."

"And I'll carve my medallion design into a tree – to mark how far it brought me from home."

Window reached for his boot knife, then stopped. His spirits fell when he remembered that his medallion was probably still stuck to the wooden frame on the wall of the Captain's office on the Dredden. Circles could tell how hurt Window was that the medallion was lost. He felt sorry for his friend from the Windlands.

Window went on, "Oh well, at least I still have my other treasures – my notebook, Panni's pin, a couple of my grandfather's coins, and a couple of Revell's Freeland coins."

"You are quite a treasure hunter, Window," Circles kidded him.

" – and Grandfather's belt and Revell's sword," Window continued to list his treasures.

"And, I have my bow and arrows and my far-scope and the jewel on my quiver – and a horse and a house!"

Thinking about all they had, Circles added, "We are rich, Window."

Window was still thinking, "And the Pixie dust, and, of course, Charm is still in my pocket."

"What are you going to do with those spurs, Window? Do you have a horse at home?"

"No, I guess that I should never have taken those from Queen Karinne. I did it mostly because she so wanted me to take a horse."

Then Window thought ahead, "The way home may take us through the Southrange in the Windlands. Maybe we can get some horses there."

"I wish I had Cameo with me now, Window."

"Yeah, but there are no roads here, Circles – and the forest is thick with trees. We would have to bring Cameo on this boat with us."

"Oh, yeah."

"Then, instead of a horse, I wish we had some springcookies. Do you think your grandmother would bake us some when we get to her house in the Windlands?"

"I am sure she will, Circles. She will probably bake you a whole batch."

Circles liked that woman.

"Okay, Circles, pick a tree and let's get carving. I want to be home by the time the sun goes down."

The two former Angel hunters each found a thin-barked tree to mark with Window's boot knife.

Circles made another pretend angel letter, and Window carved the year, W.Y. 147. Well, he started to carve 147, then he realized that the correct date of that day might actually be in year 148. He had lost track of the exact Windlands dates a long time ago. "Oh, I'll just put 147, anyway," he decided. "No one is going to be checking a calendar to see when we were here."

The two explorers stood and looked out to the Far Ocean for the last time. The sun had gone behind the clouds and it was cold and uncomfortable. Circles pushed against his friend.

"I surely never thought I would ever get this far from home, Window," Circles announced with a sigh. "You have been a great traveling partner."

Window tugged Circles tighter against his side. "You, too, Circles. You, too"

The two friends turned from the Far Ocean and started their long journey home.

Circles got in the boat and Window pushed it into the water. It was tossed quite a bit by the waves.

"I hope you like bouncing, Circles."

"I love bouncing," answered the Woot. "It is my specialty," he added as his head moved up and down along with everything else around him.

Window pulled the mast rope and the sail snapped open in the wind. Circles held the rudder bar as Window turned the sail to catch even more of the Longsea breeze.

"Goodbye, Ocean," Circles called as they moved away from the shore. "Goodbye, Angels. We are going home. Come see us when you can."

The two far-western sailors moved with the wind towards the west.

++++++++

Travel on the waters of the Longsea in their small craft was difficult and tiring for the sailors. After a few hours sailing along the tree-covered coastline, they decided to stop for the night. They worked their way to the shore and found a fallen tree they could tie up to.

Their first night on their journey home was a quiet one. Circles lit the fire and they enjoyed its warmth for the night. They shared an apple and some crackers. Circles snuggled up against Window as they fell to sleep.

The next day was a long, cold day on the water. They sailed the entire day along the coast, only stopping as the sun was going down. As they ate sparingly again, Circles tried to ask a curious grey-sparrow about the coast ahead of them, but the bird was too busy flying around from tree to tree, wasting his time.

Back on the water in the morning, the weather continued to get still colder. Window shivered through another day of steering the boat. Circles would spell him for short periods of time, but was unable to keep the craft on course.

"I'm sorry, Window," the little Woot told is friend. "I wish I was stronger."

"It's alright, Circles. I am doing okay."

Circles knew that Window was very tired, and sore – and hungry.

That night, around the fire, the travelers got Charm out in the moonlight and played Rainbow Chips for a while. That lifted their spirits. After that, since Circles was tired of singing and Window was tired of hearing stories, they just rested quietly. When they did speak, the conversation was usually about going home, getting home, and being at home – and, seeing their families, and Panni, and Rings, and the entire Oldsmith family again.

Window was missing Mary more than ever. Now that he thought he would be seeing her in a couple of months, he let himself think about her more often. Still, it was a long, cold way home. He ached for a warm bed and a warm meal, and a warm embrace from her.

"How long do you think it will take us, Window?"

"I don't know, Circles. The worst of winter is coming, and we are heading back farther to the north. We may have a lot of snow and ice that could delay us quite a bit. We will probably have to find somewhere to stay through the coldest weeks. I don't think we can travel though heavy snow, especially if there are tall mountains between the Longsea and the Windlands."

"Let's stay at a nice warm inn, Window. You can have the bed and I'll take the rug by the fire."

"Keep your eyes out for an inn, Circles. I hear that there are several nice ones in the area."

"You can count on me, Window. I am a champion inn hunter."

"I'll bet you are, Circles."

On their fourth day on the Longsea, the travelers found a low bank along the shore with just a few trees. They stopped for a very late lunch.

Well, they stopped for lunch, but the only food they had left was some stale crackers. They decided that if Window couldn't eat, at least maybe Circles could find some roots or something. Circles went searching and did find a couple of cay-roots, but they weren't very good.

"What are we going to do, Window? At home, we Woots store lots of roots and nuts and fruit for the winter, but now we have nothing."

"Why don't you ask a couple of birds if there is a city or someplace along the coast where we can get some food?"

It only took about an hour before Circles found a bird to talk to. A big, white bird, with two red wing-bars, flew right down to their camp.

It was a big Plains-dove like Sky-swift, their friend from the Grasslands. Circles said hello. It <u>was</u> Sky-swift! He had found them!

The bird did a lot of happy hopping around to celebrate his success. Then he told Circles about his search.

He had been looking everywhere along the northern Longsea coast for the two travelers. After a search of more than a week, Sky-swift finally found some gulls that liked to fly long distances across the water. They told him that they had seen a man and a small white companion on a boat on the other side of the Longsea, along its southern coast. Sky-swift knew that it must have been his traveler friends from the river.

Circles and his bird friend enjoyed their reunion. Window happily watched as the two exchanged stories. The dove told of his flight to the other side of the Grasslands, and Circles told of his trip to The Point.

"Let's just stay here tonight, Circles," Window suggested. "I am pretty tired, and not having anything to eat doesn't help."

Window and Circles built a fire and sat on some nearby rocks to keep warm. Sky-swift had never been so close to a fire before and he enjoyed its heat immensely. He was cold, and tired, as well, so he decided to stay around for a while and keep the travelers company. Apparently, he had been flying, almost without stopping, for days.

The moon was hidden behind clouds for the night, so the travelers couldn't bring Charm out to join them. But, the three unlikely campers enjoyed each other's company. Circles even sang

a few songs. Then Circles and Sky-swift played a singing game.
Window enjoyed watching and listening as Circles would sing a
line of melody and the bird would try to copy it. It turned out,
though, that Sky-swift was better at flying, and finding people,
than singing. When he tried to sing, all he could do was squawk.

Then, Circles and the dove talked for a long time by the fire.
Window leaned back against a tree and went to sleep.

"Wake up, Window. We should probably get going."
The sun was coming up and the fire had long been out.
Window looked around. "Where is Sky-swift?"
"He had to go. But he talked to a gull this morning that told
him that there is a city less than a morning's flight to the west
from here. We can be there in a couple of days."
Window was happy about the news of a city, but was not happy
he had to wait so long to get something to eat.
"I sure wish Cardette would have thrown that tin of dried meat
ashore along with our packs.
"Yeah, or some of Crossy's bread."
"Yeah."

Their day on the water was another difficult one for the sailors.
Window had lost some of his strength and it was becoming
increasing difficult to steer the boat. The wind remained good for
sailing, but it was a cold and chilling wind.

That night around their fire was dreary and lonely. Window
thought of warm nights on the porch with Mary. Circles dreamed
of jumping into a big pile of Woots to get out of the wind.

The next day on the water was much more pleasant. A warm
breeze came across from the southern forests and the clouds
stayed away. The sun warmed them quite a bit and cawing sea-
birds kept them company. The sailors felt better and were able to
enjoy their day on the water.

As they sailed on to the west, Circles got out his far-scope and
spent a lot of time looking across the water, back towards the east.
Window noticed, and asked him about it.

"What are you looking for, Circles? That city is supposed to be in the other direction."

"I know, Window, but I was hoping that Sky-swift would be coming back today.

"Where did he go?"

"He had never been all the way to the Far Ocean, so he was going to fly there and then come right back."

"Oh."

By the middle of the afternoon, the air had gotten still warmer. Window loosened his jacket and held his face up towards the sun.

Circles was again looking to the east with his far-scope. He scanned the horizon and every time he saw a gull or hawk in the sky he called out, "There's one, maybe it's him."

After a couple of hours of searching for Sky-swift, Circles was just about to give up for a while when he saw another large bird flying towards them from the east. Circles watched and watched as the bird approached.

"It's him! It's him! Window, it's Sky-swift!"

Window looked out over the water as the plains-dove grew closer.

"Hey, Circles, it looks like he brought us something to eat. He has something in his beak."

"He's got it! He's got it!" Circles went wild with joy. "Window, he's got it!"

"He's got what?" Window asked, confused by Circles' elation.

Then, with the biggest smile that Window had ever seen on his friend's face, Circles joyfully announced, "Window, Sky-swift has brought your medallion! He has your medallion!"

The big white bird glided down for a smooth landing on the side rail of the boat.

He hopped right over to Window and dropped the medallion in Window's hand.

"I told him where it was. I told him about the Dredden, and its sails, and its mast flag, and where to look for it."

Window couldn't believe it – but there it was – his rusted, faded, mysterious medallion – lying in his hand!

"Circles, this is wonderful! You are wonderful! Sky-swift, you are wonderful, too!"

He turned the medallion over and over, rubbing his thumb across its slightly raised surface. He couldn't stop rubbing it. It seemed too good to be true!

"Circles, you are the smartest, best friend in the whole world. Sky-swift, you are the smartest, best bird in the whole world."

The proud Woot and the proud dove stood up straight and bowed to Window. At least Circles did. Sky-swift was thirsty. He hopped over to an empty water cup sitting on the side-chest and squawked.

"Sure, Swifty, you've earned it." Circles opened their water tin and poured some in the little cup.

"Did you have any trouble finding the ship?" Circles wanted to know.

The bird told Circles that gulls don't care much about smaller ships, but they always notice the mighty sailing ships. They like to perch on the highest masts and riggings. Sky-swift was able to find at least one bird in every Longsea coast harbor that knew which direction the Dredden had sailed. So the ship-hunting bird just flew up the coast, stopping at every harbor until he reached one where he was told that the Dredden sailed out to sea to the north-east.

Then Swifty just flew northeast and asked more gulls along the way. He found the Dredden sailing back to the Longsea coast that same afternoon. Then, a quick hop through an open window into the Captain's office, and he found the medallion. It was still where the Captain had put it, stuck in the wooden frame on the wall.

Window's spirits were raised tremendously. He put the medallion in his pocket, but kept sticking his hand in to see that it was still there.

Circles was so happy that he had gotten Window's prized treasure back to him that he did what he said was a little sailor's dance – it wasn't.

"I wish I had something for you, Swifty," Window spoke to the bird. "Do you like really stale crackers?"

He opened the package and handed a piece of a broken one to the dove. Sky-swift took it in his beak and swallowed it right down. Then he hopped back to Circles for another drink.

The good news continued for the sailors. In just a few hours, they encountered a fishing boat coming along the shore from the west. The sailors were very light-skinned and spoke the Eastern Kingdoms language with an odd accent.

Window, though, could understand them easily. They told him that their city, which was really just a village, was only a bit farther up the coast. Before the sun had set, the happy Window and Circles were tied to a dock at the port of Darataesen.

Darataesen was a fishing village. The small harbor was filled with fishing boats and fishing people. As Sky-swift flew off to explore, Window tied up their boat at the end of a long dock, and he and Circles walked to the shops in the buildings along the waterfront.

As the hungry sailors stepped from the dock and into the street, several people stared at Circles but no one approached the strangers. Window wore his sword, but none of the local men were armed. At first Window wasn't going to wear it, but then he thought that it may be a good idea to impress the townspeople a bit.

As he and Circles had sailed into the small harbor, he had no idea how to get some food and clothes, but then he began to imagine what Captain Cardette might do, if he were in this situation. Captain Cardette would do something dramatic and unexpected.

The travelers had decided that what they needed most was some warmer clothes for Window and a blanket and some food.

"Window, all we have are some Freeland coins. What if the people here don't want any of those? How will we pay for what we need?"

"I have an idea, Circles. I hope it will work. We have no money so we have to use what we do have." He explained his idea to Circles.

"Okay, I'll try it," the Woot answered, as a sly smile came to his face.

Window reached into his jacket pocket. He felt the Pixie dust containers he had taken from his pack.

Besides looking for a store that sold food, as well as clothes, Window wanted to find a store with many customers in it.

After a brief search down the wooden side-walk, the travelers found a busy general-supply store along the wharf. As they entered the store the fishermen and merchants inside immediately stopped their shopping and conversations. Everyone turned their attention to the stranger with the jeweled sword and his odd companion. A few people on the street who had seen the pair enter the store came up to the large front window and peered through the glass to see what was happening inside.

As everyone curiously watched, Window and Circles went around the store collecting items they needed. Window chose a blanket, a heavy jacket, a pair of gloves, and food – dried meat, lots of dried fruit, and hard biscuits.

Circles picked up a long fishing pole and pretended to cast its line into some imaginary water. Then he entertained everyone by catching an imaginary fish, as Window finished their shopping.

Window piled the items on the end of the counter. It was time to pay for them. Instead of taking some money from his pocket as everyone expected, he reached down, pulled his sword from its sheath, and, with a loud thud, violently stuck the point of it into the top of the counter. The jewels on its handle sparkled as the sword stood up where all could see. The watching people were stunned. Everyone stood still, waiting to see what would happen next.

With great fanfare, Window raised his voice and announced to the people watching him, *"We have come from far-away to entertain you, Kind People. My friend is a great magician from beyond the Far Sea. If you will please provide us with this food*

The fascinated people gathered around, fell completely silent,
and listened with great interest. A few of them left the store to go
tell others about what was going on. In just a minute, the store
was full of entranced Darataesens.

Outside, the sun had started to go down. No one wanted to
miss the magic of the great magician of the east. At the insistence
of several of the men, the storeowner quickly lit wall-lamps so
everyone could see.

Circles jumped up onto the counter, bowed deeply, and sang a
few melodies of a Woot song about sunshine. Everyone was
impressed with his mysterious words. Then he bowed again and
spun around a few times. The men, and now a few women,
couldn't take their eyes off of the small, white-furred magician.

Next, as everyone remained transfixed on him, Circles ran
down the length of the counter and jumped onto a wooden potato
bin, then without stopping, or even slowing down, hopped to a
basket of dried apples, and then to a shelf of baked bread. The
crowd loved it. Circles jumped on a few more things and never
once slipped or fell.

Applause filled the store as more people were pushing inside
from the walk outside. And more townspeople stuck their faces up
to the window glass and gazed in to see the magician's
performance.

Next, with great expression, Window announced that the
mystical creature from afar would make his mystical dust float in
the air. Window was hoping that the dust would cooperate.

"We usually have had better luck with the vermillion, Circles,"
Window spoke quietly into the ear of his magician friend. "Let's
try it first." Circles jumped back onto the counter.

Holding his arms out wide, Circles recited a Woot poem about
playing in the rain and stomping in mud puddles, but of course, no
one understood what he was saying. It all just sounded magical to
the Darataesens. Window instructed everyone to watch very
closely – he warned them to not even blink. That made Circles

laugh, and he fell out of character for a moment, and had to compose himself again.

People continued to crowd into the store. Now there were more women, and several children. Window carefully opened the tin of vermillion, making sure to act as though it was very dangerous. The crowd became very quiet and intense. Circles recited a few lines of "All Roads Lead To Calisay."

Window held the dust container high over his head. He told everyone to remain silent, although no one was saying anything or making any noise at all. Everyone held their breath for whatever was coming next.

Circles carefully reached into the berry tin and took a pinch of the dust in his fingers. He slowly dropped the dust into the palm of his other hand, and held his hand out so everyone could see its many-colored sparkles.

The crowd was ready. It was time for the magic to begin. Circles glanced at Window and spoke in Atlandan, "I sure hope this works."

Circles leaned over and whispered to the vermillion, "Will you please do a trick for us?" Then he gently blew into his hand. The colorful dust puffed up into the air. It granted Circles' request!

The dust rose another foot or so into the air above his hand. The people didn't move their eyes from the floating, magic dust. Circles held his hands above his head to signify what he thought would be the conclusion of the trick. The vermillion had a different idea.

Suddenly, the dust started to float in a circular path around the room over the heads of the people. The amazed townspeople followed it with their heads and eyes as the sparkling dust moved faster and faster. Soon it was spinning around and around the room in an ever-widening circle. Some of the audience became frightened and pushed their way from the store. One mother pulled her daughter under her arm to protect her from the swirling dust.

Window was a little concerned. Circles was thrilled – he really was a magician!

As the dust spun around the room overhead, Circles bowed again to the audience. His act was a great success. Most of the audience applauded.

Then the Pixie dust decided to have a little fun. On three of the room's four walls, there was an oil-lamp lit. The dust widened its circular path until it was almost touching the walls. The people were getting a little tired of watching it fly around and were ready for another trick. They didn't have to wait long.

Without warning, the dust widened and raised its circular path even more. The spinning circle of color passed over the open tops of the three lamp-glasses and, as it did, the dust seemed to catch fire – the spinning circle of dust became a spinning circle of flames! Sparkling fire was whizzing around the room!

The townspeople were stunned and horrified. Those near the door ran outside as quickly as possible. Others fell to the floor and covered their heads. No one was happy about the magician's latest trick. They were frightened, and worried about the store, and themselves, catching on fire.

"Make it stop!" several people yelled. Circles looked at Window. Window had never thought about stopping the dust from doing anything – just getting it started. Three of the unhappy men grabbed Circles and roughly pulled him from the counter. Others surrounded Window demanding that they make the fire stop.

Circles slipped away from the men. Window pulled his sword from the counter and slid it into its sheath. More angry townspeople crowded towards them.

Circles called out to the flaming vermillion, "Please stop burning and fly away." He got part of his wish.

 All at once, the spinning, flaming, sparkling dust seemed to explode. The blast didn't hurt anyone, but scared them even more. There was a terrifically loud bang, and then a crash, as the fiery dust flew out through the front window opening, smashing the large sheet of window glass into tiny sparkling pieces. The pieces of sparkling glass landed on the side-walk and the people outside, but didn't hurt them.

Then outside, the sparkling flames of dust shot up into the air as horrified townspeople ran for safety. Inside the store, the shocked people were in stunned silence.

After such a frightening performance, it was highly unlikely that the mystical travelers from the Kingdom of the Ocean would be rewarded with any free food and clothing. A thought jumped into Window's mind, "How would Cardette handle <u>this</u> situation?"

Without taking any time to think it over, Window shouted to his magician friend, "Come on, Circles, grab that blanket and the jacket!"

Circles followed Window's instructions. Window picked up the bag of meat, and the bag of fruit, and the bag of biscuits. As he turned, he clumsily shoved the gloves under his belt.

"Come on!" Window yelled as the stunned store-people watched without reacting.

The Far Ocean magician and his assistant ran from the store, clutching their stolen goods in their hands and under their arms as they pushed into the street. Window slammed into a man and just kept running. The blanket and the jacket flew behind Circles like two kites on a windy day.

The two fleeing thieves raced down the street to the docks as angry voices called out behind them. They jumped onto their boat and frantically pushed off from the dock. But, they didn't have to hurry. No one had been brave enough to chase the strangers with the flaming, magic dust.

The air was cold but the travelers' spirits were warm. They had food and clothes to help them through the cold weather. They also had left the Darataesen villagers a night they would never forget.

As their boat moved away from the dock, out into the Longsea, Circles looked back on the village. There were several people on the shore watching them go.

"Well, Window. I guess it really is Pixie dust."

Window opened a bag and took a bite of a biscuit. He replied with a smile, "Maybe we should have used the trillion."

After the travelers' visit to Darataesen, their boat voyage west on the Longsea became a lot easier, especially for Window, who now had a heavy jacket and gloves to wear as he handled the rudder bar. Woots like cold weather, but just sitting in a cold boat for hours, Circles still got uncomfortable. So, he often wore the blanket around him.

Sky-swift sailed with the two travelers for another day, but then, that night at their campfire, said he enjoyed flying by the light of the moon, and was ready to return to the Grasslands. Window gave him the last of the stale crackers to get him ready for his trip and the big bird seemed to enjoy them.

"Come see me in the Deep Woods someday," Circles invited him. The Plains-dove said that he would do that, and he would bring some of his friends, so he wouldn't have to make the long journey alone.

Sky-swift let Circles pat him on the head. Then he jumped into the air, flew a quick circle around the camp, squawked twice, and headed back across the water to the north. Circles watched by the light of the moon with his far-scope as the big bird climbed high into the night sky and disappeared over the northern Longsea horizon.

+++++++++

[BY THE ICE-COVERED RIVER]

Far past the sea, the mountains, and on beyond the prairies of the Windlands, Mary Looking was standing by her window in the moonlight. She had gotten out of bed and didn't bother to pull a blanket around her uncovered skin. She was cold – she didn't care. She couldn't sleep – she didn't care. She was thinking of only one thing.

Mary stood by the window and looked through the glass out across the glittering scene before her. Yesterday, the river had frozen over completely. Tonight, the ice sparkled in the moonlight as though it were made of diamonds. It was a beautiful, quiet, sparkling river.

Last night, she had gotten out her notebook and started to write a letter to him, but she couldn't get beyond "Dearest Window." What could she write? How could she ever tell him everything she desperately needed him to know? How would he ever read the words from deep in her heart?

His grandmother had written to her several times and told her not to worry, that Window would be alright. Mary wasn't so sure. Now, it had been months and months since he left for the Northlands. She couldn't bear to think of him lost or hurt or captured – or worse.

And then, last night, after she had looked across the moonlit ice, instead of a letter, she had written him a verse. She had recited it over and over again as she had gone to bed. It calmed her a bit to pretend to be speaking the words to him. If only he could hear them.

Once, about a year ago, as he and Mary had sat together late into the night, Window had told her, "I will be thinking of you whenever the moon is high in the east." Tonight, as she followed its light up to the sky, she thought, "Maybe he is looking at this very same moon at this very same moment." The thought comforted her as she sent her love to him on a moonbeam.

Mary stood in the cold of her room and gazed again at the moonlight on the river. She opened her heart completely and spoke the words of her verse out loud, imagining, as she did, that he was with her, listening and holding her. Her words echoed off of the window glass and quietly bounced around her room.

> *"Stars across the nighttime sky*
> *You and I below*
> *Silent silver beams of white*
> *Moonlight in the snow*

Moonlit wish and midnight eyes
Hearts in never-ending sighs
May I kiss you once or twice
I love you always
Moon on ice"

Mary Looking was standing by her window in the moonlight. She had gotten out of bed and didn't bother to pull a blanket around her. She was cold – she didn't care. She couldn't sleep – she didn't care. She was thinking of only one thing.

+++++++++

The boat-travelers continued along the southern coast of the Longsea, stopping at night and building a campfire to sleep by.

Circles had added the matches he found in the boat toolbox to the ones they already had, so the travelers never had to go without a fire. But they didn't know when they might ever be able to find matches again, so they didn't want to use any more than necessary.

When they stopped for the third night after leaving Darataesen, Circles had trouble getting the fire to start. The wood they had found was too wet to burn easily. He had already used three of their valuable matches without success.

Circles tried one more time. This time, the flame from the match caught on a few of the twigs he had gathered. Suddenly, the breeze started to blow around the fire – not around the outside of the fire where Circles was standing, but around the inside of the stack of twigs and sticks. The wind spun within the little stack of sticks and the fire spread quickly. Then some larger pieces of wood burst into flames as though the night wind was trying to help the fire burn.

Circles watched as the flames grew. "Hey, Window. There's something very breezy around here, and I think I know who it is."

With that comment, another blast of wind hit the fire and sent flames jumping up into the sky as though they were being thrown into the air.

"I think that it's our friend, the leaf-talking wind. Except there are no leaves on most of these trees, so he can't say anything – but I think he just helped me get our fire started."

"Hello, Mister Wind," Circles spoke into the air above the fire. "Welcome back to our camp. It is nice to see you again – well, sort of see you. If it is you, blow the fire again so we will know."

The flames jumped again. It was their wind-friend!

"Hey, Mister Wind," Window joined in. "Thanks for helping us with those soldiers in the grasslands. I really appreciated that."

The flames jumped in response.

"Have you been traveling since then?" Circles asked in a rather one-sided conversation.

The flames blew towards the west.

Circles was thinking. "Window, since there are no leaves on the trees, can you think of anything else that we could use, so we could hear our visitor talk?"

Window tried to think of something that would shake or vibrate in different ways if the wind blew over it – his notebook pages, the blanket, the water – but couldn't think of anything that might work.

"I don't think we have anything, Circles. I guess we will just have to ask him questions he can answer with the fire, or maybe he can write answers in the dirt."

Circles wouldn't give up. He thought and thought about everything they had.

"I know!" Circles excitedly yelled as he jumped to his feet. "Maybe the signal flags!"

Circles ran over to the boat and brought back, from the tool box, the five brightly colored flags used by sailors to signal other boats and ships. Two were larger and rectangular. Two were smaller and rectangular. And, one was smaller and triangular. He also brought a long piece of rope from the emergency supply.

Within just a couple of minutes, Window and Circles had stretched the rope between two trees near the fire and had attached the flags. They hung straight down for the moment, but for the next many minutes, they were fluttering, and flapping, and shaking, and snapping, and talking in the breeze.

Circles had done it again! The different sizes and shapes of the flags, along with the skill of their wind-friend to blow them each with different intensities, caused the fluttering flags to give off different sounds and pitches. It took the travelers a couple of minutes to get used to it, but before too long, as the colorful flags briskly moved in the breeze, the wind was once again talking to the travelers.

Window and Circles sat by the fire. Their wind-visitor blew back and forth through the flags.

"Where have you been, Mister Wind? We had hoped to see you sooner, after you helped us in the Grasslands."

"I needed to rest for a while after that little adventure. By the time I was ready to follow you again, you were on your way to the east. I decided to go west, instead. Talking to you had gotten me interested in seeing that ocean again."

The friendly wind continued, *"I went over to the Windlands to see where you are from, Window. It is a very nice place for a wind. The breezes really have a good time blowing over there."*

"Did you go to where I live in Windtown? You should be right at home there."

"No, I went out by the coastlands. I spent a couple of days spinning the giant windmills there. I hadn't done that in a long time."

I'll bet you were over by a town called Union, where my friend Mary lives. Maybe you even blew right past her."

"I remember seeing that town, but I didn't go there."

Window suddenly had a very hopeful, and very unlikely idea. "If I wrote Mary a note on a piece of paper, could you carry it all the way to the Windlands and deliver it to her? Could you do that?"

Window waited with great anticipation, as the flags didn't
answer right away.

"*Yes, I think so. I have often carried things that I was blowing,
a long distance, but never that far. I guess I could take her a small
message without too much trouble. If I dropped it, I could just pick
it back up again and keep on blowing it until I got to wherever she
is. I might have trouble finding her though. I usually blow
wherever I want without paying too much attention to where I am.*"

"Will you please try for me? Please?"

"*I will do it for you, Window.*"

As Circles continued the conversation, Window retrieved his
notebook from his pack. He carefully tore out about a quarter of
an unused page from the back, and sat off by himself as he wrote.

> My Dearest Mary,
> A friend of mine is bringing you
> this note, from my travels far,
> far away, so you will know that I
> am alright and thinking of you.
> He may not speak to you, but
> will leave this where you will
> find it. I am sorry that it must
> be such a short message. I will
> explain when I see you at your
> house in Windtown in the spring.
> My heart aches to see you.
> My love belongs to you.
> Window

Window sighed, put his pencil away, and walked back to the
fire. "Well, here it is."

He held the small piece of notepaper out in front of him.
Without warning, the note was pulled from his fingers by the
wind. It twisted and turned and flipped in the air in front of
them. For a moment, it fell towards the ground, but then it was
picked up again by the breeze and thrown upwards.

The row of flags flapped once more. *"Goodbye friends. I will look for you again."*

"Goodbye – and thanks," Window called out towards the flags.

"Come see us when you can," Circles added.

Suddenly the camp was quiet again.

"Wow, Window. That wind-talker sure doesn't stay in one place for too long."

Window had something else on his mind. He wondered if his message would really be carried all the way to Mary.

Then Circles thought of something, "Window, he forgot to ask you how to find her."

Window let out a big disappointed sigh. "Maybe he'll come back, so I can tell him – or, maybe he can find her anyway."

"Yeah, maybe," replied Circles.

Window wasn't at all sure the note would make it to Mary.

"It's a long, long way for a piece of paper to be carried by the wind."

"Yeah," agreed Circles, "a long, long way."

The next morning, the travelers were, once again, sailing to the west. The sky was cloudy and the wind was cold.

"What will we find when we get to the end of the Longsea, Window? Are there any roads over there?"

"Why don't you use your far-scope and see if you can see anything."

Circles searched the western horizon. "Just more water," was his report. Then he turned his scope back to the east.

"Hey, Window," Circles spoke quietly to his friend. "There's a big storm coming."

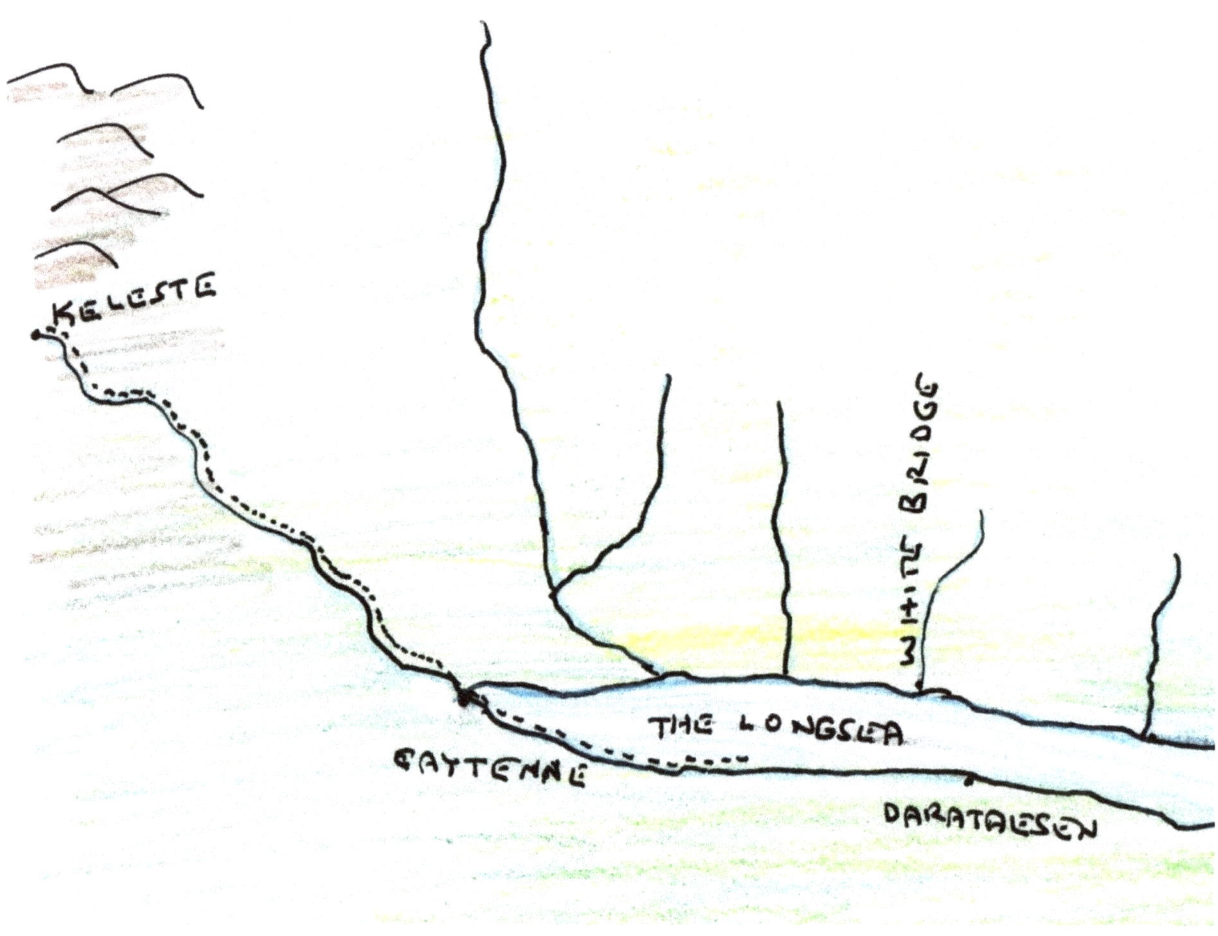

KELESTE
WHITE BRIDGE
THE LONGSEA
CAYTENNE
DARATAESEN

CHAPTER TWENTY-EIGHT

IN THE WINTER TOWN

Window looked off to the east. Across the Longsea horizon, the sky was dark with ominous clouds racing in their direction. The clouds were quickly climbing high above the water and, in a moment, had hidden the morning sun.

Circles watched the storm grow for another minute, then put his far-scope down. "Maybe we'd better go back to shore until the storm is past, Window. It looks like it is going to be a really bad one. And it is heading our way in a hurry."

"Put our packs into the side-chest, Circles. Then make sure the latches are closed. We don't want all of our things getting soaked when the rain hits."

In just a few minutes the wind picked up markedly and started to violently buffet against the sail. The icy-cold air burned Window's face. Circles pulled the blanket tighter around him. Then, in another minute, the sky was almost black. The storm seemed to pick up the boat as it threw it about on the waves.

"Circles! Help me! I can't keep the rudder turned. We are being blown farther out into the sea!"

The waves jumped higher around them, Circles put his weight against the rudder bar next to Window and pushed with all his strength. It wasn't enough. The craft was moving farther from shore.

Then, the storm was completely upon them. A downpour of
rain joined the cold wind – immediately drenching them with
near-freezing water. The sea crashed against the sides of the boat
and cascaded over the rails. The storm filled their ears and eyes.
The wind pushed them, but it was now too dark to tell what
direction they were going.

"We've got to get the sail down!" Window cried. "Can you hold
on while I try?"

Circles did his best, but, as soon as Window let go of the bar,
the little sailor was thrown to one side of the boat.

"Hang on, Circles! Hang on!" Window shouted but Circles
could not hear him. The wind carried his voice away.

With one violent yank, Window pulled the mastline free and
the sail collapsed, and flapped wildly in the wind. He struggled to
let down the topcord and the canvass fell free into a crumpled pile
in front of him. Window climbed over it as he fought his way back
to help Circles.

There was nothing else they could do. It was impossible to
control the craft, and so as Window lined up the bar, Circles
dropped the rudder peg and secured it. Now they would just have
to ride out the storm as best they could. Where they might end
up, they had no way of knowing.

An hour went by. Circles huddled against Window as they sat
in the freezing water at the bottom of the boat. The storm raged
around them. Another hour passed. They were numbed by the
cold that seemed to go right through them.

As more time passed and the storm finally quieted a bit, Circles
spoke to Window, "I'm ready for that warm room at the inn, now,
Window. Let's stop there tonight."

Window didn't reply, but put his arm around Circles and gave
him an extra tug against his side.

Almost as quickly as it came, the storm blew away to the west.
The sky cleared rapidly and the sun came out. The sailors
watched as the dark clouds disappeared over the trees. Trees!
They were near the shore! They were still near the southern

shore. The storm must have carried them exactly where they wanted to go. They were near the shore, close to the western end of the Longsea!

Window reset the sail as Circles bailed water from the boat with a metal bowl he found in the fore-chest. The air warmed a bit as Window steered them to the shore.

The cold sailors pulled their boat up onto the low, shallow seabank, and sat down. They desperately needed a fire to warm them, but there was no way they would be able to find any wood dry enough to burn.

"I wonder if the trillion would help us, Window."

"I guess that we may as well try it. Maybe it will cooperate a bit more than the vermillion did last time."

Window found some larger branches and Circles collected the smaller sticks. They were totally wet, but the campers stacked them to build a fire anyway.

"How many matches do we have left, Circles?"

"Eight."

"Okay, here we go." Window sprinkled some of the silver dust on the cold, wet wood. "Give it a try, Circles."

Circles took a match and carefully struck it on a rock. He held it to the little tower of sticks and made sure the flame touched some of the trillion dust.

"Please, Mister Trillion. Please help us make a nice fire."

This time the Pixie dust cooperated – it burst into a gentle, but very hot flame. The fire jumped between the sparkling particles and surrounded the wood. Then, with a bright flash, the wood started burning. It was a fire much hotter than what the travelers were used to. Most of the heat was coming from the dust and not the wood.

The two cold, tired travelers were thrilled. The fire was so hot that they were able to warm themselves and dry their clothes. They rested by the fire in the afternoon sun, and had something to eat.

As he ate, Circles shared his thoughts with his friend.
"Window, the next time we have an adventure, let's make sure we
do it in the summer time."

Just as Window was about to agree, Circles spoke up again –
loudly, this time. "Window, there are sails on the water!"

As they looked out on the Longsea, the travelers could see the
sails of three boats. They seemed to be fishing boats, and they
were headed to the west.

"Quickly, Circles. We have to follow them. They may lead us
to that inn you were hoping for."

"Thank you, Trillion," Circles spoke to the fire, and he spread
the burning wood on the ground with a stick. The fire cooperated,
and the flames went out. Most of the wood was still unburned.

The sailors hurried to the shore and in just a few minutes were
back on the water, following the three sails to the west. The other
boats were larger than theirs, and moved more swiftly, but the
travelers didn't have to follow them for long.

Circles got out his far-scope and discovered their destination.
Ahead of them was the western end of the Longsea and the village
of Caytenne. It was located at the mouth of a river that came
down to the sea from the mountains farther west. That was the
direction Window thought he and Circles should go. They followed
the other boats into the small harbor and tied up at a dock. The
buildings of the town were spread along the water to the north.

On the docks, there were many fishermen busily unloading
their day's catch of fish. Other men were pulling their boats up
onto the shore to be put into storage for the season. It seems that
the travelers arrived on what was, for most of the local fishermen,
the last fishing day of the winter.

The Caytennes spoke the Eastern Kingdoms language with the
same odd accent as the people in Darataesen. Window left his
sword on the boat this time as he and Circles climbed to the dock.

Everyone glanced at the strangers but no one came over to talk
to them until Circles started to do another little "sailor's dance."

One man became curious and engaged Window in conversation. In just a few minutes, Window was talking with four or five men on the dock and some others who were loading their wagons near the dock. He was quickly making travel arrangements for him and Circles.

First Window sold their boat to one man for a gold coin, three silver coins, and a barrel of salted fish. Then he traded the fish to another man for three boxes of fruit and cheese and bread. Then he made a deal with one of the wagon-masters for him and Circles to ride in the man's supply wagon up to a town in the mountain foothills to the west.

The man's wagon was already loaded and ready to leave. Window and Circles immediately collected their packs and clothes and boxes and weapons, climbed into the back of the wagon, and were soon on their way out of town. They had only been in the village for about ten minutes.

"Wow, Window. Maybe you should be a merchant."

"Well, it helps that I was underpaid for the boat and I overpaid for the other things," Window answered with a smile. But, Window didn't seem to mind. The travelers were once again on their way – and, this time, all they had to do was relax and enjoy the ride.

+++++++++

[AT THE RIVER HIGHLANDS HOUSE]

Past the head of the river and across the mountain divide, Renae Flasette was working at her kitchen cooking board. Tomorrow the girls would arrive, so today was the day. Today she was baking cookies – not the usual, ordinary, flat, brown cookies, but the thicker, softer, sweeter, lighter-colored springcookies with the raised pictures on them.

Renae usually only baked these special cookies in the springtime, but the twins had pleaded with her to bake them now as a treat for when their friend Wendy came back to town with them. Wendy lived in Riverhold, several days trip down the river near the mountain foothills. The girls exchanged visits several times a year.

Renae stood at the board, glanced out the window at the mountains to the east, and started. She beat the eggs and mixed in the powdered sugar and sifted flour – and then the lemon flavoring. As always, the dough got pretty sticky, and she got her hands just as sticky because it was so thick she had to mix it by hand – and <u>not</u> the "by hand" that used a wooden spoon, but the "by hand" that used her hands! When she finished mixing, she licked the sticky-sweetness from her fingers and set the dough in a bowl outside on the porch to cool and stiffen for an hour or so.

Renae cleaned off the counter and opened the baking drawer. She reached in and retrieved her three cookie pressing-boards. She <u>could</u> choose to use the board with the trees and flowers on it, or the board with the pictures of animals carved into it.
But Renae knew that Wendy liked Angels, so this time she would make the cookies using the board with the many different kinds of pictures on it – including the picture of an Angel. That was also the pressing-board that had the picture of the Silkie on it. Renae's grandmother had once told her that she had actually seen a Silkie when she was a girl, but Renae didn't believe her. And it was that same cookieboard that her grandmother always called "the map," but Renae didn't know why.

After about an hour, Renae brought the bowl in from the porch. She rolled out the cool dough into a flat sheet and dusted it with flour. Then she laid the cookieboard on the rolled-out dough and pressed the carvings of the board into it. She cut the pictures apart and placed them on the tray to harden overnight before baking.

As she placed the cookies on the tray, Renae looked over the pictures pressed into them. Her favorite was the tower. Her grandmother had told her that it was a carving of a real tower in the Northlands. Renae wondered if there really were any towers there.

Then Renae Flasette sat on her front porch and looked down the river road as it wound out of sight along the water. That was the direction from which Wendy would be arriving tomorrow afternoon with Annette and Audette. In the morning, Renae would bake the cookies. They would be ready when the girls arrived.

+++++++++

The trip by horse-drawn wagon to the village of Keleste took almost a week. The road wound past villages along the edge of the river and across low, frozen creeks that fed into it. As they rode, the wagon-master, Sirvenne, told the travelers about their destination.

The town was at the foot of the mountains. His would be the last wagon to make the trip to Keleste for about a month. The harshest of the winter snows would fall soon and the town would be isolated until the spring thaw.

Window had made arrangements with Sirvenne to pay for their food and lodging in the town by helping him in his woodworking shop. During the warmer months, the man carried furs and nuts and silver and newly built furniture to the sea, and returned with supplies, and salted fish. During the winter, he worked in the town making cabinets and tables in a workshop behind his house. Window and Circles could sleep on a bed in the back of the workshop.

Then when the spring thaw had opened the main pass through the mountains, Window and Circles could cross over to the western side. There were more towns on that side of the

mountains, but the people there spoke a different language.
Sirvenne didn't know much about them.

The trip to Keleste was cold but otherwise comfortable. The
travelers found a spot between the boxes and barrels in the back
of the wagon and covered themselves with their blanket. Circles
couldn't talk to Sirvenne too much but, sometimes, Window would
sit up front and exchange stories with him as they went.
As they got closer to Keleste, the road got somewhat steeper as
it began the steady climb up the outer edge of the mountains.
And, two of the days of the trip were made with snow falling on
them as they went.

The sun was shining brightly on the day the wagon-riders
arrived in the town. It reflected from the ground and houses and
gave the snow-covered town the gentle, friendly look of a Winter's
Eve town from stories back in the Windlands. Window wondered
what day it was, and if the people of Keleste also celebrated the
winter holiday.

Sirvenne lived alone so he was happy to have the travelers
keep him company for a while. Window and Circles moved their
things into the workshop and settled in for the rest of the winter.
Besides tools and wood, the room had a small bed and a fireplace.
At one time, Sirvenne's father had stayed there.
The next day, Window helped Sirvenne deliver fish and other
supplies to people and stores around the town and to clean the
wagon. It had gotten pretty dirty on the long trip to the sea.
Circles found a spot by the workshop window and sat looking
out dreaming of playing in the snow on the side of a long gently
sloped hillside nearby. He knew that the hill could provide for
some very fancy sliding.
That night, the long-expected blizzard buried the town in
beautiful white. The storm lasted all through the next day and
covered every road and building and fir tree in a beautiful white
blanket of snow.

The morning after that, the sun was out and the children swarmed the hillside to play. Circles wanted to join them. Sirvenne introduced Circles to his nephew and the two "boys" went off to play with the other kids. Everyone else had a sled but Circles said he didn't need one.

Circles had a fabulous day of slipping and sliding and skating and rolling in the snow. The town children quickly accepted him and they played for hours beneath the clear blue sky.

The kids were amazed that Circles could slide down the hill on his belly without a sled and even roll over and slide on his back as he went. Then, when Circles reached the bottom of the hill, he would smash into the snow bank and disappear in a puff of white. The kids would look for him and he would jump up and surprise them. Window came outside for a while and watched them play.

That night, by the warmth of the fireplace, Circles fell asleep quickly. He was exhausted from his day in the snow. Circles really was a champion snow-slider.

The weeks passed quietly at the winter town. Window and Circles didn't go out into the village too often. Mostly they stayed in the woodshop.

Window was happy to get to work with wood again. He spent his days helping Sirvenne build different kinds of tables and cabinets. Window learned a few things, and was also able to teach Sirvenne some things that Window's grandfather had shown him. At night, the travelers would go to sleep with the smell of freshly cut wood.

In the evening, the three of them played Rainbow Chips. Window made a bright new set of chips in the workshop and taught the game to Sirvenne. He enjoyed trying to beat the travelers, but he wasn't very successful.

Circles' job was to keep the fire going in the woodshop. Every morning he would clean the fireplace and drag more wood in from the stack behind the shop to start another fire. After the fire was going, Circles would spend a lot of time making sure that it was hot enough. He would lie in front of the fireplace, on a rug, enjoying the crackling flames for hours.

Sometimes, Window would put out seeds and corn to feed the birds. He enjoyed sitting by the woodshop window and watching as the sparrows and wrens and phoebes and swing-jays and mountain doves hopped and pecked at the pile of food he would put on the wooden shelf Sirvenne had nailed to the outside wall below the window.

One afternoon, Window and Circles went out together. Circles wanted to follow the snowtrails of some rabbits and see where they went. The rabbit hunters quickly found some tracks and followed them over the hillside and into the woods. But they never did find the rabbit's nest. The wandering tracks eventually led back to the same spot where the trackers had started, right outside of the woodshop.

It was a fun day together for the two travelers. When they got back to the woodshop's small front porch, the sun was shining brightly on Circles' fur, but the silky white of the fur had something mixed with it.

"Hey, Circles," Window pointed out. "Some of your fur is turning blue."

"Where? Where? Where?" the Woot excitedly asked.

"Well, right here on your arm, and over here on your leg."

Circles almost spun around trying to see.

"There's another spot on your back."

"It's starting, Window. My fur is changing! My fur is changing! I have been waiting for a long, long time. Now I will know what kind of Woot I am!"

"What does the blue color mean, Circles?"

"Blue? Oh, I don't know. We have some dark blue Woots back home. They are good at finding good-tasting roots and leaves."

Circles thought for a moment. "But this color is different. It is much lighter. I must be a kind of Woot that they don't need very many of. I have never seen this color fur before."

Circles was disappointed that he didn't recognize his new color. "I wish my Mama was here. She would know."

Then Circles thought of something else. "Hey, my new fur color reminds me of Raine's skin. I'll bet he would be happy to have me be the same color as him. I know I am!"

"It is a very handsome blue, Circles. You are a fine looking Woot."

"I know, Window. That's the kind of Woot I am."

The happy travelers went inside. Circles checked his fur every few minutes for the rest of the day. He went to sleep by the fire that night dreaming of returning home.

The next day, Window and Sirvenne didn't have any work to do in the shop. Window wanted to get outside again for a while.

"Hey, Circles. Do you want to go down and skate on the lake today? I'll pull you around on the end of a rope."

"No, I don't feel like it, Window. I am still tired from yesterday, even though I slept all night. I wonder if I am getting sick."

"I didn't know that Woots ever got sick."

"Not very often – but sometimes."

Over the next three days, Circles' fur continued to change. His arms and legs, and then his body, and finally his face – lost their pure white color and became light blue. But Circles couldn't enjoy his growing up as a Woot. Every day he felt more and more tired. The changes in his body, that were causing his fur to change, seemed to be taking his strength away.

After a few more days, Circles became so weak and tired that all he wanted to do was sleep.

During the day, Window would help Circles to the blanket on the rug in front of the fire. At night, Circles slept in Window's bed.

They tried to feed Circles some special broth that Sirvenne suggested, but it didn't seem to help. Window asked if there was a doctor in the town, but there was not. A doctor probably wouldn't have known what to do for Circles, anyway.

Not even the Pixie dust helped. Window had tried both kinds, but they just dropped to the floor when he blew them towards Circles. Window was becoming very worried.

The days went on – Circles' condition got worse and worse. His body became very hot, his muscles sore to the touch, and his head ached constantly. Window could think of nothing else. He had no idea of how to help his friend.

In the village, the people of Keleste were preparing for the celebration of Midwinter's Day. It was a celebration Circles would miss.

In the afternoon, on Midwinter's Eve, the townspeople gathered at the homes of family members for singing and games. They gave each other gifts wrapped in bright paper and colored ribbons. After the sun went down, everyone met on the town square to build a fire to scare away the cold of winter, so spring would come soon.

Circles could not go out to the square but Window went to watch. Before he left, Window helped Circles to a chair by the window so Circles could see the fire in the distance.

The winter town people built the biggest bonfire Window had ever seen. The fire flames jumped higher than the trees into the cold winter sky. The town kids held hands in a big circle and ran around the fire singing. Afterwards, everyone gathered at the Town Meeting-Hall for dancing and games.

The next morning the entire town met again, in the square, to build the Midwinter's Day snowman. The children rolled huge balls of snow as the adults piled them higher and higher.

Window was going to help build the snowman, but Circles was feeling so badly that Window decided to stay with him. They sat together by the window so Circles could see a little bit of what was going on outside.

"What am I going to do, Window? I am not feeling any better. My fur is almost completely blue now, but I am still getting weaker."

Tears came to Circles' eyes. "I wish I could get home. Mama would know what to do."

Window could not help his friend.

Circles continued to deteriorate. Soon, he could hardly speak.
He would smile bravely at Window, but there was sadness and
fear in his eyes. Window sat on the bed for hours and held his
hand and talked to him. Circles would drift to sleep in the middle
of the day until his discomfort would wake him up. Then he would
sleep most of the night as well. He couldn't eat very much.
Window was terrified. He was afraid that Circles might be dying.

But something else happened on a clear and cold night in the
winter town. Snow had fallen during the day, then, the sky had
cleared. Now it was a quiet, beautiful sight out from the
workshop window. The full moon was high in the sky. Its light
beamed into the woodshop and fell on the floor and the foot of the
bed.
Circles was in the bed when Window came in from the house to
tell him goodnight. As Window sat by Circles on the edge of the
bed and spoke to him it seemed that Circles' eyes brightened a bit.
They seemed to glisten and come alive. Then Window was sure –
but Circles' eyes had not brightened from the inside, but from
outside in the room somewhere.

Suddenly Window heard a tiny tapping sound. It stopped.
Then he heard it again. Window looked around the room. Besides
the moon, there was another light outside of the shop window.
He walked curiously to the window and looked through the
glass. What he saw was something he never could have expected
– something that surprised him and filled him with awe and
wonder. Floating in the air outside of the window were two tiny
Fairy-like beings, each maybe just four inches high.
Their bodies were glowing and sparkling. They wore no clothes
but were wrapped in sparking light. Two wispy wings stuck up
behind each of them. Only an occasional burst of their wings and
the delightfully charming creatures stayed aloft.
Window swung out the glass and the two sparkling Fairies
flew into the room. They had young woman faces with tiny bright
eyes and slender bodies, and were a pale green color. They
seemed to be of extremely light weight, and to float, rather than
fly.

"We have been looking for you," they addressed him, as they bowed in the air with a flash of sparkling green light.

The Fairies spoke their words in perfect unison with matching high-pitched female sounding voices that also sounded a bit like tinkling bells. Without saying anything, Window stared in wonder at his magical visitors.

Then he looked back at Circles. Circles had fallen asleep.

"Would you like to stay for a while?" he finally answered them.

"Oh, yes. Thank you," the tiny, tinkling voices replied.

The wispy little light Fairies flew to the table and landed. As they walked over its surface the light from their bodies reflected from the shiny wood.

Window's visitors spoke again. "We are twins. Caroline calls us Fairies."

Window sat down but didn't reply.

"Are you the man named Window who was near the Far Ocean several weeks ago?" the Fairies wanted to know. They still both spoke the words at the exact same time."

"Yes, I am Window. And this is my friend Circles." He gestured to the sleeping Woot. "He is ill."

"We have been looking for you," the tiny voices repeated.

"Where do you come from – and why are you looking for me?"

"You will see. You will see," they repeated, and with a single bust of their wings, unexpectedly flew back to the window, then pulled it open just a crack with their tiny fingers and flew out into the cold night.

Window gently shook his friend. "Circles, wake up. There have been Fairies here." Circles slowly opened his eyes.

"Circles, there have been Fairies here."

"Pixies?" Circles weakly asked.

"They said they were Fairies."

"Where are they?"

"They flew away, but I think they are coming back."

Circles gathered his strength and with Window's help, sat up in the bed.

"When are they coming?" Circles wanted to know.

"They didn't say. I'll see if they are still outside."

Window looked out through the ice-frosted glass. The moon shone down on the long, gentle hillside and evergreen trees. At the top of the hill something was moving. Someone was slowly riding down the hill on a horse through the snow towards the woodshop. As the rider drew closer and closer Window marveled at what he saw.

The rider was not on a horse but rode on the back of a large deer. The deer had a curled set of antlers that the rider held on to. Then Window could see that the rider seemed to be a woman, not an old woman, but a very frail woman wrapped only in a flowing dress of faded cloth. Her long hair was windblown and tangled, as though she had ridden a long way in terribly cold and windy winter weather.

Window told Circles what he saw as they waited for the woman to reach the shop. In just a minute, there was a quiet knock at the door. Circles sat up as straight as he could. Window slowly opened the door.

Their visitor seemed to be nearly frozen from the cold and appeared as if she was almost completely faded. Her face and hair and clothes were colored the lightest pink. She and her clothes seemed almost transparent.

The woman stood on the small porch. In the air by her shoulders the two Fairies were sparkling. When they saw Window they sparkled more brightly.

The woman's voice was weak but extremely clear and precise. Like the Fairies she spoke in Atlandan.

"Window, my name is Caroline. I have traveled from the Far Ocean. May I please come in and speak with you?"

"You are welcome to come in. This is my friend, Circles. He is ill and cannot speak easily."

She nodded towards Circles' direction. He nodded in reply. Circles' tired eyes were big and excited.

"May I fix some tea for you? Or get you something else, perhaps?"

"Yes, I would like some tea," she spoke with a gentle voice. "You are kind to offer it."

Window and Circles waited patiently as the water was heated in the pot at the fireplace and the tea was prepared. The two Fairies flew again to the table where Window had pulled out a chair for Caroline.

The woman's face was smooth and young looking, yet she appeared to be extremely tired.

Caroline drank the tea slowly and savored every sip. The warmth of the liquid seemed to warm her and she spoke with more energy. The Fairies flew to the counter and examined the cups and dishes kept there.

"May I get you something else?" Window repeated his earlier question.

"There _is_ one thing you could give to me, but you must give it with complete understanding. Would it be alright if I told you about myself?"

Window certainly had nothing else more important he could possibly be doing. He simply said, "Of course."

Window put a couple of more logs on the fire. The flames leaped up and shone on Caroline's weary face.

Then, as Window and Circles listened in wonder, Caroline sighed, as though she were finally at the end of a long, long journey. While she spoke, the Fairies flitted about the room, stopping to examine saws and drills and half-finished pieces of furniture.

Caroline began, "I am an Angel – one of the very few remaining in the world. There used to be many Angels, but they have been fading away. Years ago, we watched over the people of the world and gave help to those in great need – but now we can no longer do that."

The travelers watched and listened in awe as she spoke.

"The Angels live on an island far in the Eastern Ocean in a beautiful city rarely ever visited by men. We appear in your form, but we are made of only energy, and our energy is fading. Most of the Angels now are far too weak and powerless to travel much, or to help anyone. They were once powerful and beautiful but are fading away

"We have become weak and are losing our strength because we can no longer renew our power. We have lost the source of our light-energy."

Then Caroline said the most surprising thing. "But, Window, I believe that you can help us."

"A few weeks ago, my Angel friend, Valentine, was rescued from an island in the Far Ocean. Valentine had gone exploring but had become too weak and could no longer fly home as healthy Angels can do."

"Valentine was found by the man you know as Captain Cardette. The Captain was very kind and brought Valentine back to our island. During their journey, the Captain told Valentine of the spark of light you carry in your pocket. I believe that your spark may save us from fading away as so many other Angels have done. We need it so desperately."

Window and Circles sat in amazement. Grandma Windowen was right! Circles was right! There <u>were</u> Angels in the world! There was an Angel talking to them right now! Window was so excited he could hardly stay seated. Circles felt very weak, but, still, he was thrilled by their visitor and her words.

Caroline went on. "When the world was young, all Angels lived in the Ancient Lands with the Fairies and the other magical creatures."

"As men came to the nearby lands, Angels would travel to places where they lived to watch over the people and sometimes help them with magic. We tried to remain a secret, but sometimes someone would see one of us, so there were legends among men that we existed, but no one was sure."

"There are other smaller Angels in the world, but I am a Moon Angel. Moon Angels get their power from the stones that hold the moon's light for us. When the Angels were all living in the Ancient Lands the moonstones were nearby where we could restore our strength easily, but as the years passed and the world changed, the Angels left the Ancient Lands and went far away to places where men were living. The Angels would only return occasionally to renew their energy.

Then a terrible change came to the world. A terrible quake shook the Ancient Lands and all the lands nearby. The moonstones were lost.

They had been watched by towering moonplants but those plants were lost, too. Angels who returned looking for the crystal stones could not find them. The Angels returned home even weaker than before. Soon no Angels were strong enough to even look for the lost crystals. And as the Angels went longer and longer without the crystals' energy, they began to fade away and die. A few lived on, but only as shadows of Angels.

The last of us live on the Island Of Angels in the Far Ocean, but we, too, are fading away. I am the last to leave the island. Without your help I will never return. Without your help all of the Angels will soon fade away forever.

Window and Circles listened in amazement and quiet sadness to the Angel-woman. Circles held on to Window's hand and squeezed it again and again.

"So, I have only one request of you, Window. Will you give me the spark you carry in your pocket? Perhaps, with it, I may regain my power and health."

Caroline's sad, pleading, eyes looked into his. "Please, Window. Will you please help me?"

Window was stunned. Charm held the power of the Angels! Charm, the light that had been playing Rainbow Chips with him and Circles, held the power of the Angels! – the Angels they had searched for so long.

Window looked at Circles. Circles' eyes were quiet and sure as they shared the easy decision with Window.

"Yes, Caroline, we would be happy to help you. We will return the spark to the Angels."

Caroline briefly closed her eyes and sighed happily. Then, she stood up and straightened herself as best she could.

The light of the full moon was still flowing into the woodshop. Window reached into his pocket and retrieved the crystal-light. He held it up in the moonbeam that was flooding through the window. As the moonlight awoke the sleeping Charm, it glowed and flashed and shot beams of blue light across the room.

As Charm's light energy bounced around the room it flowed into Caroline's faded eyes. Instantly, they began to shine the brightest blue. The light bathed over her faded form. Her slumping body straightened. Her faded pink color and that of her clothes was replaced as she began to shine a bright blue. As the light swirled around her, her body recovered its health and beauty. Her dress became brilliantly sparkling and gently flowing. Her face became calm and strong. She was again an Angel – powerful, graceful, and beautiful.

Caroline spoke again. Now, her voice was still gentle, but stronger and clear.

"Thank you forever, Window. Your kindness has saved me." The Fairies were hopping wildly about the room.

Caroline held out her hand to Window. A rainbow of colored light arched across from her hand to his. Window felt a tingling sensation on his skin.

Window felt a loyalty to Charm, who had been so faithful to him and Circles. He spoke to the flashing spark. "Charm, we will miss you, but, if you will agree, the Angel would like you to go with her."

The light sped around the room, twisting and spinning. He agreed that he would go.

"I will try to repay you, Window. Your gift is great."

"Can you help my friend?" Window wondered. "We don't know what to do for him."

Caroline walked to the bed and touched Circles with her hand. Circles had joyous tears in his eyes. He had found the Angels at last! Well, even better, they had found him.

"Circles, I am sorry, but my power is not yet strong enough to help you. It will take some time, and more of the moon-stones, for all of my strength to return."

"That's okay, Caroline. My Mama will help me."

"Where is she, Circles?"

"She is in the Deep Woods – where I am from."

"I have never been there. Is it far?"

"It is very far."

"I am sorry that I am not yet strong enough to take you there."

Circles reached out and touched her hand to let her know he understood.

The thought of the Pixie dust jumped into Window's mind. He asked Caroline if she needed it as well. She thanked him twice, but said it would not help her – and she didn't know any Pixies.

Then Window remembered something his Grandmother said to him before he left for the Northlands.

"My Grandmother Windowen asked me to say hello if I saw any Angels while I was away from home. So, I want you to know that she will be happy that I have met you. I think she has always wished that she had an Angel to watch over her."

"Please tell her that I hope to meet her someday."

"She would like that."

Then Caroline expressed her regret that she would have to leave very soon.

"Window, I am sorry but I cannot stay to visit. While I am still somewhat strong, I must go to the Ancient Lands and try to find the lost moonstones. Only then will I and the other Angels be able to regain all of our power. I hope that your Charm will help give me enough strength to find them."

Then Circles spoke up, very quietly. His body was weak but his head was clear.

"I can do it, Window. I can show Caroline where Moonbow's crystal cavern is. I know the way to the Moonlands. I will show her."

The little Woot spoke again. "Then she can take me home. I miss the Deep Woods. I need to recover from my illness. My Mama can help me."

Window looked deep into Circles' eyes, then turned to Caroline.

"Could you do it, Caroline? Could you take Circles home if you were stronger?"

She nodded that she could.

Window turned to Circles again. "You are going to get your wish, Circles. You won't have to walk anymore. An Angel is going the take you home!"

Circles smiled, but then spoke with difficulty. "But what about you, Window? What about you getting home?" Circles' faced was filled with concern for his friend.

Window answered with the love he felt for Circles. "I will just have a bit longer of an adventure, but I will get home alright. It <u>will</u> be very lonely without you, though."

Caroline saw a way to perhaps help. "I will send some Fairies to keep you company, Window."

"I would like that." Window answered her kind offer.

Then Caroline went on. "I am sorry to hurry you, Window, but Circles and I should leave right away."

Window turned to Circles. Their eyes looked deep inside of each other. There was no way to say goodbye. There were too many things they had shared. No amount of time would ever be enough for Window to be ready to leave Circles' company.

"Perhaps a quick parting will be the easiest, after all," Window spoke out loud to himself.

Circles again joined eyes with him. Window held his gaze with his friend. They said everything in one knowing look.

"Okay, Caroline. Please take care of my friend. He is very important to me."

Circles lay back on the bed. His mind was reeling.

Window went immediately to the worktable and carefully wrapped Circles bow and arrows in a large piece of cloth usually used to cover furniture. He added one of the Freeland coins to Circles' pack, so he would have part of Revell's treasure as well.

Then he helped Circles get out of bed and gently wrapped their blanket around him.

Window could hardly think. He could hardly breathe. He couldn't bear to think of being without Circles. They had shared too many adventures. They were too much a part of each other. Window held on to Circles to keep him from falling. Circles held on to Window. They didn't want to ever let go.

Window spoke quietly to his friend. "Send a bird to bring a note to me after I get home, Circles. I will come visit you as soon as I can."

"I will do that, Window. I will see you in the Deep Woods after I am better."

"If you see Panni, or Rings, or Oldsmith, tell them..."

"I will, Window. I will."

"Tell your Mama to take care of you."

"She will, Window. She will."

Window and Circles looked into each other's eyes one more time. They could hardly see through the tears.

"Goodbye, Circles. You are the best traveler and treasure hunter of all times. No friend could ever be better."

Circles hugged Window again. "I am sorry that I got sick, Window."

Window tried, but couldn't speak to reply.

"Thanks for taking me along on your adventure, Window. You are the best friend in the world." Then he quietly added, "Bye."

The two travelers couldn't say any more. The pain was too great.

Window lifted Circles into Caroline's arms. The Fairies picked up Circles' things. Circles was covered by the blanket and the glow of Caroline's sparkling dress. He held out his hand to his friend. Window touched it one last time.

Holding back more tears, Window opened the door. Caroline and Circles floated out into the cold. The Fairies followed her, sparkling as they went.

Window stood in the doorway as Caroline floated above the ground up the snow-covered hill to the east. The Fairies pushed against the side of the waiting deer and it trotted into the pine forest. Then they followed the Angel up the hill. Window stood watching.

The moon shone all around the Angel. She stopped at the top of the hill and looked back towards Window. Suddenly, there was a bright glow of light as two sparkling wings formed on her back. Then, with another flash of light, Caroline was gone, and with her, Circles was swept away into the cold winter night.

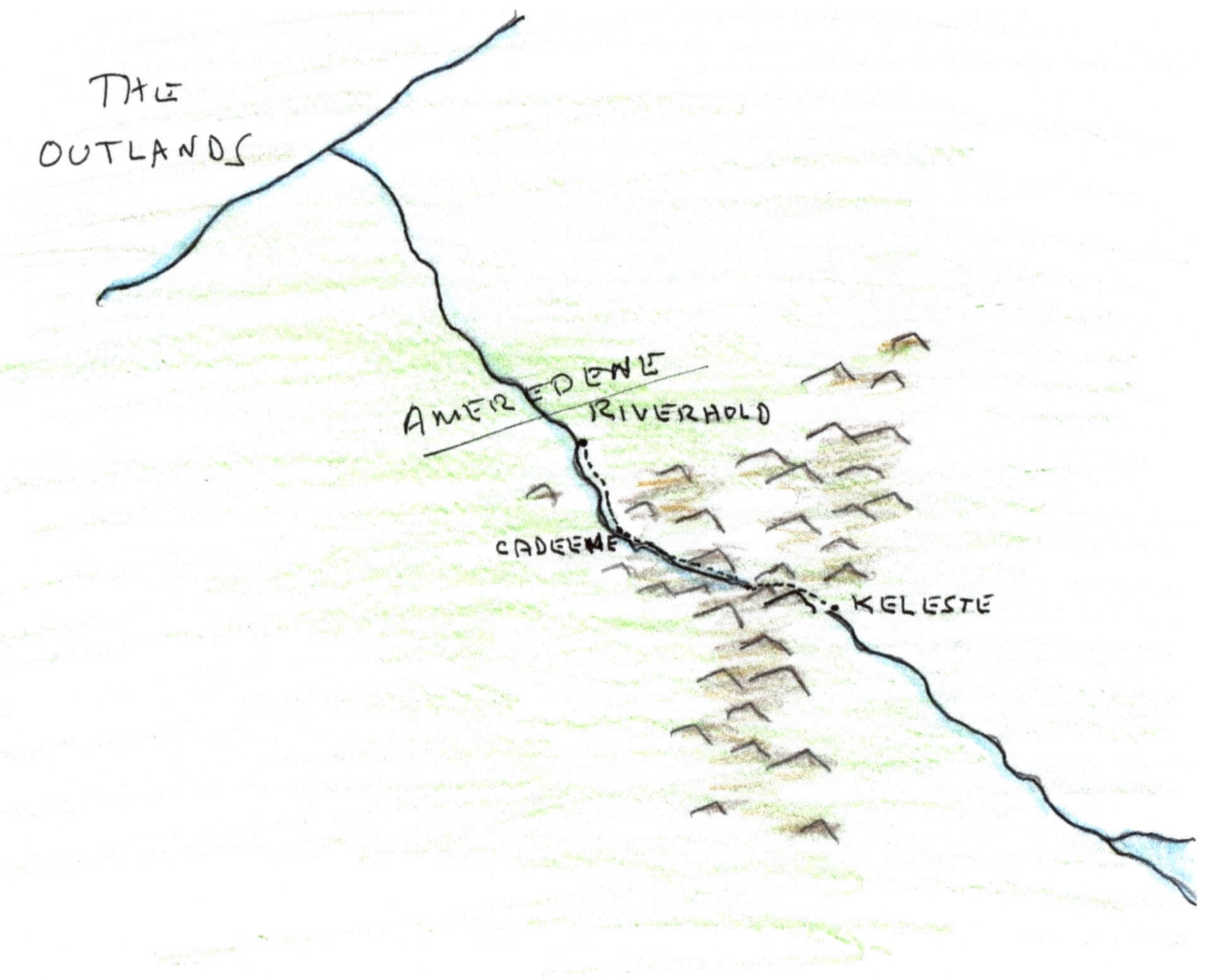

THE OUTLANDS
AMER EDENE RIVERHOLD
CADEEME
KELESTE

CHAPTER TWENTY-NINE

TO RIVERHOLD

Window stood at the edge of Keleste and looked towards the mountains. It had been a long, lonely wait for the snows to melt enough to open the high passes and allow him to travel to the west. Being without Circles had been very difficult for him. As he worried about his friend, Window spent many hours in Sirvenne's workshop, cutting and sanding and gluing and nailing as he built tables and cabinets. The work helped keep his mind off of his concern for Circles.

But now, Sirvenne felt that most of the deepest drifts would be melted and that it should only take a week or so for Window to walk across the mountain divide and reach the towns on the other side.

Window had used the rest of his Eastern coins to pay for food and supplies for the journey, and now he was ready. One quick look back towards the town and he was off. The road through the mountains was rough and little used but that didn't matter to him. He had rested far too long and was eager to begin what he hoped would be the last part of his journey home.

"Goodbye, Eastern World," he called out to the forests behind him. His mind was full of memories from his travels but he concentrated on the task ahead – and the family and friends back home he missed so much.

The late winter weather was agreeable and Window climbed the road to its crest without too much difficulty. The winter birds kept him company and he even sang a few old Northlands marching songs to pass the time. It was odd for him to travel without someone to talk to. It made him realize more than ever how fortunate he had been to find so many friends to share his adventures. Of course, he still had a long way to go to reach the Windlands.

The mountains here were many times larger than any of the others he had encountered on his travels. He had been able to go between most of those mountains. Here he had to climb high up and over them. At the very highest point of the mountain road, Window stopped for lunch and a rest.

He was higher up than he had ever been. Far to the east, he could see the river winding down towards the Longsea. To the west, were forests and more forests. Somewhere far beyond, he hoped to find the Windlands Southrange, or maybe the Outlands, on his way to the Prairies and home.

Window followed the rough road down the mountain's western slopes. As he reached the treeline he saw the first few buds of an early spring on the trees. And on the ground the ice-flowers were peeking from the melting snow and dotting the hillsides with color. It was still cold but beauty was returning to the mountain world.

On his third day on the western slopes, Window passed a couple of cabins and then some houses and barns. He waved to a man who was tending his cattle but did not speak to him. Slowly, Window was entering the world on this side of the mountains.

After just another two days of walking, Window could see the houses and buildings of a town. It was built on the bank of a small river that wound down from the woods above it. The sun was out as Window neared the village.

As it approached the town, the road turned past a small cemetery. Window decided that it was the perfect place to rest before going on.

As he walked up to the rows of grey headstones, Window noticed that above the names carved into each of the stones there was a crest or emblem cut into the rock.

"What if I can find my medallion design here?" he spoke to himself, as he slowly walked up and down the rows of stones searching for the elusive answer to his medallion's identity.

As he walked past the stones, he saw designs of flowers and animals and children's toys and bells and houses and fancy letters and designs of all kinds. The figures added a bit of individuality to each stone.

In just a few minutes Window had scanned all of the gravestones except one that was off a bit to the side of the others, under a tree.

"There it is," he thought, kidding himself. "There is the gravestone that will have my medallion carved into it."

From a distance, he imagined that it <u>was</u> his medallion design cut into the stone. But what he found was even more surprising. It wasn't his medallion carved on the headstone – it was two crossed swords with a sun between their blades! It was the Northlands Kingdom symbol that was on his grandmother's cookieboard! It was the crest of King Alezan of the Northlands!

His mind reeled. What was the crest of the Northlands king doing in this mountain village?

Window reached down and ran his fingers over the design. Then he did the same for the name on the stone. It wasn't the name of a King or a Queen. It was simply the name, "Jame Flasette," and the inscription, "Husband and Father."

Window looked toward the houses of the town. Someone there must be related to Mr. Flasette, or at least, know something about him. Why the symbol of the Northlands King was used on his gravestone, Window could not imagine.

It was the middle of the day as Window walked along the river road in front of the houses and shops of the town. Above the doorway of each building was painted the same type of design as were on the gravestones. It was going to be easy to find the King's symbol if it was on any of the houses.

Window hid the jeweled handle of his sword under his jacket so that, although the townspeople were sure to see the sword, they would not know that it was covered with a small treasure of brilliant stones.

As he approached two men who were talking outside of a small supply store, Window listened to their conversation. They were speaking in Amerand. This must be one of the areas chosen by the Amerans during the settling periods of the Newlands. Window remembered that his Grandmother Windowen's ancestors came from Ameran.

Once again, Raine's gift of language allowed Window to understand and speak with the men. He remembered that Starfin had warned him that the finger-rings' language ability might sometimes not work for him, but so far he had not had any difficulty with it. Then he wondered if Panni or Rings had had any trouble with their gifts from the starman.

Window greeted the men and explained to them that he had just come over the mountains and was passing through their village on his way farther west. They welcomed him to the land of Ameredene, and their village of Cadeene. There were several more towns of Amerans farther down the River Road, along the Bluewater. In the flatlands below the mountains, were Amerand farms and ranches and still more villages.

Window thanked the men and asked if they might know if there were any family members of Jame Flasette still living in the town. They directed him farther down the River Road to the last house on the way out of town. There he would find Flasette's widow. In just a few minutes, Window was standing before her house.

It was a small house with a wide porch and the symbol of King Alezan painted above the front door. Window climbed the porch steps and knocked on the wooden side-board.

Window's knock was answered by a light-haired woman of about age forty-five. She wore a colorful flowered dress and an apron, which suggested that she had been cooking in the kitchen.

"Hello, Good Traveler," she politely greeted Window.

The woman was curious why a young stranger would be at her door. Noticing his pack and blanket and unshaven appearance she continued, *"You must have come far. Would you care to have something to eat? I am just finishing my lunch."*

"That is very kind of you. If you could bring me some bread and cheese, or perhaps some fruit, I would appreciate it."

The woman smiled and invited Window to sit down on the porch steps. The sun was out and it was a pleasant day outdoors. Window took off his pack and sword and sat down as the lady went back into the house. In a minute, she returned with a plate of cheese and a piece of bread spread with berry jam.

"My name is Renae," the woman introduced herself with a pleasant smile as she sat on the steps next to Window. He accepted the food and ate as they spoke.

"It is my pleasure to meet you, Renae. My name is Window Breesian. I have been on a very long journey and am traveling home to the Windlands. Do you know where the Windlands are?" He asked, not knowing if the people of Cadeene knew of his homeland.

"Below the mountain highlands and far across the open lands to the west and north," Renae immediately answered. Then she noticed Revell's sword, partially hidden under Window's pack, and gestured towards it.

"You won't be needing that here, Window." She smiled gently. *"Are you a soldier?"*

"I have been in some very dangerous places," came his reply. *"I found this sword along the way."*

"They must have been some very interesting places, as well. Would you like to tell me about them?"

Renae had quickly become fascinated by her unexpected guest. She had a love of far-way places although she had never been outside of the lands of Ameredene. And, she could sense that Window was not an ordinary traveler who was returning to his shop or his fields, down-river. He appeared to be a very unusual traveler.

"I will tell you a story of my travels if you will answer a question for me," Window replied. *"As I came into your town from the east, I stopped at the cemetery and rested. One thing I saw there made me curious. If you don't mind telling me, I would like to know why your husband's gravestone is marked with the symbol of King Alezan of the Northlands?"*

Renae gasped. Her face took on a look of surprise and confusion. She didn't answer. Window could tell that she wasn't sure what she wanted to say. Then she looked into his eyes and seemed to relax. It was as if Window's question to her had opened up a new connection between the two of them and she had decided that it was safe to answer him. She certainly was correct that he was no ordinary traveler.

"I will answer your question, Window, but before I do, would you please tell me how you knew that the symbol belonged to the King? The people here in Cadeene believe that it is the symbol of my grandfather who was a metal-smith. But its true meaning has been a secret, known only to me. Even my daughters have not yet learned the truth. How could you possibly know it was the symbol of the King? The King lived so very many years ago, and so very far away.

"I have been to the Northlands. My friends there told me of the symbol. And, I have seen the symbol myself, also." Window couldn't think of a way to tell Renae about the springcookie picture so he didn't say any more about it.

"Perhaps you would like to come inside for a while, Window. It would please me to hear your stories of the Northlands."

"I would like that very much, Renae."

Renae led Window to an open-windowed day-porch off of the kitchen where he was offered a chair at a small table. The early afternoon sun was streaming in through the windows and bathing the room in bright, pleasant light. The sunlight brightened the flowers in the crystalline vase on the table.

Window was especially pleased when Renae brought lemon-tea for both of them and sat down by him to continue their conversation. Then she quickly excused herself again and went through the kitchen to a door that led to the cellar. She returned to Window in a couple of minutes with a plate of cookies – cookies with a raised picture on each of them – springcookies!

Window was speechless. He recognized the pictures on the cookies!

"Window, I thought that you might enjoy these cookies, especially this one." She smiled as she held out a springcookie with the King's crossed swords symbol on it.

Window's mind was racing. *"Are these cookies made using a carved pressing-board?"* was all he was able to ask in his excitement.

"That's right," Renae answered, pleased that the young man was somehow familiar with the cookies. *"I'll show you the board I used."*

She stepped to the kitchen and retrieved a cookie-board from a drawer. *"Although I have others, here is the board I used to make these cookies."*

She held out the pressing-board for Window to see. In his complete amazement he could hardly speak. What finally came out was, *"My grandmother has that same map."*

Renae dropped the cookie-board in shock. It clattered to the floor at Window's feet. As Window picked it up, Renae sat down and gave him the biggest smile.

It was going to be a very long afternoon of cookies and lemon-tea for the new friends.

As the pleasant sunlight fell on the table and the flowers and across her face, Renae began her story, *"Well, Window, unlike most of the people in this part of the Newlands, my ancestors did not come from Ameran. Here is how it happened. This is the story my grandmother told to me and my mother."*

"In W.Y. 65, the Atlandan Army was marching on the Northlands Kingdom castle in Calisay. As the city was about to be surrounded by enemy forces, the Royal Family was forced to flee. One of the King's three sons, Prince Raeven, escaped with his mother, Queen Cillaia, and his sister, Princess Laycelle, to the city of Meriselle on the western ocean, but found it was not safe to enter. Instead, the Prince took his family farther up the coast to the north."

"There the Royal Family came upon a ship from Ameran called the Setampa that had been blown far off course to the north by a storm. The Prince bought passage for his mother and sister on that ship which sailed from there to the Wind Lands in the south. The Prince stayed behind in the Northlands."

"On board the Setampa, the Queen and her daughter kept their royal identities secret from the Amerans. The two Northlands woman became part of the Amerand settlers who were searching for a new home."

"The Setampa settlers stopped at the harbor at Coastown, in the Wind Lands, but were not welcomed there so the captain took his ship farther south. The Amerand settlers disembarked in the southern Wind Lands at the beginning of the King's Straight Road. That was a road which was built by the Atland King to encourage settlers to travel inland and to colonize the far south-eastern parts of the Wind Lands.
The Amerans followed the King's Straight Road to the east but decided to go even farther than the road took them, beyond the borders of the Wind Lands, and so came to settle in this distant part of the Newlands. The Queen and her daughter remained part of the Amerand settlers and never reveled their true identities."

"Here, in the new country of Ameredene, Princess Laycelle married and started her own family. Laycelle was my grandmother. So, I am the great-granddaughter of King Alezan and Queen Cillaia of the Northlands!"

Window listened in wonder. He could hardly believe it. He had found part of the Northlands Royal Family – the family whose treasures he and his friends had searched for – and found!

"I guess that you are Princess Renae now, or maybe even Queen Renae," he responded to her revelation.

"I suppose so, Window, but that part of me is long past. I am happy to just be a lady in Cadeene who likes to bake. I have two wonderful daughters and friends here. I would never want to be part of Kingdom Royalty."

"I never planned to reveal my past to anyone – except my twin daughters, who are now seventeen and need to be told soon. But still, I don't care to regain my connection to the Northlands. That is something that is not a part of my life here."

Then Renae went on to another surprise.

"And, Window, I have an idea of how it could be that I have a pressing-board with the same pictures as your grandmother. I think that you are really going to like this story."

Window was sure that he would. He sat and waited with great anticipation of what Renne was about to say.

The Ameredene cookie-baker told more of her story.

"While Queen Cillaia was on board the Setampa, she hired two young Amerand women, who were sisters, as her servants. My grandmother, Princess Laycelle, who was about the same age as the sisters, became friends with them."

"But while in the port at Coastown, one of the Amerand sisters decided that she didn't want to travel beyond the Outlands and live in a settlement far from the cities and ports and civilization of the Wind Lands. She packed a few things and left the ship – she abandoned her family and remained in Coastown.

"That sister, whose name was Sevenna, must have been your great-great-grandmother, Window. That is how your

grandmother's ancestors came from Ameran. And, Sevenna must have taken a cookie-board with her."

Window was thrilled with the story – and Renae was right. He remembered his grandmother telling him that Sevenna was <u>her</u> grandmother's name.

Renee went to the kitchen and returned with more tea and some crackers with jam. While she was gone, Window thought of a small surprise gift he could give to her.

"My Dear Princess, perhaps you would like to have a few coins from the Northlands Kingdom – the faces stamped on them are probably the faces of ancestors of yours. I have a few that I found on my travels and would be happy to share them with you."
"That is very generous of you, Window, but I already have a few coins from the Northlands. Come with me and I will show them to you." Window noticed an odd, playful smile on Renae's face.

The secret Northlands Princess led Window to a door on the same side of the house as the room where they had been sitting. It was a large storage room, filled with boxes and bags of all sizes.
Beneath a window on the far side of the room, sat a large wooden sea-chest. It was wrapped in metal bands to keep it secure if dropped while in transit. The bright afternoon sun came in through the window and bathed the chest in light. Renae unhooked the latch and tipped back the heavy chest lid. Window was in for a great surprise.

The chest was filled to its top with brilliant gold and silver coins! They must have been some of the coins that Window and his friends had followed to the cannon on the western coast of the Northlands! It was part of the missing third treasure of King Alezan!
The rest of the King's treasure of coins must have stayed in the Northlands with the Prince, but this chest had traveled with the Queen on the Amerand ship.

Window slid his hands across the top of the thousands of shiny coins. He spotted a few of the silver lance coins he found with Revell's things, but also, many, many other designs and values. It was certainly a treasure worthy of a Queen!

As Window examined the coins, Renae went on with her story.

"Apparently the Queen was saving these coins until she could someday return to the throne in the north. This chest has remained unchanged for all of these years. I know that I could melt a few of these coins and sell the metals, but I intend to keep them unchanged as well. Perhaps someday, my family will return to Calisay."

There was a far-away look in Renae's eyes as her thoughts flew across the lands to the north.

"I am so envious of you to have been there, Window, while I have not."

"Perhaps one day we can go there together, Renae. You would make a beautiful Queen."

The woman smiled at her guest. Then she asked the question she had been waiting to ask. *"Window, do you know why the cookieboard is called 'the map?' When my mother taught me to bake the cookies, she always called it that."*

Just as Renae asked that question, Window dug his hands into the coins one last time and moved them around. As he did, he noticed that, buried behind the coins, next to the back-side of the chest, he could see the edge of some brownish colored paper sticking up .

"Do you know what this is?" Window asked as he slid his fingers along the folded edge of the paper.

"I have never noticed it before," Renae answered. *"Pull it out and we will see."*

Window used both hands to pull more coins away from the back wall of the chest and carefully tugged the paper from behind those coins still holding it. It was a piece of heavy, darkened paper, folded twice to about the size of his outstretched hand.

Before examining their find, the two treasure viewers returned
to the day-porch and sat again at the table. Window slowly
unfolded the paper. It crinkled as he opened it and smoothed it
flat on the tabletop.

Before Window and Renae on the table was the outline of a
map of the Northlands Kingdom. There were no names of cities or
any other places written on the map – there were no words at all.
Instead, drawn on the map, in their correct locations, were the
same pictures as on the cookieboard! Window recognized it
immediately as a map to the treasures of King Alezan!

The Queen, or the Prince, must have feared that the map
might be captured by the Atlandans so it was drawn to keep its
true meaning a secret. Only someone who knew that it was a map
to the King's treasures would have had any idea what it was

It now made sense to Renae why the pressing-board was called
"the map." She spoke to Window. *It seems to be a map of the
location of different things to be found in the Northlands,* Renae
observed. *I am surprised that anyone would bother to make such
a thing.*

Window's thoughts went way beyond Renae's understanding of
their discovery. He was thrilled to, at last, understand the
connection of his grandmother's cookieboard to the Northlands
Treasures. But, he decided to not say anything about it to his new
Ameredene friend just yet. He would surprise her later with the
story of his adventures of following "the map."

Renae went on with her speculation. *The Amerans loved
making springcookies and had collections of different carved
pressing-boards. Even now, most of my Amerand neighbors bake
the cookies here in Ameredene. While on board the ship, some of
them must have passed the time by carving new boards.*

*Perhaps Princess Laycelle and her two Amerand friends wanted
some ideas of pictures to carve into a board and the Queen gave
them this map to copy from. Or, maybe the Queen just wanted a
pressing board that would make cookies that would remind her of
her lost homeland. However it happened, the pictures were taken*

from this map and carved into my cookieboard – and your grandmother's board as well."

Renae's guesses made sense to Window. It must have happened that way. He smiled to himself. At last, the mystery of his grandmother's cookieboard was solved. And, apparently, his grandmother never knew that the board was called 'the map' or she would have told him.

"I have one more surprise for you, Window."
Window couldn't imagine being any more surprised by the woman than he already was. He looked at her and waited for her to continue.
Renae smiled as she told him, *"Tomorrow you will meet your cousin, Wendy."*

Window stared blankly at the lost Northlands Princess.
"Here, have another cookie while I finish the story of my family's coming to Ameredene."
Renae explained her final surprise. The Amerand sister who stayed on board the Setampa as a servant of the Queen was named Verlesa. She remained a friend of Princess Laycelle after their families settled in the Newlands. As years went by, their families continued to stay close and now the great-granddaughters of those girls were friends.

Renae's twin daughters, Annette and Audette, were returning the next day from a visit to Wendy's home in the town of Riverhold. As she often did, Wendy was coming back with them to visit for a week or so in Cadeene.

Since Wendy was the great-granddaughter of Verlesa, and Window was the great-grandson of Verlesa's sister, *Sevenna*, who left the Amerand ship and remained in Coastown, tomorrow, along with meeting Renae's daughters, Window would meet his distant cousin, Wendy!

So Window's adventures would soon take still another turn. And, so, he had still another thing to thank his Uncle Breeze for.

Window and Renae spent the rest of the day talking and planning. Window hadn't had any springcookies for a long time and so he really enjoyed every one he ate. He and the Princess sat by the fireplace that evening and talked still more. Window didn't know what to say about all of his treasure hunting in the Northlands so he spoke mostly of his friends he met there, and his other discoveries.

As Window sat by the fireplace, Renae brought him a small, hinged, wooden box and opened it for him. The box contained jeweled rings and jeweled chains and jeweled pins.
"These are what remains of the Queen Cillaia's personal treasure from the Northlands Kingdom," Renae explained. *"Window, I would like you to have one of these as my gift to you."*
Window was touched by her offer. Renae went on. *"Perhaps you have a lady friend who would enjoy wearing something once worn by the Queen."*
Window's thoughts jumped to Mary and the jeweled treasures he had left behind in the North. He had not taken anything from the treasure there except the pin from Panni.
"It is so kind of you, Princess. I am honored to accept your offer."
He searched through the twenty or so items and found the perfect gift for Mary. It was a bright, light-green jewel in a silver mounting that hung from a silver neck-chain.
"My friend, Mary, will love to wear this, Renae. It is beautiful. And I will forever remember your kindness."
The Windlands traveler leaned forward and gave the Northlands Princess a kiss on the cheek.
Window was invited to sleep on the day-porch for the night. He went to sleep tired and happy with thoughts of Mary in his mind.

Wendy and Renae's daughters were to arrive late the next morning by wagon from Riverhold. Window anxiously waited on the front porch steps, looking constantly down the road to the west. He had just closed his eyes and let the sun warm is face when he heard the clopping sounds of two horses drawing nearer.
"Renae, they are here!" he called into the house.

Renae came out onto the porch and waved to the girls. Wendy, who, like the twins, was seventeen, stood up in the back of the wagon and waved wildly back to Renae and the stranger on the porch. The first thing that Window noticed was how much Wendy resembled pictures of his mother when she was about that same age. Wendy's eyes were dark brown and her hair dark brown and wavy as it fell in front of her eyes. And like his mother, Wendy wore a happy smile along with her blouse and skirt.

The twin girls sat more calmly, but still greeted Renae and Window with enthusiasm. Annette and Audette were identical twins, at least to Window. Their light-brown hair and smooth faces seemed to be copies of each other. Only Audette's bright red jacket helped Window tell them apart.

"Hello, Mama, Hello Mrs. Flasette," the girls called out. *"Did you bake picture cookies for us?"* Annette happily added.

The girls jumped down from the wagon and grabbed their bags from the back. *"Thanks, Mr. Wheeler,"* they called as the wagon-master continued on to deliver supplies he had brought from Riverhold for the stores in Cadeene.

"Welcome home, Girls. Hi, Wendy."

The three young friends couldn't take their eyes off of the handsome, young man standing on the porch next to Renae.

"Ladies, this is Window. He has come from far, far away to visit."

The girls straightened their clothes and brightened their faces.

"And he has a story to tell you – especially you, Wendy."

Wendy looked oddly at Renae, then at the man at her side.

"Window is your distant cousin, Wendy," Renae started to explain.

"From Silver Falls?" Wendy responded.

Renae chuckled at Wendy's interpretation of her comment, and answered her accordingly. *"No, even more distant."*

"From Liberties?"

"No, Window is from the Windlands, but he has traveled much farther than that."

Wendy could hardly believe it. She had often dreamed of traveling far from home, but she had never even met anyone before who had been outside of Ameredene.

"Have you ever been to the Northlands plains?" Wendy excitedly asked Window.
"Yes, Wendy, I have been there."
"Have you ever seen a Silkie?" She was remembering her grandmother's stories.
"I have even ridden on one."
Wendy's eyes opened even wider. She knew that she was really going to like her new cousin.

The new family spent the next week learning more about each other and enjoying the cool highlands weather. In the mornings, the girls would run around Cadeene as they usually did. In the afternoons, everyone would meet in the open-porch room and Renae and Window would tell stories – well, mostly Window would tell stories. Wendy sat enthralled as he told of some of his adventures across the lands.

The springcookies soon were all eaten so everyone helped make another double batch. The flour and powdered sugar flew around the kitchen as the girls carelessly poured, sifted, and mixed the ingredients. Renae hadn't laughed so hard in years. She even asked Window if she and her girls could be his "cousins" too. He happily agreed.

Window noticed that as she worked in the kitchen, Renae whistled just like his Grandmother Windowen always did. He remembered Panni whistling like that, too, at Oldsmith's. It gave Window a feeling of joy and comfort to hear Renae do that same thing as she worked. He felt closer to her than ever.

One morning, while the girls were out, Window thought that the time was right to tell Renae the rest of the story of his grandmother's cookieboard, and his treasure-hunting adventures. The Ameredene Princess sat in awe as she learned the entire story of Window and his friends searching across the Northlands and finally finding the King's Treasure at the Eastpoint Gate.

Her eyes grew big as she admitted to him, *"I am not surprised, Window. I can tell that you are just the person to be able to find a treasure, even without a cookie-board map."*

Then he told her of the plans his friends had, to use the treasure to try to reestablish a new, fair, and just Northlands Kingdom.

The Renae loved their idea and wished them well. *"You and your friends are welcome to the treasure, Window. I have all I need here. But,"* she added with a smile, *"if you ever need any Queens or Princesses, perhaps my daughters or I might agree to help you out."*

Window thought that that was an excellent idea.

Window's visit had awakened in Renae the sense of adventure that she had forgotten. She had begun to think about doing a little traveling of her own. Perhaps she and the girls would start with a trip to visit their relatives at Liberties in the lowlands. There they could ride horses and travel even farther to the edge of Ameredene if they wished.

Window had insisted that Renae accept a gift from him – the spurs from Queen Karinne of the Hearts. Renae held them up in the sunlight and spun the eight-sided stars. They lightly clanked against the spur-bar and made a pleasant spinning sound.

Renae watched with fascination as the shining stars went around and around. They seemed to take her thoughts far away for a moment. She thanked Window and promised that after she and the girls learned to ride that they would travel to the Windlands and visit him.

"Make sure that you bring me along," Wendy insisted.

"Okay, I will," Renae promised the girl.

Window's thoughts now turned every day to the Windlands and to Mary. It was decided that when Wendy returned home to Riverhold in two more days, she and Window would travel together, not by wagon, but would travel downriver on one of the flatboats that carried supplies and goods to towns along the water.

So it was at the river dock where they would say goodbye to the Flasettes.

The boat they would ride on was flat and rectangular and had been stacked with boxes and barrels to make the trip. Near one end of the boat, there was a small cabin section to sleep in.

Annette carried Wendy's bag and Audette carried Window's pack. Renae had given Window a narrow bag to carry his sword in, but the girls had sneaked a look at it one afternoon while he had gone to the supply store for Renae. The twins didn't care about it much but Wendy was fascinated. She planned to ask Window about it when they were alone and she had the chance.

Window stored their things on board and stepped back onto the dock. *"Goodbye, Ladies. I hope to see you again."*

Renae held out her hand. Window held it in both of his. He was so appreciative of her kindness and the secrets she had shared with him. She was thankful for all he had shared with her as well.

"You are welcome here always, Window."

Renae reached into her pocket and took out a small package wrapped in paper.

"You don't have to share these with anyone," she whispered in his ear. Window saw the sly smile on her face and slid the springcookies into his pocket. He would enjoy them later.

There were hugs all around, then, the travelers stepped onto the boat. Annette held her mother's hand as Audette leaned against a dock post. Wendy blew a kiss to her friends.

Window took one last glance at Renae. She nodded her final goodbye to him. The boat-master pushed off from the dock and the boat moved into the current. The girls yelled to each other but Window and Renae remained silent. It was another sad parting for Window.

Two jays cawed overhead as the current swiftly carried Window and Wendy around a bend in the river and out of sight of the Northlands Princess.

+++++++++

[IN THE DEEP WOODS VALLEY]

Across the low-mountain forests and the Outlands, and near the Deep Woods path, Runner, the Woot, was waiting. He had been up since before the sunrise – waiting – waiting for something to do. He was a Woot who was not used to waiting. He was a Woot who was used to traveling – and exploring.

His Mama told him that, at least for a while, his traveling and exploring days were over. Now, he had something else to keep him busy.

"That's what happens, Runner, when your fur turns light-blue," she had told him. But then, she didn't tell him what he was supposed to be doing instead.

And anyway, he didn't like it when his Mama called him Runner. He liked to be called Circles.

Ever since his return from his travels, Circles had been the center of attention in the Woot valley. No one could ever remember a Woot whose fur had turned light blue. Even the Grand-grandma Woot had never heard of it.

"Maybe you're a Woot Prince," Lilli had suggested. We've never had one of those.

"Maybe you are a Woot who likes to stand on one foot," Dotter guessed. Dotter was not very good at guessing.

Circles was pretty disappointed. Now he would probably never find out what kind of Woot he was really supposed to be.

Circles had a friend, though, from a far-away world, who once told him that he was a very special Woot.

"What's so special about a Woot who has traveled across the lands and seen two oceans and an Angel? I had friends who helped me," he explained to his Mama.

*And, of course, only a few of the Valley Woots believed
that he had done those things. Most of them thought that he
had just wandered off into the Woods and gotten lost – and
had been afraid to come home for a long, long time.*

*Some of the Woots, though, did wonder where Circles had
gotten an arrow weapon, and a shiny round stick that he
would hold up to his eye. Others wondered why, sometimes,
a bird would fly down and sit on the ground next to him.
Maybe he was a special Woot, after all.*

*Powder believed in Circles completely. She loved the
idea of having an adventure and wanted to go along with
him next time he decided to see the kites.*

*"What are kites, Circles?" she had asked him one night
while they were sitting together on a hillside.*

"I will show you, Powder. You will see."

*"Are they colorful birds? That's what an Owt told me
once."*

"You will see, Powder. And you will like them.

"Will we see the kites tonight, Circles?"

*"Tonight, we will see something else. Someone is coming
to visit me."*

"Will we see the Angel?" the Woot girl excitedly asked.

"Listen, you can hear them coming."

*Then, from behind the trees and rocks, the Fairies started
to appear – twenty, or so, tiny, sparkling, flying creatures.
Each glittering a different color, and each making a sound
like a tinkling wind-chime, or a tiny bell, as they flew out in
front of the bright-eyed Woot.*

*There were Sun-fairies that watched over the world by
day, and Star-fairies that watched over the world by night.
There were Forest-fairies that watched over the trees.*

*There were River-fairies and Music-fairies and Sky-
fairies and Flower-fairies and Rain-fairies and Wind-fairies
– Fairies of every kind that helped the Angels watch over the
world.*

Rainbows of color bounced between the beautiful creatures as they floated in front of the two Woots. The hillside was alive with sparkling light.

"We have come from Starland to see you, Circles," the Night-fairy spoke in a tiny voice. "We have come to honor the Saver of the Angels and thank you for your help."
Circles bowed to his visitors. "It is kind of you to visit me. I am pleased to see you."
"Where is Starland?" Powder wanted to know. "Can we go there?"
"It is a secret place that only believers can see," came the tinkling reply.
"I would like to go there. Circles, can we go to Starland?"
Before Circles could answer, the Fairies all flipped their wings once and jumped up higher in the air. Then, as suddenly as they came, the Fairies flitted into the forest.

Once again, the night was quiet. The moon was high above them as Circles and Powder sat on the hillside. Powder didn't care what the others thought. She knew that Circles was a very special Woot, indeed.

It was late, and time to go back to the Valley, but Powder wasn't ready to go home just yet. She sat and looked up at the moon. Circles' thoughts turned to his friends, far away.
Then Powder took a deep breath, sighed, and whistled a little melody as she sat on the hillside with her special Woot friend.

+++++++++

The weather was turning to spring. The nights were cool but the days were pleasant. The early mountain highland flowers were all in bloom as the boat travelers sat on the top of the flatboat cabin and watched the riverbank go by.

Riverhold would be about a three-day trip downstream. As they got farther from Cadeene, the trees thinned out somewhat but still the travelers were in forest country. They stopped overnight in the town of Krystenille, but only stayed in Otter Bend for a few hours.

Window and Wendy were the only passengers on the river flatboat. Except for the boat-master, who kept to himself, they were alone. They mostly dangled their feet over the edge of the wide boat-house and talked.

"Window, where did you get your sword?"

Window had been expecting the question. He pulled Revell's sword from its bag and handed it to her. Wendy carefully drew the blade from its sheath. The sword's jeweled handle gleamed in bright colors as it always did. The afternoon sun reflected them into Wendy's eyes.

"It once belonged to a friend of my grandfather's. I found it in the far, far East."

Wendy ran her fingers over every stone and along the smooth, slippery sides of its sharp blade.

"I wish I could find a sword."

"You will someday, Wendy," he encouraged her. *"Never give up looking for adventure."* Window felt like his Uncle Bill must have felt talking to him at the Summer Breeze.

"Oh, I won't, Window, I won't."

Resting the sword on her lap she asked, *"May I hold it for a while?"*

"Sure."

Window watched as Wendy kept her hand gripped tightly around the sword's hilt. The Bluewater continued to wind through the forests of Ameredene.

After a while he asked her, *"Wendy, would you like to see the maps and pictures I have drawn of places I have been?"*

"I would love that!"

Window got out his notebook and handed it to her. She reluctantly returned the sword to him and sat in the sun examining every page of drawings and notes, except a few he

asked to keep private, as they continued on their way to
Riverhold. They would reach the town later that day.

As the afternoon sun was starting to go behind the trees along
the Bluewater, Wendy couldn't wait any longer to share the idea
she had been working on. It would be her only chance to continue
what she thought of as her adventure with Window.

She leaned over the side of the boat and watched the water
rush by as she got up her courage to ask him something. Then she
looked straight into his eyes.

*"Window, would it be alright with you if you didn't meet my
parents? I know that they are your relatives, too, but if you come
home with me and meet them, you will have to spend most of your
time visiting with them and I wouldn't have time with just you."*

*"This could be the only night I ever have when I don't have to
share you with someone. I would so like to have time with you just
to myself."*

Window was flattered, but understood exactly what his cousin
was feeling. He knew very well what it was like to be excited by
thoughts of adventure.

Wendy went on, *"Besides, neither of my parents, or my brother,
ever even thinks about adventure or traveling far away. They
would just think that you are strange and be happy when you went
on your way."*

*"Couldn't we just camp out in the woods near Riverhold for one
night? Then I could see what it is like to sit around a fire with you
and tell stories and make plans to find treasures."*

*"I even know a place where we can set up our camp. I have been
there before with some of my friends. It is close to the river – and I
have my blanket and jacket with me."*

Window was about to answer when Wendy continued her
request.

*"Please Window, it would mean a lot to me. I have been
dreaming my whole life about far-away adventure and – is it true,
Window, do Angels sometimes ride on Silkie in the moonlight?"*

In her excitement, Wendy's mind raced on.

*"I even dream about Angels sometimes – usually the same ones –
Caroline and Valentine."*

Window thought that it was odd that she dreamed about an
Angel named Caroline.

*"Did you see any Angels while you were in the far-away lands,
Window?"*

Wendy's eyes were excited and pleading. But she would have
to wait until they were sitting around the fire to hear the answers
to some of her questions. Window only replied to one of them.

*"Yes, Wendy, we can make a camp and sit around the fire late
into the night. The boat-master can let us off before we reach the
Riverhold docks. Your family will not know that you are back from
Cadeene yet, so they won't miss you. I will even teach you a song or
two from the Northlands."*

Wendy was thrilled. Her small adventure was continuing.

In just a few hours, the two campers had climbed from the boat
onto the shore and made the short walk to Wendy's campsite.
Window collected firewood and Wendy built the fire. She had
built fires here before and was happy to do it this time for her
Windlands cousin.

Then, as the world grew dark around them, Window and his
adventurous cousin sat and watched the flames jump high into the
sky. Wendy shared a small stack of crackers she had wrapped in
thin paper and stuffed into her pack at home. Window enjoyed
the feeling of sharing the fire as much as Wendy did. He missed
his days of traveling with his friends.

It was such a peaceful night, Wendy forgot all about Window
telling stories or singing songs. She just looked into the flames
and dreamed about far-away, magical places. Then, Wendy
happened to look over to where she had laid Window's notebook on
her blanket under the trees.

"Window, do you believe in Fairies?"

"I have seen Fairies once."

*"Well, you are going to see them again. There are two Fairies
reading your notebook!"*

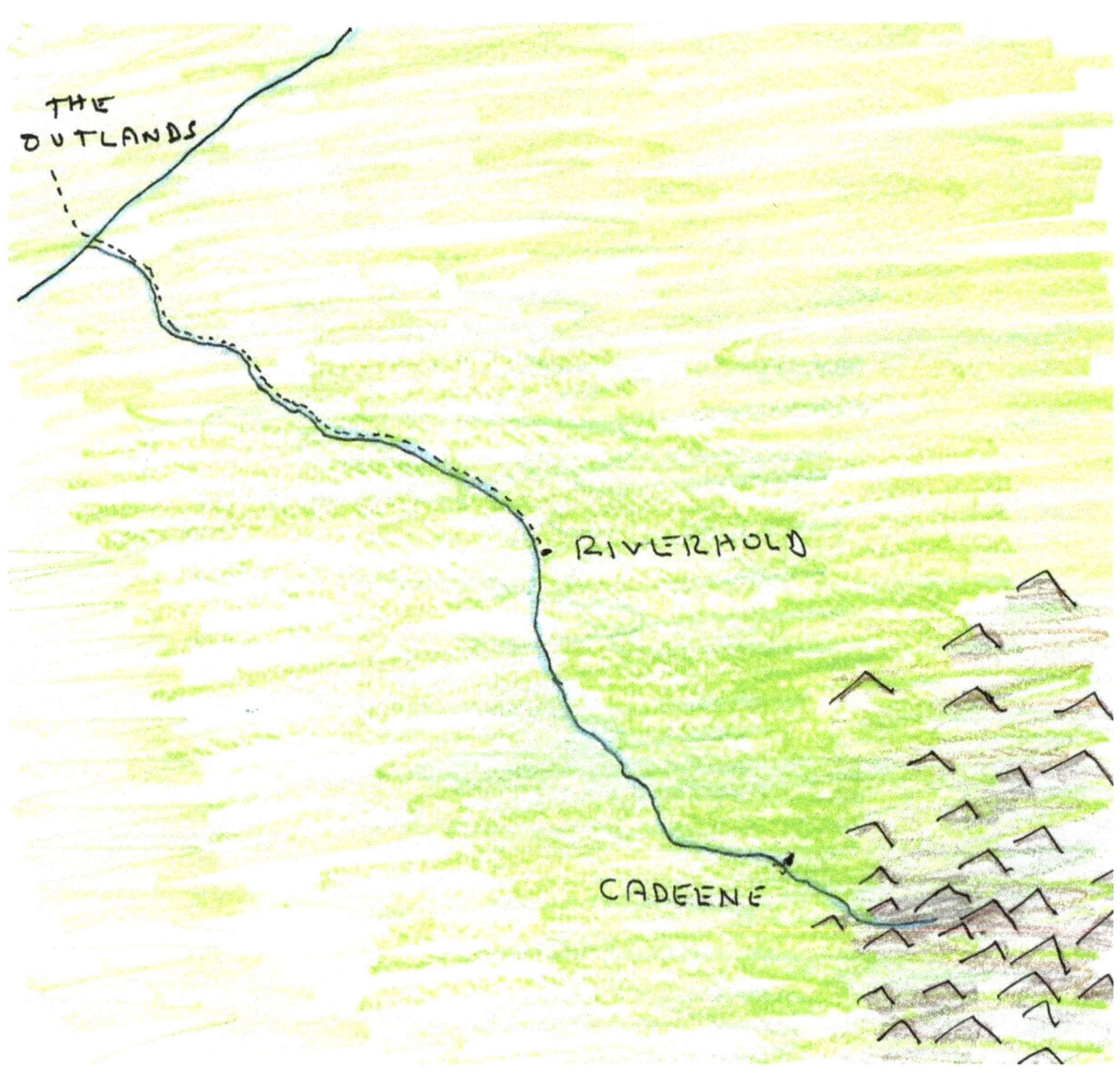

THE
OUTLANDS
RIVERHOLD
CADEENE

CHAPTER THIRTY

ON THE WOODLANDS ROAD

Window turned and looked over to his side towards Wendy's blanket under the trees. There he saw two Fairies glowing in the darkness. Their tiny bodies were wrapped in sparking pale-green light and their wispy wings were motionless behind their backs. They were walking across the pages of Window's open notebook – lighting it up and reading as they stepped back and forth across its pages.

The two cousins just quietly watched them.

"Oh, Window, this is wonderful," Wendy whispered. *"They are beautiful."* Her eyes shone almost as brightly as the magic creatures before them.

The two campers quietly turned around and sat on their log seats facing the Fairies. The little creatures were intently reading Window's notes and looking at his pictures. When they finished looking at a page, they would flit their wings and fly up into the air just far enough so one of them could reach down and turn to the next page of the notebook.

Suddenly they seemed to sense that they were being watched and turned to face the campfire. Window recognized their soft young faces and tiny bright eyes. They were the Fairies that had found him at the workshop in Keleste – the Fairies that had brought the Angel, Caroline.

The two sparkling creatures jumped up from the blanket and flew over towards the fire. There they stopped and floated in the air in front of the campers. As before, the Fairies spoke their words exactly together. Their tiny voices reminded Wendy of wind-chimes or an orchestra of tiny bells. They spoke in Amerand so she could understand.

"Hello, Window. Caroline has sent us to keep you company, but you have been hard to find. She sends her greetings and her thanks for your help."

Before he could ask, they went on. *"She wanted you to know, Window, Caroline has taken Circles home to the Deep Woods and he has recovered completely from his illness. He is now healthy and fine. He misses you but knows he will see you soon."*

Window quietly sighed and breathed happily. It was exactly the news he was hoping for.

"Thank you for your welcome message. That is wonderful to hear."

The amazed Wendy watched and listened to the conversation in awe.

The Fairies bowed to the girl. *"Hello, Wendy. We are pleased to meet you."*

Wendy smiled and nodded her head. *"What are your names?"*

The magical visitors spoke again. *"We are twins."*

"I am Tresette," one of them answered. *"And I am Vermillion."*

Again the creatures spoke in unison. *"Caroline calls us Fairies, but we are really Forest-angels. We watch over the trees and streams – and while we are here, we will watch over you. We can see that your heart is pure and brave."*

Wendy smiled broadly.

"Is Caroline a Forest-angel, too?" the girl wanted to know.

"Caroline is a Moon-angel. She gets her strength from the moon, but she watches over people. The moon doesn't need anyone watching over it."

"Tresette, I have dreamed of an Angel named Caroline. Do you think that the Angel in my dreams could have been your Moon-angel friend?"

The sparkling-green Fairy landed on the curious girl's hand to answer.

"When a believer looks up at the Moon and makes a wish, that night she sometimes dreams about what the Angels are doing."

Wendy was sure. She really had been dreaming of the Angels!

The two cousins and the two Forest-angels sat by the fire late into the night. Well, the Fairies didn't sit very much, but, a couple of times, they did alight on a log or a rock. Mostly they just flitted around being beautiful – and comforting to Wendy and Window.

Finally, Window and Wendy wrapped themselves in their blankets close to the fire. The light and the sound of the Fairies lulled the campers to sleep.

In the morning the Fairies were gone. The distant cousins packed their things and had a quiet breakfast of crackers and conversation.

"I wish I could go with you, Window. I would love to see the Windlands."

He dug into his pack and found his silver Windmill Dollar.

"Here is something to remind you of me and the Windlands – until you have a chance to see it for yourself."

"Thanks, Window. You have brought a shining light into my life. I hope I can repay you someday."

Then she thought of something. *"Hey, you are going to need some food for your trip. And I have an idea."*

About twenty minutes later, they were standing in front of the great wheel of a Bluewater river mill.

"This is Riller the Miller's place. I come out here and talk to him sometimes. He doesn't have a family so he enjoys company. I am sure that he will give you some food for your trip."

Then Wendy added, *"Well, Riller had a brother who used to help him at the mill, but I guess he moved out of town a few years ago. I wonder what ever happened to him."*

"I think I know," answered a smiling Window.

Wendy looked at him questioningly, but Window didn't say anything else.

Wendy was right. Riller was a friendly and generous man. Window's pack was soon filled with cheese and bread and dried meat. He also reminded Window that the spring berries would soon be out. Window offered him a Freeland coin but Riller wouldn't accept it.

After a quick thank you, the cousins were on their way. They reached Riverhold as the mid-day sun was breaking through the clouds.

Then, once again, Window would soon have to say goodbye to someone he cared about. As Wendy walked with him along the river to the western edge of town, she asked if she could wear his sword for a few minutes.

He buckled his grandfather's belt around her waist and she let the jeweled handle flash in the sun as they went up the street. Two women who were sitting on a bench by the park watched curiously as the cousins walked by.

"I love this town," she said to Window. *"But I could love some other places, too. And I plan to find them someday. Now, whenever I look down the River Road, I will think of you and all of the places you have been. I want to go to those places too."*

Window hugged her and kissed the top of her head. *"I believe that you will, Wendy. There are adventures down every road. All you have to do is go find them."*

"Thanks, Window. I'll see you."

"Goodbye, Wendy. I am proud to be in the same family as you. You will be a great explorer."

She squeezed his hand.

Window and Wendy walked silently the rest of the way to the edge of town. There, sitting on the riverbank, were two girls about Wendy's age, flying a kite out across the water. Its blue

226

paper rattled in the wind as the girls watched it flutter above them.

The Riverhold girl turned and walked towards the water. She stopped and looked back, then went to talk to her friends. The Windlands traveler returned his sword to his side and started on his way to the Ameredene lowlands. A light breeze pushed through his hair. It was a beautiful day for an adventure.

++++++++

Window's journey along the Bluewater to the flatlands below the mountains was a pleasant one. The nights were cold, but the days were comfortable as each mile brought him closer to home. He wondered about Circles and he wondered about Panni and he wondered about Cardette and he wondered about Mary. He hoped that Mary had gotten his wind-carried note. She and her father should be moving back to the town of Station about now. Then, by the time Window got home, while Mary's father remained in Station, she should be living in their house in Windtown.

But things got interesting again. Three days after he left Wendy, as Window walked on the road beneath the trees along the river, he was happily surprised to see the Fairies, Tresette and Vermillion, fluttering up the road to join him, out of breath as though they had been hurrying.

Window was very glad to see his new visitors. "I didn't know that Fairies came out in the daytime," he told them as he pulled off his pack and the two shining creatures joined him for lunch. "Here, have a piece of this bread."

"We usually sleep during the day, Window," they answered him. "But we needed to catch up with you. We promised Angel Caroline to keep you company, but we haven't done such a good job so far."

Tresette tugged on the bread Window had given them and a tiny piece pulled free. She handed it to her sister.

"We are sorry that we left you so soon when you were with Wendy, but we had something important to do."

"And what was that?" Window wanted to know.

"You will find out tonight."

Window didn't ask any more questions. He was happy to have their company.

Around their campfire that night, Window put his blanket out on his pack to make a playing surface for Rainbow Chips. He thought that maybe his bright, little companions would like the game. And, he missed his games with Circles and Charm.

The Fairies said that they loved games and stood still in the air as Window explained how Rainbow Chips was played. Things started off okay but then there were some problems.

First, Tresette kept forgetting how many chips she needed in each row and was constantly starting her turn over again. Then Vermillion knocked over a big stack of green chips and they fell in the dirt. Then, Tresette played three of her chips to make a pretty pattern rather than to try to earn any points. Window just started putting chips anywhere as a joke to confuse them and soon all three of the players were just seeing how high they could stack the chips rather than trying to actually play the game.

Vermillion won with a stack twenty-six high. Then the two Forest-angels built more tall stacks of chips and tried to stand on the stacks without them falling down. Window enjoyed the big splashes of color each time the Fairies and their chips fell to the ground. Vermillion started laughing wildly and pretty soon the other two game-players joined her.

Suddenly, in her small voice, Tresette cried out, "Milli, she is here!"

Window turned towards the trees. Standing above the ground about twenty feet from him was an Angel – a woman surrounded by brightly glowing, red light. Her silky dress-wrap shimmered against the dark of the trees.

The visitor's face was smooth and calm. Her hair was a very light red, and fluttering. Her skin and silky wings were also red – and shining as the rest of her.

This Angel was not weak and struggling as Caroline had been – but was healthy and powerful. Her eyes were piercing but kind.

Window stood up to meet her. As she spoke, the red Angel's voice seemed to float across to him.

"Greetings, Traveler Window. I am Veronica. Caroline has sent me to thank you for helping her – and all of the Angels."

"Hello, Angel Veronica," answered an astonished Window. "Welcome to our camp. I am pleased that you have come to visit."

"It is my honor to speak to you, Window. You are forever a friend of the Angels."

"I am honored as well, Veronica. Your words are kind."

"Window, when they hear how you have helped the Angels, the Fairies will be coming, also."

"Tresette and Vermillion?"

"No, other Fairies

"Coming where?"

"Coming to thank you."

"If they can find us," Vermillion added. Tresette tinkled with laughter.

Veronica ignored the Fairies and continued.

"I hope to repay you someday, as I can, Window. If you are in desperate need, call for me. If I am nearby, I will come."

Window was thrilled at her message. "Thank you, Veronica. I happily accept your offer of help. It is an unexpected, generous gift."

The Angel nodded, and her wispy, red hair fluttered around her.

Window's thoughts jumped to the question that had brought him so far on his travels. He reached into his pocket. Surely, if anyone would know of his medallion, it would be the Angel.

"Veronica, if you could answer my question, I would greatly appreciate it. Do you recognize this medallion from the Windlands?"

The Angel looked at him with kindness in her eyes. "I have never been to the Windlands, Window. I am sorry to disappoint you."

As he heard Veronica's answer, Window thought that the Angel's calm face had changed to a look of sadness.

"Where is your home, Veronica?"

"I used to live beyond the Eastern Plains, near the Far Ocean, but, except for me, all of the Angels there have faded away. I am uncertain where I live now."

Window felt the great sadness in her heart and joined her in her sorrow. "You are always welcome to live by my home in the Windlands, or in the Deep Woods. I would come visit you when I could."

"Thank you, Window. It is kind of you to invite me."

"I could show you Signal Hill, where some say the Angels used to live."

"I would like that very much, Window. Perhaps someday I will come visit you, but for now, I have other concerns to attend to."

Window was sorry to see that the Angel intended to be leaving soon.

"Couldn't you stay with us for just a bit, Veronica? I would so love to visit with you for a while."

The beautiful red Angel sighed. She was drawn to Window and the campfire. She felt an overwhelming desire to let go of her Angel duties for a short time and share in his quiet world. She realized that she may never have the chance again.

"It does look so comforting and inviting, Window. Perhaps just for a bit I could join you. I have never sat around a campfire before. I have never done that."

So that is just what happened. The powerful, magic Angel, Veronica – one of the few remaining Angels in the world – sat

down on a fallen tree trunk by the fire. Window pulled some more
dry limbs onto the flames and sat next to her. The Windlands
Traveler and the homeless Angel warmed their hands and faces as
they listened to the popping and snapping and hissing of the blaze
before them.

As the two fire-lovers enjoyed the flames, Tresette and
Vermillion found their way to Window's blanket and curled up on
top of it and closed their Fairy eyes.

Window and Veronica didn't talk or tell stories or anything like
that. A couple of times Window hummed a short melody and
Veronica copied it. She had never sung with anyone before. She
had never shared a peaceful night like this before. She had never
felt such comfort.

Window thought about the wonder of it all. It was so oddly
calm and beautiful. The breeze washed across his face and hair
and then did the same to the Angel. She gazed at the stars and
the moon and the fire. She was changed. She would never be the
same again.

Window felt it also. His friends back home could never imagine
such a thing – him sitting by the fire with an Angel. He wanted it
to never end.

The peaceful magic lasted for a couple of happy hours. Finally,
as the fire was burning down, Veronica could wait no longer. She
sighed as she stood up and stretched her arms and hands and
straightened her flowing clothes. She took Window's hands and
looked deep into his eyes. She didn't need to say anything. It was
understood. He knew it was time for her to go.

Then the beautiful magical creature crossed her hands over her
heart in a sign of caring and spoke in a quiet voice. "Thank you,
Window. All that you are is so important to me. May you always
be safe from harm and sadness. I give you the wishes of all the
Angels of goodness and magic. And, Window, I give you the magic
from deep within me as well. I will never forget this night. You
are forever a part of me."

Window nodded his head in appreciation and shared one last
look into her eyes. Veronica smiled deeply to him and he returned

the smile to her. Then she stepped back, and with a flash of
brilliant red light, the powerful, beautiful Veronica disappeared
into the Woodlands night.

Window was overwhelmed. His mind was filled with feelings of
all he had been through on his travels. He became very quiet and
just sat down without speaking.

He stared into the crackling fire as he had done so many times
before. His thoughts turned to home. Suddenly, Window felt
more lonely than he had ever felt before in his life.

Tresette and Vermillion woke from their rest and quietly flitted
past Window and picked up the Rainbow Chips they had been
playing with earlier and, one by one, put them back into his pack.
Then they sat on a rock next to him and sang. It was a simple,
comforting melody. The light from their sparkling bodies joined
with the light from the fire and washed across Window's face. He
listened to the beauty of the Fairies as they sang song after song.
He sat up late into the night.

The Fairies traveled along with Window through the forests of
Ameredene for two more days. They were pleasant company as
they flew alongside of him and talked about nothing in particular,
or chased birds and butterflies. But sometimes they flitted around
nervously and Window could tell that they were getting anxious to
go.

The twins had each started speaking more for themselves, so
Window addressed just one of them. "Are you looking forward to
getting back home, Tresette?"

"We live on the other side of the mountains to the east,
Window. That is where Caroline found us. But our world is
changing, too. We have decided to look for a new place to live."

"Why don't you go back to the camp where we stayed with
Wendy? That was a pretty nice spot. Maybe you could even
surprise her with a visit."

The little Angels whispered to each other for a moment.

"We like that idea, Window," announced Tresette. "But we
promised Caroline that we would keep you company."

"It is alright. I will miss you whenever you go, but I will be fine. I can see that you are ready to be on your way."

"Let's go now, Settie," Vermillion suggested. "I want to get there before the sunrise tomorrow."

"Okay, Milli. Let's do."

"Thank you both for traveling with me. Please tell Wendy that I miss her, too."

"We will, Window. We will," came two happy voices in unison.

The two Forest-angels each flew up and gave Window a kiss on the cheek. Then, with a final flit of sparkles and a flash of pale-green light, they disappeared into the trees.

+++++++++

A few more days of travel along the Bluewater brought Window to the end of the forests. He stepped out from under the trees and saw the flatlands of Ameredene before him.

He walked on – past farms and ranches, across bridges and through towns. At one farm, he passed a fenced-in yard that was home to a light-brown pig lying in the sun. He called out to the pig and it returned his greeting with a bored look.

He walked on. He talked to ducks and birds and squirrels and rabbits. None of them spoke back to him. He saw kites in the sky as village children enjoyed the winds.

One night, after about a week in the flatlands, Window stopped at the edge of a small forest. He was about to get one more visitor on his long journey home. As he sat by the fire, remembering his nights with his friends from Windtown, the full moon was overhead – lighting his campsite and brightening his spirits. The wind was light and the fire crackled in the quiet.

Then he looked towards the trees and saw something standing in the moonlight. His heart took a happy jump. A wispy shadow, like the silhouette of a tall, thin man, was floating above the grass. It was the Watcher – his shadow friend from the Deep Woods!

Window was thrilled. The creature was back! It was the first thing he had encountered at the beginning of his adventures, and

now it may be the last. But how could it be? He was far, far from
the Deep Woods.

"Hello, Shadow. It's nice to see you again," Window called to
the wispy form, expecting that once again, the shadow would
remain silent. But the traveler was in for a happy surprise.
"*Hello, Window, I have been looking for you,*" the shadow
answered – not with a voice, but with a thought that Window
heard in his head, soft and clear.
Window excitedly answered right back to the voice, talking out
loud towards the creature. "Shadow, can you talk to me now?"
The shadowy form fluttered a bit in the breeze, the moon
lightening its dark color.
"*Yes, Window, I am sorry that I couldn't before. Caroline found
me in the Deep Woods when she was returning Circles to his home.
She shared the moon-crystal light you had given her. I have
regained some of my powers.*"
"Are you an Angel?" Window asked, surprised and wanting to
make sure.
"*Yes, Window. I am an Angel. I was the first to travel from the
Ancient Lands to build the stone Angel City in the Deep Woods. I
was also one of those who built the Signal Hill to help watch over
the people of the Windlands when they arrived.*"
"*When most of the Angels went to other places around the world,
I stayed in the Deep Woods for I loved it there. Then my Angel-
form started to fade and I was unable to leave. For so long I have
been the only one remaining, unable to form except in the
moonlight, and unable to talk to anyone. I have been very lonely.
But now, although I will always remain faded, I can speak again.*"
"Will you come by the fire with me? We could visit for a while."
The Angel-shadow drifted above the grass nearer to Window
and the fire. The firelight flickered from his dark silhouette.

Window was full of happy questions. "Tell me a story of the
Angels, Shadow. I would like to know all about you. Why did the
Angels come to the Ancient Lands?"
"*When the world was new, the Angels came to help people
against the evils that were here. I am afraid that our work is still*

234

unfinished. There is much evil in the world. And, our faded magic may never return completely to as it once was.

"Do you know of the Cat-eyes creatures in the Ancient Lands called Cadence and Arrow?"

"Oh, Yes. They are the secret keepers."

"What secrets do they keep?"

"Even the Angels do not know. Cadence and Arrow are very good at keeping secrets.

"Yes, I have discovered that myself."

"Some Angels think that the Cat-eyes watch over us all."

"Are the Cat-eyes Angels, too?"

"They are very, very good at keeping secrets."

The shadow went on, *"But the Cat-eyes do help the Angels sometimes. And so do the Fairies – like the Forest-fairies that brought me to you. They are messengers for us."*

Window's curiosity continued. "My friends and I found Pixie dust in the Ancient Lands. Do you know of the magic Pixies?"

"Well, the Pixie-angels are supposed to help the other Angels also, but they usually only do what they want."

"As does their magic dust," Window added.

The odd friends sat by the fire late into the night.

"Do Angels ever talk to the wind?" Window wanted to know.

As before, the answer floated into Window's mind. *"The Wind-fairies sometimes do – at least they used to. The world is changing, Window, and some things are not as they once were."*

Shadow went on, *"I am afraid that even with the moon-crystals that the Angels may fade from the world."*

"I hope that you never fade away, Shadow."

"It is a bit too late for me, Window. I will someday be gone completely."

Window sat sadly thinking for a minute, then his spirits lifted. "Would you like to travel with me for a while? I am going back home near where I first met you."

"I would like that very much, Window. The Fairies who brought me here will return in a few days to take me back to the Deep Woods. Until then, I will travel with you."

The Angel-shadow went on, speaking though his thoughts, in a happy voice.

"Perhaps as we travel, you could tell me some more stories like the ones you told me in the Woods before."

Window answered his welcome companion. "I even have some new stories, Shadow. I have been traveling to the far lands."

"Did anything interesting happen on your journey?"

Window just smiled. "A few things."

"Good. I will listen as we go. You are a good story-teller, Window."

"And you are a good listener, Shadow – a very good listener. I'll bet that you could listen to the stories of my Uncle Bill long after I had fallen asleep."

"I would like to hear his stories, Window."

"Can you come with me all the way to Windtown?"

"Not this time, Window, but maybe someday."

"I would like that."

"So would I, Window. So would I."

The Deep Woods friends talked on and on.

Even as Window finally pulled his blanket around himself to sleep, he thought of something to ask. "What is your Angel name, Shadow?"

"I do not remember my name, Window. That part of me has faded away."

"Then would you like a new name?"

"I like the name you have already given me."

"So do I, Shadow, so do I."

Window closed his eyes and drifted off to a happy sleep. Shadow happily drifted with the breeze by the dying fire.

For several days, the Windlands traveler and the Angel-shadow walked down the road from the edge of the Ameredene forests. If anyone had been looking in their direction, they might have thought it strange that the young man carrying the jeweled sword seemed to be talking as though there were someone walking with him. They would probably not have been able to see the very faint, shadowy shape of a man walking in the sunlight beside him.

On their third happy night together, Window sat by the fire as Shadow drifted near him. They had been talking quietly. It was almost time for Shadow to go.
"They will be here soon, Window."
"Yes, I can hear them in the trees – here they come,"
In a soft flash of light, a dozen sparkling Fairies flew out of the darkness, up to the fire, and stopped in front of Window. They bowed and glowed and sparkled as they tried to form a straight line in the air. They were only partly successful.

"We have come to thank you for saving the Angels, Window," they called out together. Their tiny voices bounced from the trees.
"You are welcome, and thank you for bringing the Angel-shadow to me."
"You were a hard traveler to find, Window," a beautiful golden-colored Fairy complained to him. "We had to search for a long time."
"Well, I guess that I <u>have</u> been a few places the past few months."
The Fairy didn't reply.

Window turned to his forest friend. "Goodbye, Shadow. Thank you for your company."
"Thank you for your stories, Window. You can finish them another time."
"I will do that."
Several of the Fairies held tiny silver wands into the air. In an instant, the Angel-shadow faded into nothingness – and then, with a soft flicker of light, Window was alone.

+++++++++

After the visit of the Fairies, it was just one more day's journey, until, at last, Window reached the river that marked the end of the lands of Ameredene. Beyond the river were the flat and lonely Outlands which would take him back to the Windlands Prairies and home.

Off to the side of the road, as it approached the river bridge, there were a few final Ameredene trees. Under one of the trees was a stone table and several stone benches. Renae had told Window that the table was built years ago to welcome Amerand settlers. Window stopped to rest before he pushed on across the Outlands.

Window sat on the top of the table with his feet on a bench and thought ahead to the last part of his journey. As he sat and felt the breeze on his face a small bird jumped from a branch of the tree onto the table.

It was a small pinkish bird with red wings. Window recognized it right away. It was his mother's favorite bird – the one that his grandmother had asked him to look out for. It was a red-winged flower wren.

"Here, have some bread," Window called to the happy, little bird. The wren hopped over to him and pecked at the bread. Then it picked up the whole piece, and in a flutter of pink, flew back into the tree.

"Well, I guess that now I can go home," Window spoke to himself. "My Grandma told me, 'come back home when you have found everything you hope to find – but not before'."

"I have found so much more than I ever hoped."

Window dug into his pack and found the Windlands coins he had brought with him on his journey. He chose a silver Kitepiece and placed it in the middle of the tabletop. It flashed in the mid-day sun. The flower wren flew back down to the table and pecked at the coin a couple of times.

"Watch over that coin for me until I get back," Window spoke to the bird. "I'll look for it when I come here again someday." The bird bobbed his head a few times, let out a little whistle, and flew back into the tree.

Then the Windlands traveler rubbed his fingers over the jewels on the handle of his sword and tied the sword next to his blanket on top of his pack. He pulled the pack over his shoulders and stepped across the bridge into the Outlands. The sky was clear overhead. He would be home in a couple of weeks.

Then, as Window walked through the rough grass of the Outlands, his thoughts drifted out across the miles.

+++++++++

[ACROSS THE ADVENTURELANDS]

In Coastown, Kathryn Breesian was running down the dock towards her husband. The ship of Captain Ernest Breesian had just arrived in the harbor.

In Windtown, everyone was preparing for the Spring Holiday celebration.
This would be the first year that Davey and his friends would be in the races without Window. So this year, someone else would win for a change.

In the back room of the Summer Breeze, Bill Breesian was holding a glass of water he had just ladled from the bucket he pumped from the well that morning. He was watching the little bits of iron and other stuff floating around in the water. He was thinking of his nephew, Window.

A couple of streets away, Sally Resand was at her Grandmother Breesian's house having lunch.

In the Town Park, young girls were jumping rope and singing about a princess jumping on her bed.

On the side of Kite Hill, near the Windlands Tree, older girls and boys were trying out their latest creations. Window's cousin, Johnny, was there. The kite judging would be in the afternoon.

On their farm north of Windtown, Grandma Windowen was excitedly telling her husband what had happened the night he was away. It all started when she glanced out the window and saw a brilliant blue light shining in the yard — the light of a brilliant blue visitor named Caroline.

Farther to the north, on the top of Signal Hill, Shadow, the faded Angel, was looking out over the trees as he traded stories with Duster, the Owl. Shadow had a lot of missed storytelling to make up for.

In the moonlight of a Deep Woods clearing, Charm, the crystal-light, was waking up. Before he returned to the Moonlands, he wanted to find someone.

In a Deep Woods valley, Circles, the Woot, was saying goodbye to his mother. He and his friend, Powder, were leaving for the Northlands in a few minutes. She wanted to see the kites of Calisay.

In her Calisay bakery, Rayard Oldsmith's daughter, Sara was finishing another batch of her sugar-sticks. Next, she was going to bake some picture-cookies.

At the Matenne Palace, Rayard Oldsmith was talking with his horsemen friends. He needed their help with a little project his grandson had uncovered in a Cairiston Tower tunnel.

In an alley near the Cairiston Tower, Oldsmith's grandson, Rook, was busy planning for that same project with his band of Calisay street children.

On the western Calisenne grasslands, Royal Feyette, the shepherd, was packing his things. The Owts were going to have to watch the sheep for a while. Because Royal used to be a soldier in Calisay, his friend, Rings, the Brarrie, had asked him to return there and help Oldsmith with that same little project.

Off on the far western Atlandic Ocean coast, six, silver-grey Pinnipeds were sticking their lucky noses out from the water and calling a couple of "Waay" sounds. There was no one on the shore to answer them.

In the Ice Lands, Dester, the Brarrie, was sliding down a big hill in the snow. He was thinking of making a trip to the south. Maybe he could find his cousins in the Deep Woods.

On the far Northern Plains, Fireback, the Silkie, was still tired. The week before he had been racing with his Brarrie friend, Rings. Rings was a very fast Brarrie.

On the road to Laveselle, Rings, was trying out his gift from the starman. It was amazing! All he did was look into the eyes of the two soldiers he just passed and they forgot he was there. This was going to come in really handy!

At the Laveselle inn, Dawson Oldsmith was dealing out another hand of Northdraw to his wife, Polla, and his daughter, Mellie. In two days, Dawson and Rings, and several riders from the castle of Noble Paris, were leaving for the Gate To The Angels. There was something there that they wanted to bring back with them.
Mellie had insisted upon going along.

Nearby, in the day-room of the Pariselle Castle, Pantine Tresette was sitting in the sunlight. Noble Paris had invited her to live in the castle until she could return to her family in Traepelle. With her lightest-blonde hair falling across her soft shoulders and chest and down her silky-white dress, she looked like a Princess. Panni was a Princess.

In the Traepelle Province Castle, Feather Blonde and April Moon were singing on the evening-room balcony. April's hair fell in gentle waves around her face. Feather's hair was flying wildly. The young women had been talking of serious things lately. Perhaps they should run away from the castle as their friend had done.

In the Traepelle Province Woods, the Pixies, Pinkie and Kisses, were returning to their tree-house, exhausted, but howling with laughter. They had been out all night scaring chickens.

In the forest of the Ancient Lands, the Cat-eyes, Cadence and Arrow, were having a conversation.
"So, Arrow, are we Sun-angels or not?"
"I think that, maybe, we used to be," Arrow replied. "Hey, pass me one of those cookies, will you?"
"Do you want a plain one, Arrow, or one with a picture?"
"Better make it two cookies, one of each."

A thousand miles above Tessimaysan, Raine, the starman, turned off his picture screen. He had just spoken with the most beautiful blue-skinned woman on a million worlds. In a few minutes, and after a trillion, trillion miles, Raine was returning to Nikee Like.

On a hillside near the Moonlands, a plant was growing. It was not an ordinary plant – it was a plant with a name. It couldn't remember its name, but it would when it was older. Now, it was trying to rub its leaves together. It

*couldn't remember why it was doing that, either. "Oh, well,"
it thought, "maybe tomorrow."*

*Running up the hillside were two tiny, red, dog-like
animals. They had come to visit the plant.*

*Near the western shore of the Middle Sea, Flitter, the
feather-dove, was busy finding more trees. He found them
over by all of the other trees.*

*On the southern shore of the Middle Sea, Re-Enne, the
Sea-True, was sitting on the sand in the sun watching the
waves. Later that day, she would go under those waves to
the City.*

*Near the western bank of the Great Grasslands River, the
wind was blowing through the trees. Although no one was
listening, the leaves seemed to be saying something.*

*High above the Eastern Grasslands, Sky-swift, the plains-
dove was scanning the horizon. He was looking for the
Kingdom of the Hearts. His Woot friend had told him he
should visit there sometime.*

*In the Grasslands castle of the Hearts, Anna Bliss was
painting a picture of an ocean shoreline. She didn't know
which ocean it was. "I will have to visit them all to see
which one I have painted," she joked with her mother.*

*Then the Princess went outside and practiced with her
sword.*

*On the castle side-porch, Queen Karinne was looking at
the Pixie key in the hand of the Queen on her deck of playing
cards. The more Karinne thought about it, the more she
thought that maybe her friend, Circles, was right. Maybe
the cards <u>were</u> a map to a treasure.*

*On the north-western coast of the Longsea, two boys from
the River Kingdoms were climbing on the beams of the White*

Bridge. In a few minutes, they would make a surprising discovery.

On the Far Ocean coast, north of Oceienne, Reed Cardette was leading the first of the horses from the ship. His sister was running down to the water to meet him.

In the harbor at Varadeyyes, Elle Cross had thrown on her sea-blouse and was leaving in a hurry. She had to find Cardette. The Piks had found <u>her</u>.

On the Far Ocean Point, Casse Sarenne, Captain of the Dredden, was angry – very angry. Two things that belonged to him were missing.

On the Island of Everland, Veronica and Arcadia were sitting by the water waiting for Caroline to return from the Windlands. The ocean breeze cooled their smooth, beautiful faces.

In the southern Longsea village of Darataesen, several fishermen were sitting in a harbor shop arguing about what really happened on the night that the Far Ocean magician had come to their town.

In a woodshop in Keleste, Sirvenne Daetond, the wagon-master and woodworker, was admiring the cabinets he would soon deliver to the shops of Caytenne near the Longsea. The stranger from the west, with the odd little friend, had done an extraordinarily fine job when he built them.

Across the mountains, in the highlands town of Cadeene, Renae Flasette, descendant of the King, was running her fingers through a chest of coins and thinking. Perhaps it <u>was</u> time for a trip to the Northlands.

In Riverhold, near the Bluewater, Wendy Kesselle was making cookies to take with her into the Ameredene wilds. Two pale-green Fairies were helping her.

"Settie! Milli! Stop that!" Wendy yelled at them. There was sifted flour and powdered sugar flying everywhere.

At her house in Windtown, Mary Looking had finished her sewing, read the note again, and was waiting. She wouldn't have to wait too much longer.

And, in the wide, desolate Outlands, Window Breesian was pressing on through the sparse grass and lonely dust-flowers. He was thinking of her.

+++++++++

THE WINDLANDS
THE OUTLANDS
AMERREDEWU

CHAPTER THIRTY-ONE

TO WINDTOWN

The sun had gone down and the moon was rising as Window saw the trees of Windtown on the far horizon. He had pushed across the rough grass of the Outlands and the soft grasses of the outer Prairies. He had reached the low, rolling hills and the small forests of the eastern Windlands. Then he came to what he was sure was the southern branch of the Near River. From there, he knew exactly which direction he needed to go.

And now, Window quickened his pace even more, and in just a half hour, he could see the Windtown watertower sticking up above the willows and oaks around it. In a few more minutes, he could see the houses at the edge of town.

Mary's was the last house on the Town Road East. Window's heart jumped as he looked through the poplar trees at the edge of her yard and saw lights burning in her windows.

The streets of Town were quiet and the night air was cool and fresh. The Windlands traveler took the last few steps of his long journey and crossed the road into Mary's yard. He took a deep breath and tried to slow his breathing. He could not.

Window took off his pack and untied his sword and blanket. Then he wrapped the blanket around the sword. As he walked up to the house, he laid them both down in the grass by Mary's wide front porch. He didn't want to have to think about his sword right now.

Then with another deep breath, Window started up the steps. The inner-door was open so he could see into the house through the screened door. The light from within was comforting and compelling. It was calling to him.

As he stepped onto the porch, Window could hear Mary's voice through the screen of the outer-door. Her voice took his breath away. She was humming a quiet melody as she sat on the couch – he could see her in the soft light of a table lamp!

With the sound of Mary's voice, a great wave of happiness and relief swept over Window. He had been away from her for such a long time. She was beautiful in her silky, white, night skirt and open half-blouse, and a light blanket around her shoulders. Her eyes were quiet and her face was soft. The light-brown of her hair glowed in the lamp-light.

For maybe a minute, he stood and silently listened to the voice he had longed to hear over all the miles of his journey. Then he lightly tapped on the screened-door frame.

"Window?" came her hopeful, pleading voice, as she looked up towards the tapping sound. "Window, is it you?"

"Mary!"

"Window!" she screamed as she ran to the door. She was, now, also wearing the happiest smile in the world.

Mary threw open the screened-door and threw herself into his arms. Window pulled her close and they both held on as if they would never let go.

"I have missed you so much Window. I have missed you so much."

She kissed him again and again. He returned every kiss with another. His mind and heart exploded with happiness. His long, long wait was over!

"Come inside. Come inside so I can see you better," she implored. "I want to <u>see</u> you."

The happy young woman pulled Window by the hand through the front room and into the brightly lit kitchen. She looked into his dark eyes and knew that her wait was worth it. He was there. That was all that mattered.

Again she wrapped her arms around him. Window closed his eyes and floated across the room with her. He could hardly speak. He could only say, "I was afraid you wouldn't be here. I was afraid that I wouldn't find you."

He couldn't say much more. Mary wouldn't let him. She just wanted to hold him. She just wanted to know that it was really him. It was a sweet reunion that would last long into the night.

"Tell me, Window, tell me," Mary excitedly implored. "Where have you been? I have missed you so."

"I have been a long, long way from home, Mary. And, it will take a long time to tell you about it."

"Tell me something – tell me anything. I just want to hear your voice. I just want to see you, right here, by me. I just want you here with me. Oh, Window, I am so happy you are back."

For an hour or so, they sat at the kitchen table, holding hands, as Window told his very best friend of his travels. He told her about finding his medallion, and talking with his Uncle Bill, and going into the Deep Woods. He told her about meeting Circles, and a little bit about the cookieboard map, and searching for treasures. He told her he had met many new friends – even some magic ones – and one of them even tried to bring her a note.

She had gotten it! The ancient wind had found her and left Window's message where she would see it on her porch-table at her house in Union! Mary was thrilled. She didn't know how it got there but she didn't care. Since then, she was so excited that she had done little but think about coming back to Windtown, so she would be here when he returned.

Here in Windtown, she told him, she would sit on the porch each evening, wrapped in a blanket, thinking of him. Then, before bed, she would mark off that day on her calendar.

Window saw the calendar on the kitchen wall above the counter. "Mary, what day is it today?"

She pointed to the day. "Averil, twenty-fifth."

"Then it has been exactly one year since I left for the Northlands. I last saw my Uncle Bill at the Summer Breeze a year ago today!"

"Well, let's see your treasures, then, Window. In a year, you must have found a lot of them."

He set his pack on a kitchen chair and took out the Pixie dust tins and placed them on the table. Mary opened each tin and announced what she found inside.

"A matches tin of silver dust and a berry tin of different colored dust – are these two of your treasures, Window?"

"Yes, they are each a very special dust."

"They are pretty, Window. Do you do something with them?" she asked as she poured the trillion between her fingers, catching what slipped through her hand in her sleeping-skirt.

"They can help you do things," Window explained.

"Like what?" the pretty young woman wanted to know.

"Well, it is hard to be sure. Sometimes, they don't help all that much."

"Sounds like quite a treasure," she said with a smile in her eyes.

Window took more things from his pack.

"Are these coins part of the treasure you found?" the happy girl asked.

"Well, those Windlands coins I took with me when I left from my Grandfather's house for the Wilds."

Mary took a silver Willowix coin and spun it around on the table. "And you've been carrying them with you for a whole year?"

"Well, yeah."

"And these coins – " Window continued, "they are Northlands coins from near a sea by the far Eastern Plains."

"Northlands coins from the East?" Mary teased him.

"There's a story that goes with them," Window tried to explain.

"I'll bet there is," Mary replied with still another smile.

"And here is my Grandfathers belt. I found <u>it</u> in the East, too."

"You are a fine treasure hunter, Window." She kissed him twice on the cheek.

Mary went to her covered back porch and filled two glasses with water from the bucket on the table there. When she returned, Window had laid out the necklace he had for her on the table.

"Wow, what is this, Window?"

She held the silver necklace up in the light. It's bright, light-green jewel flashed in her eyes.

"This is beautiful, Window. Where did you get it?"

"It is a necklace from the Queen of the Northlands that I got in the lands far to the southeast of the Windlands.

"Did you sleep a lot in geography class, Window?"

She couldn't help teasing him. She was so happy to have him back that everything he said made her smile.

"And, it is for you," he said with love and softness in his voice.

"Oh, Window," was all she could say. "Oh, Window."

He put the chain around her neck. The beautiful stone gleamed against her soft skin. She stroked the side of his face with her fingertips.

Mary dug into the pack looking for more treasures.

"Where is this beautiful rose-diamond pin from, Window?"

"I met a girl," he answered.

"Was she pretty?" Mary teased him, wondering what he would say.

"She was beautiful."

"Did you fall in love with her?" Mary asked, with a twinkle in her eye.

"Just a little."

"When you told her about me, what did she say?"

"She said that you were the luckiest woman in the whole world."

"I like your girl-friend, Window. She may be beautiful – but she is also very smart."

"And I am very, very lucky," Window admitted.

Mary replied with certainty in her voice. "So am I, Window. So am I."

Then Mary's face brightened again. "I have a gift for you, too, Window."

Mary went to a counter drawer and dug beneath some wooden spoons. Smiling proudly, she held a springcookie pressing-board out to him.

"This is for you."

Tears came to Window's eyes. Mary had remembered his love of the cookies. It was the perfect gift.

The cookieboard was like his Grandmother's, but with different pictures. On this board there was a wagon, and a gate, and a well, and a goose – and his favorite bird, a willowix – and seven other carvings.

"I found it in a shop near the King's Straight Road. And, last week, I went out to the farm, and your Grandma showed me how to bake the cookies."

Window ran his hand over the carvings, feeling each one with his fingertips.

The loving young woman's eyes glowed as she announced to him, "Tomorrow, I will bake you some cookies."

Window looked again at the pictures on the board and smiled at his friend. Then, he thought of a question to tease her. "I wonder what adventure this cookieboard could be a map to. Perhaps I should try to follow it."

Mary took the board from Window's hand and set it, out of his reach, on the counter.

"Perhaps another time, Window, in a thousand years – but not until then."

Again, she wrapped her arms around him as though she would never let go.

Window dug into his pocket. "And here is the medallion I found that started it all." He handed her his mysterious, rusted medallion.

"Have you ever seen that design before?"

A gleam came to Mary's eyes. "Yes, I have, Window, about five minutes ago."

Window was sure she was kidding him again. "What do you mean?"

"Come with me," she replied. His year-long search for the identity of the medallion was about to be over.

Mary took Window by the hand and led him out to her back porch. There on the table was the bucket of water she had drawn from her well that afternoon. It was shiny white, with a thin red ring around the rim. On the side of the water bucket was a small metal emblem that said "Newtown Metal Works."

And there, above that emblem, was a larger emblem — rectangular, and painted in one corner with a little picture of Windlands grass and, in the opposite corner, the shining sun. And, diagonally across the emblem were three light blue bars. In the center of the bars was a circle with a star inside!

There it was! – Window's mysterious medallion design — welded to the side of Mary's water bucket! He held his own medallion up to the bucket. It was the exact same emblem!

Window was speechless. Mary shared her thoughts of an explanation.

"I wouldn't be surprised if the water bucket in the back of Breeze's tavern has the exact same emblem on it. I'll bet that your Uncle knew, all along, that your medallion came from a water bucket!"

Window could hardly believe it. "I guess that <u>could</u> be true. I suppose that Breeze <u>might</u> have known."

He rubbed his fingers over the emblem on the bucket as Mary continued.

"And I wouldn't be surprised if your uncle made the whole thing up about a mysterious, traveler stopping at the Summer Breeze, too."

Window didn't know what to think. There <u>must</u> have been a traveler. His uncle wouldn't have sent him into the dangerous wilds otherwise. But, Mary could be right. Breeze could have just made the whole thing up! Window thought quietly for a minute.

Finally, Window said to her, "Yeah, maybe there never was a young treasure-hunting traveler who stopped at the Summer Breeze."

Window sounded pretty disappointed. Then his loving Mary reminded him of something.

"Well, whether there was one before or not, Window, by tomorrow afternoon, when you go to see Breeze, there <u>will</u> be one for sure. It is going to be you. <u>You</u> will be the young treasure-hunting traveler who stopped at the Summer Breeze."

Window's face broke into a big grin. "Breeze told me that I could make my own adventures. Either way, he helped me do just that. I have certainly have had some great adventures."

Mary got quiet again. She pushed against Window and shared another kiss. She didn't care about traveling across the lands and finding treasures right now. Window was here – she was satisfied to stay home for a while.

Then, Window remembered something else.

"I wrote you some notes while I was apart from you, Mary. You can read them all later, but maybe you would like to see one or two, now."

He took his notebook, turned the pages to near the back, and handed it to her.

Mary read the beautiful words he had written – words of love and hope – words from deep inside his heart connected to hers. "You are my magic," he had written to her. She wiped the tears from her eyes.

"The Fairies read these notes one night, and they seemed to like them," he said with a smile.

"Well, I like them, too, Window. I will treasure them always."
She closed the notebook and set it on the table.

Mary took Window's hand. Without another word, she pulled
him into the living-room, grabbed her blanket from the couch, and
led him onto the porch. She sat down on the wide porch-swing
where they had spent so many nights together, and pulled him
down next to her. It was late, but the moon was still in the sky.

"This porch is where I have been spending a lot of my time
since I got back to Town, Window. One morning, I sat on the steps
and watched the sun come up, and wondered where you had been
sleeping that night."
"In the afternoons, I would sometimes sit on the railing and
watch rainstorms come across the southern fields, and remember
when we did that together."
"In the evenings, I liked to wrap myself in a blanket and sit
here on the swing and talk to the moon or watch the stars – and
wonder where you were – and what you might be doing."
"Some nights, I would listen to the wind blowing through the
trees. Then I would pretend that the wind was talking to me –
telling me that you would be home soon. I guess that the wind
was right."

Just then, a gentle breeze blew across the yard and across their
faces. Mary pulled the blanket tighter around them. Window
heard a tiny tinkling sound and turned to see if, perhaps, the
Fairies had found him again. It was Mary's wind-chimes, hanging
from the side of the house behind them. They were singing quietly
in the cool night air. Window felt Mary against him and listened
to the gentle melody of the wind.
"I love this place," he thought.

Suddenly, Window saw something bright, out across the yard,
coming from beyond the trees.
"Hold out your hand, Mary. We have a visitor."
As Mary held her open hand before her, she saw it coming. A
bright, sparkling, blue light was flying through the darkness

towards them. It spun and twisted around in the air as it came closer. Then it flew right up to them and landed on Mary's outstretched hand.

Mary felt a slight buzzing on her palm as she looked in wonder at the beautiful flying-light. She turned towards Window to share the light with him and saw deep into his eyes as he returned the glance.

"Hello, Blue Light," Mary spoke to their visitor. "How are you tonight?"

The light flashed more brightly in her hand for a moment.

"Do you live around here?" Mary asked politely.

The blue glow dimmed a bit.

"Well, please come see us any time you are nearby."

Again the light flashed brightly. Then it suddenly jumped up from her hand and buzzed lightly against her cheek. Window held his hand open and the sparkling light hopped onto his palm for a moment. Then, with another flash of blue light, and, spinning in loops as it went, their wondrous visitor silently flew back between the trees and out of sight.

Mary was smiling. "Oh, he is so beautiful, Window. Is that light one of the magic friends you found on your travels?"

"Yes, it is," he answered quietly. Then he spoke in almost a whisper. *But, you are _my_ magic.*

Mary took her fingers and slid them inside Window's hand. She sighed as she leaned her head against his shoulder. Window pulled her still closer. Mary closed her eyes.

"And you are _my_ treasure, Window."

Window looked across the yard and across the road and out over the fields. In the distance, clouds were forming above the horizon. The wind rustled gently through the poplar trees and softly brushed Mary's hair against his face. Beyond the fields and woods, the heat lightning flashed silently in the far southern sky. It was a beautiful night for the end of an adventure.

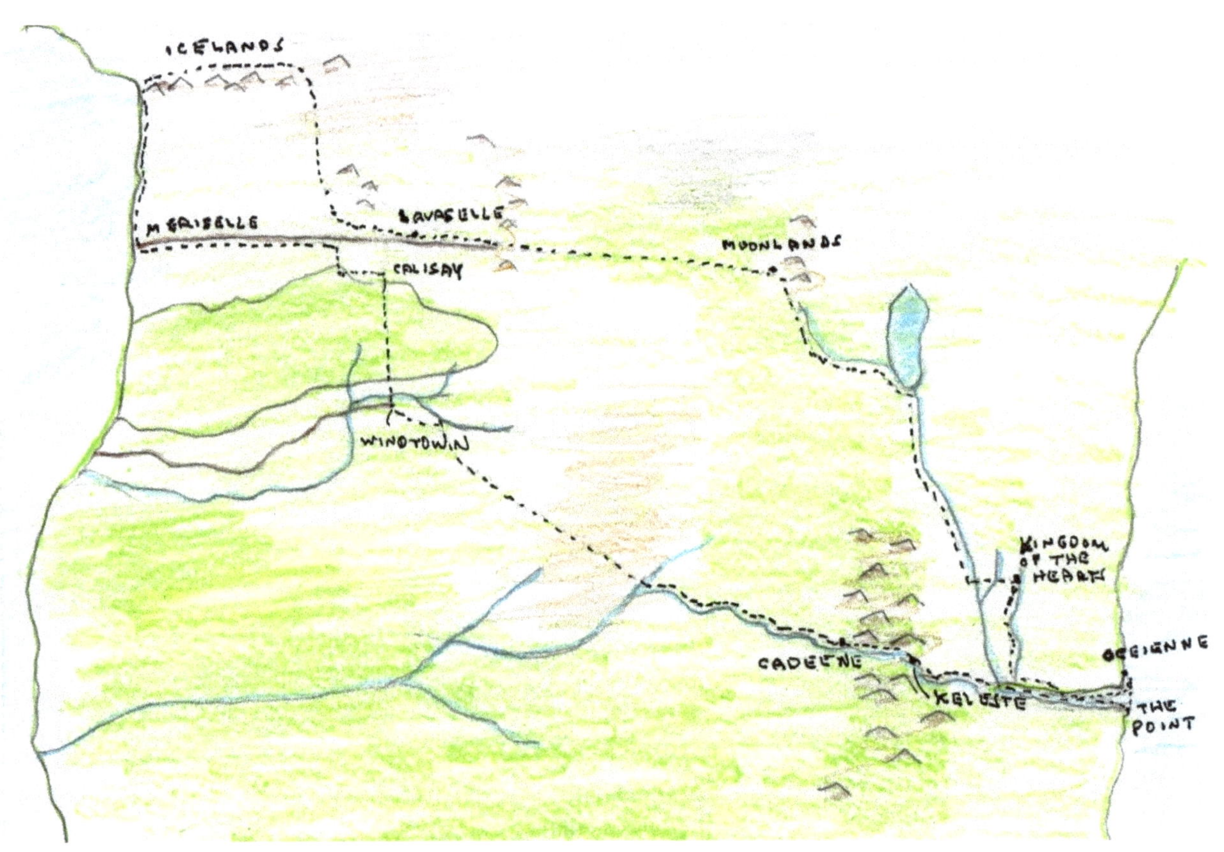

ICELANDS
MERISELLE
SAVASELLE
MOONLANDS
CALISAY
WINOTOWIN
KINGDOM OF THE HEART
CADELNE
KELESTE
OCEIENNE
THE POINT

CHAPTER THIRTY-TWO

AT THE SUMMER BREEZE

Window Breesian stood in the doorway of his house and looked out down the path toward the Town Road. The bricks of the path were old and pale and almost buried beneath the leaves that the spring winds had blown from their winter resting place below the big willow trees that stood alongside the path. Window's eyes followed the curve of the path down the hill and across the bridge to where it met the Road, and then followed the Road as it peeked through the trees, all the way into Windtown. Above the Road, the sun shone brightly down from the midmorning sky. It had been a cold night last night, but today was warm, and a perfect day for an adventure...

EPILOGUE

+++++++++

[IN THE LAND OF DREAMS AND ADVENTURES]

Somewhere across the lands from the Windcoast, to the Northlands, and far to the Very East, the moon was shining, as it often did, into the bedroom window of Tresette and Vermillion. It was a tall, wide window with a rounded top, and was framed by soft curtains quietly moving in the warm summer breeze.

The breeze came in through the window and gently caressed the faces and ruffled the blonde-brown hair of the twin girls as they lay on their bed, in their sleeping-shirts.

"It had been a cold night last night, but today was warm, and a perfect day for an adventure..."

"Thank you for reading to us, Mama," Veri said, with sleep in her eyes. "We love that story."

Tressi yawned and struggled to stay awake.

Their mother stood up from the edge of the bed and shifted her white-lace night-dress. The bright light of the table lamp reflected from the jeweled pin in her hair and flashed on the ceiling like stars in the warm night sky.

Her face was smooth and calm. Her eyes were quiet and bright. She lay the book down on the clothes-stand.

"Did Window have more adventures, Mama?" Veri wanted to know.

"Oh, yes, many more. It would take another book to tell about them all."

"Will you read us that book, too, Mama? Please?" Tressi asked politely.

"Not tonight, Dear. Perhaps, sometime," her mother answered as she straightened the covers over the girls.

Tressi was waking up a bit. "I like adventures, Mama. Can Veri and I have one sometime?"

"Yes, Mama. May we have an adventure like you and Window?"

"Certainly, you will have adventures – but not tonight, My Darlings. It is too late for an adventure tonight."

The loving mother looked into the eyes of her questioning children. "Tonight, you should just <u>dream</u> of your adventures. Then when you are older, you can have one of your own."

"Okay, Mama. We will," Tressi promised.

"What adventure do you want to have, Tressi?" Her mother asked.

"I want to travel to..."

"Oh wait, don't tell us, Tressi. I want to be surprised."

"Okay, Veri. But I want you to come with me."

Veri turned on her side and looked at her mother. "Did you get surprised in your adventure with Window, Mama?"

"Oh, yes, Veri. That always happens with adventures. They never turn out just as you planned them."

"Is that a good thing, Mama?" Tressi wondered.

"That is very good thing. If you knew everything that was going to happen on your adventure, you would never have any surprises. And surprises can be the best part."

"I hope I dream about a surprising adventure tonight, Mama."

"I hope you do, too, Veri. You can tell me about it in the morning."

"I will tell you my dream, too, Mama."

"Okay, Tressi.
"I hope I dream about finding...
"Oh, wait, Tressi. Don't tell us, now."
"Okay, Veri. I'll tell you in the morning."

"Do you still have dreams about adventures, Mama?"
"Yes, Veri. I will never stop that."

Their mother thought back to the days of the story she had just finished reading to them. Those adventures were so important – but now she was having new adventures. She loved them all. She looked out through the window at the bright, white moon and made a wish that her girls could be so fortunate as she had been.

Then, she reached over to the table-lamp and put it out. The girls settled themselves under their covers. The moon was shining through the window onto their bed.
With one hand, their mother pushed her hair behind her ear. Then she leaned over and gently kissed each girl.
"Good night, My Darlings," she whispered to her two new adventures.

On their pillows, Tresette and Vermillion had closed their eyes. The breeze came in through the window and brushed across their quiet faces. Tonight they would dream of their <u>own</u> adventures. And maybe, someday, they would have the adventures of their dreams.

+++++++++

REFERENCES

**CHARACTERS, PLACES, AND THINGS
IN PARTS ONE, TWO, AND THREE
AND THE PAGE WHERE INTRODUCED**

+++++++++

A Mallen went to Calisay… – The first line of a Windlands
    children's rhyme. I : p. 20

A rumbling stumbling tumbling Zumbler… – The first line of a
    Windlands children's rhyme about a Deep Woods creature. I
    : p. 63

A star for the Old Countries and three stripes for the new… – The
    first line of a Windlands children's rhyme. I : p. 45

Ace – One of the Atters, a Calisay band of street children. III : p.
    85

Ajer Hollen – Grandson of R. Holland of Grandfather Windowen's
    Northlands Expedition, from Ameran. II : p. 43

Alana – An angel friend of Caroline and Valentine. II : p. 27

Alezan – The last king of the Northlands, who gave his kingdom's
    treasures to his three sons to hide. I : p. 168

All Roads Lead To The King – A Windlands children's rhyme
    about the Northern Wars. I : p. 124

Alysse – A dancer at the Traepelle Castle. II : p. 133

Amarie – A dancer at the Traepelle Castle. II : p. 133

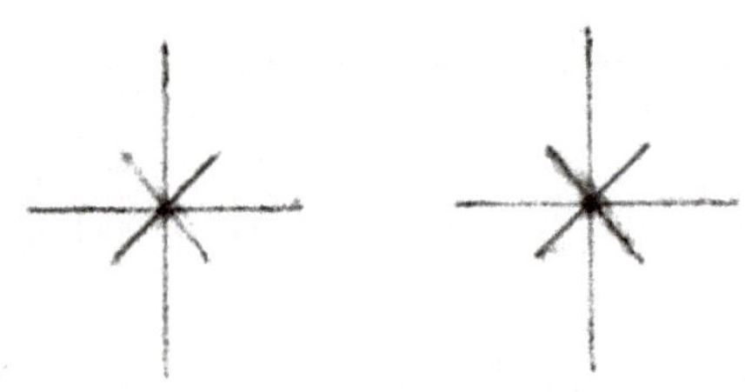

xxii

Silkie [pl. Silkie] – Tall, long-legged, long-necked, silky-furred
     animals from the Northlands plains. I : p. 45

Silver Falls – An Ameredene river-town far below Riverhold on
     the Bluewater. III : p. 211
Sirvenne (Daetond) – The wagon-master who gave Window and
     Circles a place to stay the Keleste for the winter. III : p. 179
Sky-fairies – One of the types of Fairies that came to honor Circles
     in the Deep Woods. III : p. 216
Sky-Swift [Swifty] – A plains-dove befriended by Circles on the
     Great Grasslands River. III : p. 36
Skyflowers – The tall flowers, with pointed leaves and petals,
     common in the Eastern Mountains. II : p. 107
Slack-lizards – Long, slick-skinned, Deep Woods creatures. I : p.
     198
Snackers – Long-necked Deep Woods Talkers. I : p. 193
Snowrunners – Tall, deer-like snow creatures with large padded
     paws. II : p. 54
South Cape – The Atland-settled region at the southern tip of
     South Continent. II : p. 231
South Continent – The huge, jungle-covered part of the Newlands
     Continent south of the Windlands. South Continent was
     settled by the Old Countries in only four places: Greyport – a
     wild, ungoverned city of pirates and other criminals, to the
     south, down the western continent coast from the Windlands
     – The Horselands – a large region of open grassfields and
     beautiful horses still farther down the continent coast –
     Sanarelle – a port used by traders who braved the jungle

+++++++++

John Ernest Briggs

Some of the storytelling influences which
are reflected in John's writing are:

His Uncle Bill
Robin Hood
Prince Valiant
Treasure Island
Sherlock Holmes
Disney's Uncle Scrooge Adventures
Tolkien's Lord Of The Rings
Isaac Asimov science fiction

Master's Degree in Mathematics
Mathematics Teacher - College and High School
Vietnam War Era Veteran
Singer, Songwriter, Guitarist
Music Producer, and Recording Engineer
Author and Illustrator of Fantasy/Adventure

johnernestbriggs@gmail.com

The Adventures of Window Breesian